BLUE MURDER

LORD & LADY HETHERIDGE MYSTERY SERIES BOOK #2

EMMA JAMESON

LYONNESSE BOOKS

For everyone who read Ice Blue and waited, patiently or impatiently, for book two. Thank you from the bottom of my heart.

CHAPTER ONE

Anthony Hetheridge, ninth baron of Wellegrave and chief superintendent for New Scotland Yard, contemplated the engagement ring nestled inside its velvet-lined box. Both the ring and the silver-plated box were vintage —*like me*, he thought with a slight smile.

Many years ago, when art deco designs were all the rage, some marriage-minded Hetheridge had commissioned the ring. It was magnificent. Its solitaire—a cushion-cut diamond of at least two carats—was set in platinum, the metal of choice in that prewar era. Fixed on either side of the diamond were two identical sapphires. Inside the box they looked subdued, but in the correct light, on a woman's third finger, those sapphires would rival the diamond for drama and fire. Hetheridge, who'd concealed the ring inside his desk at New Scotland Yard for more than a week, did not know its present-day value. Growing up surrounded by heirlooms, he found one was very like another; rarely, if ever, did their market value cross his mind. He *did* know that his marriage-minded forbearer presented that particular ring to a blond bombshell on St. Valentine's Day, 1926. And received an immediate and emphatic answer: no.

But that's the upside of having been turned down once already, Hetheridge thought, leaning back in his executive armchair, one perfectly polished wingtip braced against the desk's bottom drawer for an anchor. *If Kate refuses me again, at least I have some experience taking no for an answer.*

But he didn't care to take no for an answer. This time he didn't want to take anything less than an unqualified yes. Hetheridge, who rejected all forms of superstition and had zero patience for talismans, horoscopes and what Detective Sergeant Bhar called "bad ju-ju," regarded his old family ring with grudging suspicion. Suppose the damned thing was cursed?

Of course, Hetheridge didn't have to present Kate with this ring. He could pop round to Tiffany's and purchase a brand new solitaire. A ring with no history. No character. No connotations of bold extravagance and doomed romance ...

But that would never do. Hetheridge and the ring were too much alike. If Kate wouldn't have the antique ring, what use would she have for a sixty-year-old detective? His fate was bound up with the ring's, that much was clear. Even if he didn't believe in fate.

Hetheridge supposed this was the sort of dilemma other men discussed with friends. Bleating about personal matters, however, had never been his way. Professionally, he believed in open channels of communication. He wouldn't dream of working a murder case without sharing every relevant fact and opinion. But in his private life he kept his own counsel. That meant he was never forced to endure the scorn or pity of those who witnessed his failures. But it also left Hetheridge wondering, in the silence of his own mind, if he were on the right track or barking mad.

It's too soon, Hetheridge told himself for the hundredth time. *Kate and I have known each other fewer than two months. Attempted exactly one ridiculous "date," if it can be termed that, with her entire family in tow. Kissed only once. And never more than a kiss.* Even when Hetheridge had been engaged years before, couples didn't embark on marriage without discovering if they were sexually compatible. And that had been ...

Dear God. That brief engagement to a gold digger named Madge had been more than twenty years ago.

Eyes still on the ring, Hetheridge ceased to see it, distracted by an increasingly graphic train of thought. He knew Kate found him attractive. Although neither tall nor handsome, Hetheridge had grown into his looks in middle age. Still fit and trim with a full head of steel-gray hair, he had no trouble commanding the attention of desirable women, at least when he put aside his duties long enough to seek them out. But with Kate, the frisson of uncertainty tormented him. Hetheridge didn't doubt his ability to hold her attention for a night, or for the sort of three-week affair he'd once preferred. But a mini-break in Paris or a romantic dinner or half a dozen shags—that was worlds away from for better or for worse.

A polished wingtip still pressed against the desk, Hetheridge tilted back another centimeter or two, ignoring his armchair's creak of protest. He often balanced this way when he was deep in thought, trying to tease together the individual pieces of a case. And much to the dismay of his young subordinates—most notably Detective Sergeant Deepal Bhar—Hetheridge had never overbalanced and toppled over.

But really, how had he found himself in such a position, besotted with a junior officer under his direct command? It was highly improper, especially given the Met's latest round of internal studies and investigations. A battle-scarred old beast, the Metropolitan Police Service was determined to claw its way into the modern era, not die buried under an avalanche of civil rights lawsuits. In light of the Met's new rules, Hetheridge's only defense was technical; he wasn't having it off with Kate, wasn't even dating her, not in the accepted sense. And mere gossip wasn't enough to damage him—even in New Scotland Yard's increasingly egalitarian environment, the old guard held silent sway. Technically, an affair between Hetheridge and Kate could earn him forced retirement and Kate the sack. In reality, no matter what the Internal Police Complaints Commission decreed or the commissioner vowed on BBC1, Hetheridge knew he'd never get the boot for pursuing an intra-office romance. Not unless every one of his male superior officers disappeared off the face of the earth. The old guard simply wouldn't stand for such a thing.

That didn't mean Hetheridge wouldn't endure a certain amount of disapproval behind closed doors should his pursuit of Kate become common knowledge. Most of his fellow chief superintendents had been married for ages, their children long since grown. During each decade of Hetheridge's career—his twenties, thirties, forties and fifties—a superior had at some point steered him toward a drinks trolley, intoning over a Scotch and water, "You need a wife, Tony. It'll do wonders for your career. And surely it's expected, hey? You must be under pressure to beget the next Lord Hetheridge."

But Hetheridge had resisted—laughing off the suggestions, or pretending to give them due consideration, or digging in his heels and resorting to the authoritative demeanor that was his birthright. When Hetheridge's gaze chilled and his voice rang out like lord of the manor, even Assistant Commissioner Michael Deaver got in touch with his inner peasant. It was a cracking good trick, and one Hetheridge rarely used on his fellow officers. But the necessity of his selecting a wife—more specifically, a correct wife for a correct marriage—had long been a sore point with him.

What did he truly owe the barony of Wellegrave? Hetheridge's often-absent father and cool, distant mother had loved their eldest son as they'd never loved him. And so the older son's accidental death had saddled Hetheridge with all the responsibilities but none of the familial pride. He'd come of age determined to choose his own road, the Peerage and his family hierarchy be damned. He'd even joined the Metropolitan Police Force (in the years before the term "force" was replaced by the more politically correct "service") over his father's threats to disown him. That had not happened, alas, although the ensuing breach had been almost insurmountable. Hetheridge hadn't cared. He'd immersed himself in his work, rising quickly within the Met to earn his place within New Scotland Yard. There he found deep pleasure in the minutiae of detective work, connecting the tiniest dots to reveal larger truths. It was a career he loved unreservedly. But he did his best to keep that love decently concealed so it would embarrass no one, least of all himself. And before he knew it, Hetheridge was forty, fifty, and now sixty, at a time of life when he should have been contemplating grandchildren, if not the *Sunday Times* and a spot of tea. But inside he felt as young and vital as ever.

More vital, truth be told, after meeting Kate. She deserved far more from him than his usual three-week fling. And for a man of his generation, the intrusion of so many wildly erotic thoughts could be answered just one other way: marriage.

The door to Hetheridge's inner office banged open. Startled, Hetheridge closed his fist, snapping the jewel box shut. As both feet hit the floor, his armchair's front legs struck with an echoing *crack*. It was the closest he'd ever come to losing his balance, and the moment's significance wasn't lost on Detective Sergeant Deepal Bhar. He grinned at Hetheridge from the doorway, black eyes alight.

"Yes?" Hetheridge strove to look composed.

"I do apologize, Chief Superintendent Hetheridge," announced his administrative assistant, Mrs. Snell. Although cadaverous, with graying flesh and thin wrinkled lips, she'd been at the Met only as long as Hetheridge, making her no more than sixty. Tall and bony, with gray pin curls and a habitually suspicious expression, Mrs. Snell glared at Bhar like the Shadow of

Death in sensible shoes. "When I left my desk to water the plants, DS Bhar took it upon himself to break in uninvited."

"I see." Opening a desk drawer, Hetheridge tucked the jewel box away with what he hoped was seamless nonchalance. "No fault of yours, Mrs. Snell. Thank you."

Mrs. Snell's eyes, huge behind her thick magnifying lenses, showed too much white as she turned to Bhar, vibrating disapproval. He gazed back innocently. Defeated by Hetheridge's dismissal and Bhar's Teflon charm, Mrs. Snell exited with stiff dignity, closing the door behind her.

"So." Bhar was still beaming. "Alone in his office at half-eight. Lord Hetheridge."

At New Scotland Yard Hetheridge loathed the use of his hereditary title, where it was only invoked as a form of reverse snobbery. Still, he didn't bother correcting Bhar. He knew the detective sergeant didn't call him "Lord Hetheridge" to provoke him. On the contrary, Bhar committed most of his verbal sins for the same reason a small boy, warned not to swear, shouts curses at his schoolmates—for the simple thrill of transgressing.

"Just clearing up." Hetheridge indicated his almost bare desk. "Answering emails and finishing reports. Why did you burst in?"

"Hoping to catch you asleep at your desk."

"I do not sleep in this office." Hetheridge had made a career out of interviewing liars. And made a surprisingly good liar himself, when it suited him. More than once it had occurred to Hetheridge that if not for the triple accident of birth, breeding and ethical indoctrination, he might have climbed to the very top of the corporate crime ladder. God knew a position of authority within New Scotland Yard required a flexible interpretation of right and wrong, not to mention the truth.

"So you say. But I'll keep an eye out all the same." Bhar dropped into one of the chairs positioned opposite Hetheridge's desk. "And what was in that silver box? The one you stashed when you thought I wasn't looking?"

Hetheridge affected not to understand.

"Won't come clean? Fine, I'll guess. Snuff box? Pillbox? Face powder?" Bhar grinned. "No? I've got it. It's an engagement ring. You're making an honest woman of Mrs. Snell at last!"

Hetheridge studied Bhar. He'd served as the junior officer's guv for almost five years. At their first meeting, Bhar was an absurdly confident, mouthy nerd, afflicted with overlong hair, cheap suits and a weakness for beautiful, heartless females. Now he'd matured into a justifiably confident, mouthy detective with impeccable hair, well-tailored suits and a weakness for beautiful, heartless females. He could still do with some evolution, but on balance he'd changed for the better.

Can I say the same? Hetheridge wondered. *Or did turning sixty turn me soft?*

Opening his desk drawer, Hetheridge withdrew the jewel box. Bhar's expression changed from joking to carefully neutral. The man might be a habitual clown, but he was no fool. Hetheridge didn't open the box. When Bhar finally dared put out a hand, Hetheridge nodded.

Bhar withdrew the antique ring from its velvet lining. Turning it this way and that, he smiled as the diamond and twin sapphires sparkled. "Talk about posh. When will you ask her?"

"Tomorrow. Or next year. Or never."

"It's a big step. I didn't reckon things were moving so fast." Bhar returned the ring to its jewel box. "Has Kate even cracked the seal on the crypt?"

Hetheridge sat up ramrod-straight. "Is that your way of asking if she's spent the night with me?"

"No!" Bhar looked horrified. Then before he could stop himself, he emitted a high-pitched cackle. "I *meant*, have you taken Kate to see your family estate in Devon. Maybe it wasn't the clearest reference to a cobwebby old ancestral manse," he gasped, beginning to choke on his own laughter, "but for you to assume … assume …" He broke off, eyes closed, shaking with mirth.

Hetheridge could do nothing but wait the younger man out. Fortunately, he wasn't the sort to turn pink from embarrassment. The heat creeping up his throat was surely due to an over-starched collar—courtesy of his old-fashioned manservant, Harvey—not physiological proof of internal discomfort.

"Besides your stated ambition to catch me sleeping rather than working," Hetheridge ground out as Bhar's laughter subsided, "have you some other reason for disturbing my peace?"

"Murder." Bhar's eyes shone. "Assuming we still handle that sort of thing, in between love connections?"

CHAPTER TWO

The police constables charged with securing the scene at 14 Burnaby Street, Chelsea, had performed their duties heroically, given the challenges the townhouse contained. Those included fourteen male university students, most intoxicated and two unable to stop vomiting. Even less composed had been the sixteen females—crying, texting, Tweeting and calling for Mum. Almost two hours later, most of them still looked like first-week prossies, hair mussed and mascara bleeding as they shivered in the late October chill.

"They must be freezing to death out here," Hetheridge told Bhar as two uniformed officers dragged aside the plastic crime scene barriers to let their vehicle—Hetheridge's silver Lexus SC 430—through. "When did Halloween costumes for young women become nothing but lingerie?"

"Right around the time Halloween became my favorite holiday." Bhar smiled at the line of young women dressed in what appeared to be all of Victoria's secrets, including red satin teddies, black garter belts and stiletto heels. "And I'll have you know those girls are wearing more than just lingerie. That one's got devil horns. And that one? Cat ears, see, and look at her bum! A cat's tail. Proper costumes, thank you very much."

Hetheridge studied the males, dressed in T-shirts, hoodies, jeans and trainers. One had a rubber gorilla mask tucked beneath his arm; that was the most the male contingent had done to mark the occasion. How had the younger female generation let it come to this? The males milled about as slouchy and shoddy as ever, whilst the young women tarted themselves up in heavy makeup, camisoles and lacy knickers? Shouldn't the females at least demand a commensurate amount of nudity? A bit of beefcake to balance the cleavage and bare thighs?

If I had a daughter, Hetheridge thought out of long habit, then stopped. As a matter of fact, he did have a daughter, courtesy of a long-ago liaison. Hetheridge and Jules Comfrey, having met only four weeks ago, were still struggling to come to terms with each other. And whether he liked to admit it or not, Jules was undoubtedly the sort of girl who would attend a Halloween party stark naked if she thought it might attract the right young man. Thus, self-righteous thoughts about imaginary daughters now went directly into the mental rubbish bin. Hetheridge had a real daughter, and her behavior was no better than this crowd of miserable, half-dressed girls.

"Moving on," Bhar sighed, tearing his eyes away from the lingerie-costumed females to consult his iPhone. "The officer in charge of the scene emailed me the stats. First victim, Clive French. Twenty years old, Caucasian. Resident of London, enrolled at University College. Second victim, Trevor Parsons. Caucasian, twenty-two years old. Resident of Manchester but enrolled at University College. Each vic was killed by—" Bhar broke off, glancing at Hetheridge. "It's true. An axe to the head." He snorted. "Talk about a Halloween bash."

"Please refrain from saying that to the victims' families."

Bhar scrolled farther down the report. "Thirty-nine party guests have been detained, including the hostess, Emmeline

Wardle. Her parents own the house." Bhar pointed at 14 Burnaby Street, three stories tall and black-shuttered, before continuing. "Two males and three females did a runner and were brought back. Detained just there." Bhar indicated a small, miserable group corralled by two women PCs. "One male was arrested for attempting to flush his cocaine down the karzie. Another snorted it all in one big line and was rushed to hospital. Expected to live," Bhar added with a shrug.

"I presume all mobiles were confiscated," Hetheridge said. CCTV cameras were a boon to modern-day police work, but mobile phones, with their cameras and video recorders, were an ever-increasing detriment. It was devilish hard to secure a scene when the myriad players—witnesses, bystanders, perhaps even the murderer—could send unexpurgated bits of the investigation out into cyberspace.

"Mobiles collected," Bhar said. "It's estimated no more than fifty calls went out. Efforts to trace those calls will begin on the next business day."

Hetheridge sighed. The next business day was forty-eight hours in the future. And suppose even one of those calls had been placed to the *Sun* or the *Daily Mirror*? In Hetheridge's youth, newspapers had felt a certain responsibility to Scotland Yard, printing only details preapproved by the commissioner. But for modern editors, nothing mattered but sales, circulation and the worldwide scoop. If one of Emmeline Wardle's guests sold the case's salient details to a tabloid, New Scotland Yard would soon be flooded with pseudo-confessions from all the usual psychotics and fame-seekers. Without a few key facts held back—details only the actual killer could verify—it might take months to separate the phony murderers from the real culprit.

Hetheridge eased his Lexus forward as another police barrier was dragged aside. "What more do we have on the victims?" he asked, but Bhar's attention was elsewhere.

"Will you look at that? Typical."

Glancing the way Bhar indicated, Hetheridge saw a handful of dark-suited individuals, mostly male, kept at bay by blue and white crime tape and two uniformed PCs. One was shouting at a constable, stabbing his finger just centimeters from her tight-lipped, impassive face. Others vented into their handhelds, texting or phoning with furious intensity.

"Family solicitors, I'll warrant," Hetheridge said.

"Arrived double-quick, didn't they? Don't know why I'm surprised. This is Chelsea, innit?" When irritated, Bhar sometimes forgot his adopted manner of speaking—the Received Pronunciation favored by newsreaders and actors. In those moments he fell back on the cadence of Clerkenwell, where he'd been born. "Naturally the family lawyers rush in to comfort the kiddies long before their blood relations turn up."

"I'll not say you're wrong." Easing his vehicle into the narrow space between two panda cars, Hetheridge ignored the police captain attempting to direct him with exaggerated hand motions. "Just keep your opinions between your ears and off your face. These people are accustomed to having every social entity in their corner. If they sense disapproval from you, they'll turn to stone before you can cough up the first apology."

"I know, guv. And I'm ready." Bhar produced his old-fashioned leather-bound notebook. Flipping back the cover, he turned it so Hetheridge could read the block-printed words inside.

DO NOT SCARE THE WHITE PEOPLE

"Let the wrong pair of eyes see that and you'll be on report for racism." Hetheridge was only half-kidding. Generally speaking, he approved of the Met's recent efforts to change its deep-seated culture. But as a Caucasian male of a certain age, he also knew the worst offenders had thus far evaded detection. Outspoken jokesters like Bhar, on the other hand, were frequently hauled in for sensitivity training.

"Oh, it's a goal of mine to be branded an official racist," Bhar snorted. "Just as yours seems to be to grow more eccentric with every passing year. You do fancy your uphill battles, don't you, guv?"

Hetheridge raised an eyebrow.

"C'mon. You had newly promoted detectives queuing up to join your team. Most of them white, male and highly recommended. Yet you chose me. And the moment I show my mug at a crime scene," Bhar grinned, "half the posh types you're meant to pacify get their backs up. I'm detrimental to soothing the gentry, and that's precisely what Assistant Commissioner Deaver expects you to do. Appease the titled and influential."

"Indeed. Though I daresay he wouldn't object if I occasionally saw justice done." Opening his car door, Hetheridge emerged into the cool, windy night. The scent of wood smoke was overpowering, but not unpleasant. Someone on Burnaby Street had recently enjoyed an autumn bonfire.

"Good evening," Hetheridge called to the uniformed PC who'd sought to oversee his parking. "Hetheridge here. Chief superintendent. You're Kincaid, are you not? Jolly good. Put me in the picture, won't you?"

"Double murder, sir," the constable said, removing his cap like a Victorian schoolboy called to account. "Bloody mess of a scene, if you'll excuse my saying so. Mass hysterics amongst the guests. You'll have your work cut out, making sense of what that lot tells you."

Nodding, Hetheridge started toward the Georgian house, DS Bhar on his right and PC Kincaid following on his left. "The hostess's name is Wardle, you say?"

"Ms. Emmeline Wardle," Kincaid said. "Her father owns the house. Rupert Wardle. You may have heard of him, sir. Made his fortune in frozen foods, he did."

Fourteen Burnaby's front garden was encircled by a low fence. Another uniform opened the gate for Hetheridge and Bhar, hastily pulling on gloves before touching the wrought iron.

Once upon a time, New Scotland Yard detectives and even police constables had been expected to gather evidence; Hetheridge still had a box of blue latex-free gloves in his car's boot just in case. But nowadays every crime scene was documented, catalogued and analyzed by specialists—sometimes the Forensic Science Service, sometimes private scene-of-crime officers for hire. There was even a small, unpopular contingent who believed the crime scene should be secured not only from the public but from the police themselves until the SOCOs completed their efforts. But the day *that* passed into law, supposing it ever did, was the day Hetheridge buggered off for good. Modern science was an integral part of most investigations, but no matter how neatly crimes were solved on television —often with just a drop of blood and an errant twig—in the real world, it took a detective to weave an investigation's disparate threads into a solid case. Hetheridge rarely felt more needed— more alive—than he did at that moment, arriving at the scene of a fresh murder.

The Wardle house was three stories tall, with a peaked roof and old-fashioned leaded windows. Its pale brick exterior was trimmed in black; its red door boasted a brass knocker and twin brass lanterns. Closer, Hetheridge noted synthetic cobwebs stretched between the lanterns. A jack-o'-lantern sat on the porch. It had been carved with some skill—slashed eyes and no nose, just a wide, ravenous grin. Far above the door, at least three meters up, sat a CCTV camera.

"Kincaid! Point your torch there, will you? There's a good man."

The camera's status light was blinking red. It had been knocked askew, probably by a rock or similar projectile, and left pointing at the sky.

"I want that camera's orientation photographed. Tell the SOCOs to check the ground for whatever might have been tossed at it, in case there are prints," Hetheridge told the nearest uniform before pivoting back to Kincaid. "Where was French discovered?"

PC Kincaid blinked, then began patting himself down. "French … French … beg pardon, sir, let me find me notes …"

"The first victim to be found. Clive French," Hetheridge said, not requiring a glance at Bhar to know he'd remembered correctly. In general Hetheridge preferred to work without a notebook, relying on memory alone. "Where was his body discovered?"

"Oh. Yes, sir. Back garden, sir. A girl called Sloane said she smelled something bad. Followed the scent and found a fellow with an axe in his skull. Only sensible bird in the whole bleeding lot, if you ask me. Managed to answer a few simple questions without babbling or bleating for Mummy."

"Rich, privileged uni kids. I love 'em, don't you?" Bhar asked heartily.

"Oh, aye," the constable sighed, his latent Scots accent breaking through. "The lasses get themselves up like prostitutes, probably because the lads mince about like poofters. Some generation. You catch the killer, you ask him why he stopped at two, all right?"

"Is there an entrance to the back garden from out here?" Hetheridge asked.

"On the side. Oi! Merton! Show these detectives into the garden!"

"Thank you, Constable," Hetheridge said. "May I borrow your torch?"

Looking pleased to assist, the man handed it over. Training the beam over the house-hugging boxwoods—like the brass lanterns, they too had been decorated with artificial cobwebs as well as giant plastic spiders—Hetheridge used the light to examine the smaller plants hugging 14 Burnaby's east side. Nothing seemed out of place.

As they entered the walled garden, its wrought iron gate

creaked. The noise was loud enough to make Hetheridge and Bhar exchange glances. Withdrawing a silk handkerchief, Hetheridge wrapped it around his hand before pushing open the gate a few more times. No matter how he did it—slowly, quickly or in stages—the gate's dry hinges emitted a sharp squeal every time.

"Hard to miss," he told Bhar, leaving the gate ajar so no additional manipulation would loosen the hinges and degrade the effect. FSS would record the sound, true, but only if requested. It was yet another small detail among thousands, inconsequential to scientists overwhelmed by a double-murder scene but obvious to a detective.

Bhar considered the gate's elaborate wrought iron scrollwork. About eight feet tall, it boasted numerous hand and footholds. "I could climb this, no problem. Any reasonably agile person could."

"But would the murderer know to climb it?" Hetheridge asked, as much to himself as Bhar. "Would he or she be aware the gate squeaked?"

A flagstone path led into the back garden, a verdant space that was quite large for Chelsea. It boasted two oak trees, each past a hundred years old if Hetheridge was any judge, and a burbling stone fountain at its very center. Beside that fountain another uniformed constable waited, no doubt advised of their approach by police radio. As Hetheridge and Bhar moved closer, the constable angled his torch at the ground, illuminating a fallen figure. The beam passed over a white face, open eyes and parted lips. Torchlight glinted off the axe blade protruding from his skull.

Squatting a judicious distance from the body, Hetheridge ignored his arthritic left knee's twinge of protest. The moment he admitted that twinge could more properly be labeled pain, he would begin to settle for stooping, or perhaps even insist his younger colleagues, like the thirty-something Bhar, perform his crouching for him. And that would never do.

In death, Clive French looked younger than twenty, and not just because he'd died wearing his backpack. He had a round baby face with chipmunk cheeks and protruding front teeth. In addition to the backpack he wore a fleece zip-up, jeans and trainers that had seen better days. The axe in the back of his head was buried deeply in sparse dark hair. Had Clive French lived, he would have been bald by thirty.

Hetheridge wasn't sure how long he remained in that crouch, studying the body. As he arranged the details of the crime scene in his mind, cataloging each possibility, he heard a distant clack on flagstones. Bhar didn't visibly react, but the two PCs did. Kincaid drew himself up to his full height; the other uniform made a nervous sound in his throat. The clack on the flagstones came closer, closer, until a soft hand fell on Hetheridge's shoulder.

"Starting the party without me, guv?"

Forgetting his left knee altogether, Hetheridge rose in one smooth movement. Turning, he gave Detective Sergeant Kate Wakefield a carefully professional smile. She wasn't meant to be back from medical leave; by rights, she had another week. Not that she appeared to need it.

Kate had taken Lady Margaret Knolls' fashion advice to heart, at least for the most part. Gone were the inexpensive frilly suits, the costume jewelry, the cheap scent. Her tailored jacket-and-skirt combo was the model of career sobriety, her understated 14-karat gold hoops the only concession to femininity. Well— that and her knee-high black leather boots and masses of wild blond hair. Lady Margaret would never approve of the boots; to her they would be dangerous, signaling youth, sexuality and an adventurous nature. As for the shoulder-length blond hair—Lady Margaret had already suggested Kate cut it all off, opting for a career-elevating pixie or bob instead. Hetheridge knew better to advise any woman about her wardrobe. But he hoped to God Kate never cut her hair.

"Just waiting for you to catch up, DS Wakefield. I had a notion you wouldn't take your full medical leave."

Kate gave him that familiar sideways smile, hazel eyes snapping with amusement. "Nope. I'm fine. Though I meant to creep close and give you a start," she admitted, disappointed.

"I heard you walk up. Not a tremendous leap of logic to guess the constables wouldn't let anyone but a member of my team stroll into the scene. Besides," Hetheridge moved incrementally closer, stopping just short of a nearness that would strain the bounds of propriety, "Bhar didn't react, but these male PCs went quite rigid. Had to be you."

Kate leaned closer, leaving only a centimeter or so between their lips. In moderate heels she was exactly Hetheridge's height, making the proximity of their lips a constant danger.

"Have a care. One fine day, I *will* surprise you. Now." Her tone shifted, suddenly businesslike. "Is this poor blighter the first of our two dead partygoers?"

"Yes," Hetheridge said. "Apparently another guest found him after ..."

"Sorry," the constable blurted, sounding eager. He straightened nervously when Hetheridge, Kate and Bhar turned as one to face him. "Don't mean to speak out of turn. It's just that you have one bit wrong, if you'll excuse my saying so. Clive French was known to the partygoers, but he wasn't a guest. He wasn't invited."

CHAPTER THREE

"You mean he crashed the party?" Kate asked.

The PC tried to give Kate attention without giving her too much attention, Hetheridge noted with amusement. He understood the dilemma all too well.

"Yes, according to Ms. Wardle, Mr. French must have crashed. Seems he wasn't quite her sort, if you know what I mean."

Hetheridge nodded. No doubt Emmeline Wardle, as the daughter of a frozen foods baron, felt a solemn responsibility to be particular about those she called friend.

"Ask my opinion," the PC continued, emboldened by Hetheridge's nod, "it seemed like Ms. Wardle was less upset by the fact Mr. French was dead than by the fact he'd set foot on her property at all. Told me at least five times that he wasn't a friend and he had no business here. Mind you, she was off her nut with grief. The other murdered bloke was her boyfriend. UCL rugby star called Trevor Parsons."

"Hang on. I knew that name sounded familiar," Bhar said. "He was expected to make a brilliant pro career, wasn't he?"

"Not sure. Prefer proper football meself," the PC said. "Anyhow, according to witnesses, the party was in full swing when

Mr. Parsons staggered down the stairs, an axe sticking out of his skull. He pointed at Ms. Wardle. Tried to say something. Dropped dead. That's when Ms. Wardle started screaming blue murder." The PC's eyes widened slightly. "And was still at it when I arrived. One of the women PCs—Buckley—slapped Ms. Wardle across the face to make her stop. Now the poor girl's as hoarse as if she sucked a whole crate of fags. Sight of so much blood made her go starkers, I reckon."

Hetheridge nodded gravely. He wished the PC hadn't offered that last opinion, but it couldn't be helped. "Give me a moment with my team, will you? There's a good fellow."

As the PCs obligingly stepped back, Hetheridge steered Kate and Bhar closer to Clive French's body. "Impressions. DS Bhar?"

"He was taken by surprise, almost certainly from behind. His fingernails look grossly clear. No contortions, no signs of a struggle."

"I agree. DS Wakefield?"

"Body's been moved."

He met Kate's eyes. "Because?"

"There's almost no blood. Scalp injuries tend to bleed like mad. Blood should be everywhere. But the ground's more or less clean."

Hetheridge smiled, hoping Kate hadn't been prompted by the PC's comment. "Yes, indeed. I was given to understand the girl who discovered Mr. French—Ms. Sloane, I believe—responded to a bad odor. What do you say to that?"

"All I smell is wood smoke."

"Same here," Bhar said. "I think—hang on. Borrow your torch, guv?"

Hetheridge handed it over, suppressing a smile as Bhar used the light to pick out something Hetheridge had already noticed— a yellow plastic garden hose among the drifts of fallen leaves. His junior officers followed the hose to a still-damp pile, grinning like schoolmates. Bhar called, "The fire was here, guv! Snuffed with a bit of water."

"Kincaid." Hetheridge turned to the uniformed officer. "Please be so kind as to direct the SOCOs to that area the very moment they arrive. I suspect Mr. French was killed there, and traces of his blood may lie beneath the burnt leaves. With any luck FSS will be able to—"

From his coat pocket, Hetheridge's mobile vibrated. He sighed. But one glance at the INCOMING screen told him the interruption was unavoidable. The caller was Assistant Commissioner Michael Deaver.

"Excuse me." Turning his back on the other officers, he walked as far away as the walled garden permitted before saying: "Hetheridge."

"Tony, your scene is out of control. You need to lock it down. Now."

"I've only just arrived. Everything looks reasonably secure. What's wrong?"

"The young woman hosting the party, Emmeline Wardle, rang 999 a quarter hour ago." Deaver sounded harried. "She accused the Met of brutality and false arrest. Psychological torture, if you can believe it, because the PCs detained her inside the house with her dead boyfriend."

"I see. Very well, I'll have a woman PC escort Ms. Wardle to the Yard. Set up a private interview—"

"That's just the tip of the iceberg," Deaver cut across him. "A snout at the *Daily Mirror* tells me mobile phone pictures of Trevor Parsons, dead with an axe in his skull, have been transmitted to his editor-in-chief. Tomorrow morning they run in full color. Care to imagine the media firestorm after Mummy and Daddy see their son on page one, lying in a pool of his own blood and piss?"

Hetheridge bit back a protest. It was useless pointing out that anything witnesses did before the police arrived was not the fault of the Metropolitan Police Service, much less New Scotland Yard. Somehow the instant 999 was engaged, the Met became responsible for every eventuality that followed, right or wrong.

"Let's hope the photos are low quality, without much detail."

"Doesn't matter." Deaver heaved a sigh of mordant triumph. "The *Daily Mirror* knows perfectly well who lives next door to the Wardle house. They'll flog this horse for a month or more. At least until a pop star overdoses or an MP is caught buggering a farm animal. Please God."

Hetheridge felt as if he'd lost the thread. "Michael. Why is the Wardles' next-door neighbor relevant?"

"Because he's Sir Duncan Godington."

Hetheridge drew in his breath. For a moment he couldn't speak at all. But when he did, he kept his voice level. Unlike the assistant commissioner, Hetheridge didn't believe in signaling his frustrations, either by tone or expression. Particularly when the situation was grave. "Which house?"

"Sixteen Burnaby."

Hetheridge turned it over in his mind, weighing every reasonable course of action. Then he chose.

"Never fear, Michael. Leave this to me. I'm sending the majority of partygoers to the Yard at once, so if you'll designate a unit to take preliminary statements, I'd be grateful. In the meantime, I'll interview the two key witnesses on-scene. I'll ring back once I've signed the scene over to the FSS."

"I presume one of those key witnesses is Ms. Wardle. Do you think that's wise, Tony? Courting a formal complaint?"

"I have a folder full to bursting with them," Hetheridge said truthfully. "You know as well as I do—it takes at least forty-eight hours to emotionally process a loved one's demise. If Ms. Wardle is already complaining about being shut in with her boyfriend's corpse—if she wants to escape the body rather than be near it— her reaction is atypical enough to be worth my time. Not in a sterile interview room but here, within sight and scent of where the crimes took place."

"And the other witness?"

"Ms. Sloane." Hetheridge couldn't stop himself from pacing, piles of brittle leaves crunching with every step. "She discovered the first victim's body and possibly lied about the circumstances. I need to interview her before she has time to compose herself."

"Fine. But you do understand what the proximity of Godington means to your team?" Assistant Commissioner Deaver asked.

"I do."

"Good. Because it would seriously displease me to see a conviction sidestepped or overturned because of blind loyalty on your part, Tony."

Hetheridge pressed his lips together, letting the remark pass. He knew himself to be a loyal man. But his loyalty was never blind, though he occasionally envied those who were capable of following only their hearts.

"I'll keep my head, sir. That much I can assure you."

"Good." Deaver rang off.

Tucking away his mobile, Hetheridge walked back to where Kate and Bhar waited. "DS Bhar—change of plans. I now require you to organize the relocation of the party guests, with the exception of Ms. Wardle and Ms. Sloane, to the Yard. Be certain none are permitted access to mobiles or the Web. Act as liaison to solicitors and family members. Be polite," he emphasized, letting the directive hang between them, "and take a break for sleep when necessary. But as soon as possible, I want a list of those witnesses who merit a second interview. Tomorrow I'll have a research project for you, once you're rested enough to begin."

"Research?" Bhar looked mutinous.

Moving close to the younger man, Hetheridge whispered in his ear. When he stepped back, he saw his detective sergeant's expression transform from disappointed to startled—and from startled into stone.

"Of course," Bhar muttered, refusing to meet Hetheridge's eyes. "Yes, sir. Thank you, sir." Without a backward glance, he hurried away.

Hetheridge pretended not to notice. "DS Wakefield?"

"Guv?"

"Division of labor. Please coordinate with PC Kincaid. Tour the scene and conduct Ms. Sloane's preliminary interview. I'll handle Ms. Wardle."

"But what about DS Bhar? Why send him to do scut work?"

Hetheridge lifted an eyebrow. It was beyond cheeky of Kate to pose such a question. Did she have any notion how it affected him, to be questioned—challenged—after more than thirty years of authority within the Yard? The strange current of excitement her rebellious nature produced?

Studying Kate's face, Hetheridge decided she did. If not intellectually, then viscerally, on some deep primal level. And one fine day, to co-opt Kate's phrase, he'd answer in kind. Not intellectually, but physically.

"DS Bhar is already on the case. I suggest you follow his example," Hetheridge snapped, enjoying the look of surprise as he dismissed her, turning to the nearest uniformed PC. "Please escort me to Ms. Wardle."

CHAPTER FOUR

Detective Sergeant Kate Wakefield followed PC Kincaid into the Wardle house, using the entry designed for deliveries, service technicians and maids. It didn't strike her as undignified. In well-bred English households, police always entered through the back door.

That back door opened into the Wardle family mudroom. It was a stark white rectangle, unadorned except for macks hung haphazardly on pegs, a line of Wellies in various sizes and an umbrella stand. Dutifully, Kate glanced about, finding nothing to flag for the FSS. Strange that people who led such antiseptically clean lives used a "mudroom" to prevent the spread of the world's inevitable filth. In the very worst parts of Britain, family dwellings opened directly into the front lounge. In those places, a bit of tracked-in mud was the least of anyone's worries.

After the Wardles' mudroom came the Edwardian scullery, now converted into a pantry. Kate was startled to find the shelves stocked with so many of her favorite brands. Prawn crisps. McVitie Digestive biscuits. Mr. Kipling cakes. Beef jerky, tinned beans, Marmite spread ...

Having been assigned to Hetheridge's team for only a short

time, Kate was still gobsmacked by the occasional parallel between herself and the impossibly posh types her guv investigated. Well—not just investigated. Belonged to. By any yardstick he, too, was impossibly posh. And that was a truth Kate had difficulty processing.

Surely he isn't really one of them, Kate told herself. *Not in the ways that count.*

Hetheridge was her guv, yes, but she could forgive him that. Despite numerous rocky relationships with authority figures over the years, Kate genuinely respected Hetheridge as her chief. He was a policeman first, a detective second and a bureaucrat only a very distant third. Furthermore, Hetheridge was something those "authority figures" from her childhood had never been—a man worthy of the term.

Raised by females, some of them miserable examples, and viewing males only from afar, Kate had once doubted the existence of worthwhile men. Hetheridge, Bhar and others from her police training had taught her differently. These days, Kate accepted the reality of good, trustworthy males as a matter of course. But warmth and respect for Chief Superintendent Hetheridge wasn't at issue. Every junior detective idolized his or her guv to some degree. Yet Kate found herself preferring Hetheridge when he wasn't her guv. When he let slip the mask of authority. And she suspected Hetheridge revealed those rare glimpses of the authentic Tony to Kate and Kate alone.

"Detective? What is it?" PC Kincaid asked.

Kate realized she was staring at a jar of Marmite spread like it was a signed confession. "Nothing. Lead on," she said, trying to sound as unruffled as Hetheridge when a subordinate caught him wool-gathering. If the guv never perspired in public, neither would she.

Beyond the pantry was the Wardles' kitchen, spotless and fitted up with all the "mod cons," as Kate's mum liked to say. The white-tiled floor shone like glass; the white walls looked as clean as if they'd been scrubbed mere hours before. Equally immaculate was the stainless steel refrigerator, except for one faint smear near the handle.

Kate moved closer to the granite countertops. The area near the fridge was bare except for a sprinkling of crumbs and a second smear so faint, she had to squint to assure herself it was real.

"Just a tick," she called to PC Kincaid.

Pulling on blue latex-free gloves, Kate opened the fridge. Aware she was under general orders not to photograph any facet of the crime scene, Kate nevertheless used her smartphone to document the fridge's interior. Photos captured via personal handhelds fell into an investigative gray zone. Bedeviled by the ubiquity of image-manipulating software like Photoshop, the Met frowned on phone snapshots; introducing them into evidence could torpedo a case. But Kate didn't intend on showing these pictures around. They were simply a new way to catalogue a scene, quicker and often superior to her haphazard written notes.

Most of the fridge, like the kitchen, was clean and boring. Kate snapped pictures of yogurt, milk, orange juice and strawberry jam. On the second shelf, someone had pushed aside a bagful of veg to make room for two open bottles of Stella Artois. Pink lipstick marked the rim of one. Kate photographed them.

Beside the open beer bottles sat a messy sandwich. Sliced meat and cheese piled high between slabs of rye bread; mustard and mayonnaise seeped out one side. Reexamining the smears on refrigerator panel and countertop, Kate decided they were a combination of those two condiments. Someone had stashed the sandwich and beers, then hastily tidied up, leaving behind only faint traces.

Y not pour out the Stellas? Xpecting the owners 2 reclaim them? Kate texted to herself. It was her new method of taking incidental notes; she would type them up in the Queen's English the next day. It beat her old habit of struggling with a stylus to access her phone's clunky word processing program.

Nothing else about the kitchen struck Kate as worth flagging, so she followed PC Kincaid into a small dining room originally meant for the servants. In the days before labor-saving devices like washing machines and vacuum cleaners, a staff of at least twelve had been required to maintain a townhouse the size of 14 Burnaby. Those maids and footmen had needed a place to eat—preferably behind a green baize door so the sight of servants at rest didn't put the gentlefolk off their own food. Here, that iconic green door had been replaced by a tasteful oak version. And judging from the modern décor—gilt-flecked wallpaper, an antique sideboard and an array of family photos—the Wardles had claimed the former servants' chamber for their own use.

Not so much as a dust mote out of place, Kate thought. Turning to PC Kincaid she asked, "I thought there was a party on. Is the whole house this spotless?"

"God no. Mostly it looks like a bomb went off," he laughed. "Vomit on the walls, pig snacks ground into the carpet and fag burns everywhere. To hear the guests tell it, all that damage happened before the murders."

Kitchen + dining nook apparently out of bounds to guests, Kate texted to herself. She was about to pass into the next room when she caught sight of something metallic lying on the Turkish rug.

"What do you make of it?" she asked PC Kincaid, pointing at the object resting just beside a table leg. It was a metal ball with a seam in the middle but no visible hinge. A short length of chain was curled beneath it.

"My girlfriend has one of those. Lip balm inside," the constable said. "The ball unscrews into two pieces."

"Yeah. Well. Make sure the FSS bags it."

Kate followed PC Kincaid down a narrow passageway that wrapped around the back stairs, depositing them into the townhouse's enormous drawing room. Done up in soft pinks and creamy yellows, the room was dominated by bookshelves covering an entire wall. More than half empty, the alcoves were artfully sprinkled with a few picture books devoted to fashion, fine dining and travel. Kate also spied dried flowers, framed miniatures and—just off-center—an empty space. The alcove's recessed light shone on nothing, as jarring as a missing tooth in an otherwise bright smile.

Kate took in the rest of the room. A red garter belt dangled from a lampshade. Soda cans, empty crisp packets and beer bottles were scattered everywhere. The coffee table was covered with crushed cigarette butts and soiled napkins. To one side, Kate spied a steel straw and a trail of white dust.

"That there's Ms. Sloane." PC Kincaid indicated a girl sitting alone on the long brocade sofa. He pawed at his notes. "First name. Um. Kyle …"

"Kyla," the girl corrected, fixing Kate with steady brown eyes.

"Ms. Sloane, my name is Detective Sergeant Kate Wakefield." She offered her hand, which Kyla accepted. "I'm sorry for what you've gone through this evening."

Kyla shrugged. She wore a white silk dressing gown over what was probably yet another lingerie-based costume. The short robe barely covered her to mid-thigh, revealing long, shapely legs. Even seated, the girl was clearly six feet tall or close to it, with a model's angular bone structure. Her dark brown hair had been accented with a zigzagging white skunk streak; a choker with plastic bolts, a la Frankenstein's monster, was fastened around her throat. Kyla's corpselike makeup—green eye shadow, blush and lipstick—should have detracted from her good looks, but the gangrenous tones actually enhanced her high cheekbones, firm chin and well-shaped lips. Kate made a mental note to check and see if Kyla Sloane had done any professional modeling. Even in costume, something about her seemed oddly familiar.

"May I ask you a few questions?"

"Of course." The girl's hand trailed along the hem of her dressing gown, pulling it down another inch. Not that her attempted modesty made those long legs, pressed together and turned slightly, any less impressive.

"Tell me what happened," Kate said, noting Kyla's dry eyes. If the young woman had shed any tears, they had been few, and quite some time ago.

"I heard a sound, like a twig popping. I thought it was a neighborhood cat. I called out, 'Is anyone there?' Then—"

"Wait." Kate held up a hand, startled by the way the young woman launched into her recitation. Had Kyla Sloane actually skipped right to the moment she discovered Clive French's body?

"Let's start at the beginning," Kate said, putting on what she hoped was an encouraging expression. "You were invited to this party by Emmeline Wardle, correct? Are you particular friends with Ms. Wardle?"

Kyla Sloane blinked. Clearly in her world, that was the stupidest of all possible questions.

"Yes. Em and I have been friends since we were babies," Kyla said. "I can't remember a time when I didn't know Em. When she throws parties, I help organize them. Handle the decorations. Plan the menu and the games. Even tend bar, if it comes to it."

"Do you also select the guest list?"

Kyla blinked again. "Em doesn't usually need any help with that."

"I suppose not." Kate tried not to sound as curious as she felt. Kyla was an extraordinarily poised witness. She was as calm as if she underwent questioning by New Scotland Yard every day and twice on Sunday. "So just for the record, how was tonight's party going, before it all went awry?"

"Perfect. Absolutely perfect."

"You were enjoying yourself?"

Kyla pressed her lips together. Kate had the suspicion the young woman had bitten her tongue. "Of course."

"Then why were you alone in the back garden? When you discovered Mr. French's body, I mean?"

Kyla hadn't expected that. Kate worked hard to keep her own face blank. Astonishing how most witnesses assumed the police incapable of guessing anything at all.

"Because." Kyla took a deep breath. "I went outdoors to check on something. The decorations. I wanted to be sure the jack-o'-lantern candles hadn't guttered ..."

"No jack-o'-lanterns in the back garden. No party decorations, either. I was just there." Kate offered a friendly smile.

Kyla's left fist clenched. With her right hand she tugged harder at the hem of her dressing gown, covering another millimeter of well-shaped thigh. "I don't see how my reasons for going into the back garden are relevant to your investigation, detective."

"With two young men dead, and me responsible for finding out how and why, I'll be the judge of what's relevant." Kate kept her voice soft. It was a trick she'd learned from Hetheridge. Express a reasonable expectation in a reasonable tone, and then dissect the response.

Kyla's green lips twisted scornfully. A momentary flash of truth, it was gone almost as soon as it appeared, swiftly replaced with false contrition. "Of course. I'm sorry, DS Wakefield. I don't mean to be obstructive. I went into the back garden for some fresh air. I have asthma—cigarette smoke indoors makes me wheeze. While I was outside, I found Clive."

"I understand he wasn't invited to the party."

"No."

"But you knew him?"

"Of course. We go to uni together. Share class—" Kyla stopped. "*Went* to uni. *Shared* classes."

"So why wasn't he invited?"

Scorn flashed in Kyla's eyes again, though she kept her voice level. "I realize you're several years beyond your schooldays,

31

detective, but surely you don't believe us kiddies all play nice together? Just because we're technically adults?"

Kate was struck again by Kyla's poise. Everything about her seemed decades beyond her years. And where had Kate seen Kyla before? Why did she seem so familiar?

"So if Clive didn't make the cut, what was he doing in Ms. Wardle's back garden?"

"I have no idea. You know, detective," Kyla strove to sound politely imploring, "I'm very uncomfortable. If I could be allowed to wash off this makeup and put on some decent clothes—I can borrow some of Em's upstairs—I'd be far better composed—"

"Just another minute," Kate lied serenely. In reality, Kyla Sloane would be packed off to New Scotland Yard before she knew it. That green makeup would be on her face for hours to come. "Now that we've established the basics, tell me how you discovered Mr. French."

"I heard a sound, like a twig popping. I assumed it was a neighborhood cat. I called, 'Is someone there?' Then I turned around and saw Clive. Dead with the axe sticking out of his head. It was horrible."

Kate let Kyla's declaration hang between them, making no comment, keeping her face bland. Possibly the discovery of Clive French's body had gone exactly as Kyla described. Nothing in the narrative was remarkable, except for its brevity. Witnesses who discovered bodies tended to go on and on, describing each step, sight or sound in excruciating detail. Not only had Kyla neatly summarized her discovery, she'd used more or less the precise words as her first recital.

"I wish I could tell you more," Kyla said after what felt like a full minute's silence ticked by. Again she tried to surreptitiously wrangle another millimeter of coverage out of that short, thin robe. "But that's all. Nothing more. I found Clive and I went back inside and the next thing I knew, Em was screaming her head off. Then chaos. Then this."

Kate said nothing.

"So if I'm free to go ..." Kyla started to rise.

"Now, miss. You've not been dismissed," PC Kincaid said, waving Kyla back onto the long brocade sofa. The sound of his voice nearly made Kate jump out of her skin. She'd been so focused on Kyla, she'd forgotten Kincaid's presence.

"Just a few more questions." Kate smiled again. "Would you say the party got out of hand?"

Kyla folded her arms across her chest. "No."

"Think Ms. Wardle's parents will object? When they see ..." Kate trailed off, indicating the room's disarray.

"No."

"Just no?" Kate was used to witnesses lapsing into monosyllables when they felt misused. The best response was to just keep smiling, and just keep asking.

"No." Kyla's brown eyes narrowed again.

"So they prefer the house this way?"

"No."

"They gave permission for their daughter to have a huge party whilst they were out of town?"

"No."

"They won't object to fag burns on the carpet or a broken—" Kate was going to say lamp, since all the best parties in her own youth had involved broken lamps, but Kyla cut across her.

"Who cares about a vase? Two people are dead! Are you from Scotland Yard or Lloyd's of London?"

Kate fought to evince no surprise. Kyla, however, looked startled enough for both of them. Surprised and suddenly no older than her age—perhaps twenty-one—as her eyes filled with tears. Biting her lip she looked away, muttering, "Everything comes down to money in the end."

Kate turned to PC Kincaid. "See that spot?" She pointed at the mammoth bookcase's empty alcove with its spotlight shining on nothing. "Have a look at it, will you?"

Even as he moved closer to the shelves, Kyla's head came up. That remarkable poise was shattered. Sniffing, she wiped ineffectually at her eyes as fresh tears appeared.

"Is it dusty?" Kate asked. She thought there might be a fine layer of dust, except for the imprint of what had, until recently, occupied that space.

"No, ma'am. Every shelf is neat as a pin." PC Kincaid made a slow circuit of the room, shuffling his feet. Several meters away he stopped, dropping to one knee.

"Wait! Ma'am … down here …" Instinctively Kincaid poked with a finger, then guiltily drew his hand back. "Something in the carpet here. Glittering. Bits of glass."

Kate turned back to Kyla. The young woman sniffed again.

"It was an accident. Not that it will matter. The amphora was Hellenistic. From ancient Greece," Kyla added, misreading Kate's expression as ignorance. "But it's gone now and Em and I might as well be dead. Because her parents are going to kill us."

CHAPTER FIVE

Emmeline Wardle *looked* like an Emmeline Wardle, if such a thing were possible, Hetheridge caught himself thinking. Seated in the townhouse's formal front parlor, she was exactly what the pampered daughter of a frozen foods magnate should be—trim and stylish in a magazine-ready sort of way. Blue-eyed and spray-tanned, her long blond hair was equally flawless, falling down her back in a straight, shimmering mass.

As Hetheridge approached, Emmeline sat whispering furiously to a middle-aged man in a three-piece suit. Clearly the Wardle family attorney had wormed his way inside the scene before the Met secured it. And now, Hetheridge thought, cursing the officers responsible for the breach, the wretched man was part of the investigation. Sending him away was out of the question; on the contrary, he too would need to be interviewed. From the lawyer's point of view, being questioned by Scotland Yard was doubtless a small price to pay after filling his young client's ear with potentially game-changing advice.

"Who are you?" the lawyer asked, his tone wary but not overly sharp.

"Chief Superintendent Anthony Hetheridge, New Scotland Yard." Hetheridge passed over his credentials, waiting patiently while the lawyer examined the warrant card minutely enough to commit it to memory. Once the card was returned to him, Hetheridge advanced on Emmeline with a smile.

She stared back at Hetheridge from her place on the antique Queen Anne sofa. Like the rest of the parlor, the sofa had suffered during the party. A fresh stain marred the cushion beside her; cigarette butts had been stamped directly into the blue Turkish rug. Over the course of his career, Hetheridge had toured the remnants of many parties. This one had been well and truly out of control. Emmeline, by contrast, was not. Not at present, at least. The girl Hetheridge had first glimpsed, stabbing a finger at her attorney while hissing commands, had disappeared. This girl was crying prettily, wiping away each tear as it fell with that same perfectly manicured finger.

"I can't answer any more questions," Emmeline told Hetheridge in a breathy whisper. She wore the lawyer's boxy gray coat buttoned over what must have been another skimpy costume. "My throat hurts. I can barely talk. I want my mum."

"Of course you do." Hetheridge sought to radiate firm authority rather than false paternalism. Over the years, he'd dealt with more than one Emmeline Wardle. Threatening and coquettish by turns, females like her knew how to induce two responses: lust and fear. Only by avoiding the appearance of either could he keep her off-balance, and thus hope to glean what he needed. "Tell me what happened and I'll see that you're reunited with your parents as soon as possible."

Emmeline's teary look turned sullen. For a long moment she said nothing, giving Hetheridge time to register the fullness of her displeasure. Then she spoke.

"What happened? I'll tell you what happened. Someone killed my boyfriend and no one will do anything about it. Someone *killed* Trevor with an axe and ran off to God knows where and the police are making me a prisoner in my own home." Her voice rose, scratchy but still strong. "In case everyone's forgotten, I'm the victim here! Not the suspect! *The victim!*"

"Ms. Wardle, I'm well aware of your loss," Hetheridge said. "Another young man, Clive French, is also dead. Can you think of any reason someone would attack those two men? And risk doing it here, at your party, with dozens of potential witnesses about?"

"It was an axe murderer," Emmeline all but screamed, her already weak voice breaking. "A nutter! Why do nutters do anything?"

"Do you consider any of your guests potentially unstable?"

"Of course not. They're all the best people. Well—not Clive. Obviously. But all the rest."

"With regards to Mr. French. Why is he not one of the best people?"

"Because he's a slimy blackmailing little toad!"

Hetheridge blinked, amazed by her vehemence. Emmeline, too, looked equally shocked, as if unable to believe the words that had come out of her mouth.

"Chief Superintendent, we need to take a break," the Wardle family attorney broke in. "My client is overwrought. I'm her barrister. Lionel Oliphant." The man put out a hand.

Hetheridge raised his eyebrows. He'd been reared never to ignore an offer to shake hands. Most importantly, never to be rude. Never unintentionally.

"Well. You prefer to take that sort of attitude, do you?" Oliphant withdrew his hand. "I suppose you think I have no business here. Very well, take it up with your subordinates; they were all so busy collaring the party guests who fled, they did a poor job securing the rest of the house. I realize it must be a great disappointment for New Scotland Yard, to barge in and find these frightened children protected by legal counsel." Oliphant's tone grew colder. "However, at least in Ms. Wardle's case, that's exactly what you face. I won't stand for intimidation tactics from you or anyone else, Chief Superintendent. My client will answer questions for ten more minutes. Then we'll—"

"I won't! I know my rights!" Emmeline leapt up. Oliphant's borrowed overcoat tangled beneath her feet, tripping her and sending her reeling into Hetheridge's instinctive grasp.

"Get off!"

Pulling herself away from him, Emmeline tore off the gray wool coat and tossed it aside. As expected, she wore lingerie underneath—a white camisole, lacy knickers, matching stockings and four-inch heels. Crushed against her back were two pieces of cardboard pasted with white feathers. It took Hetheridge a moment to realize they were meant to be wings.

"Emmy, calm down." Oliphant tried to place a restraining hand on her shoulder, but she shook him off with surprising strength. Without the coat, Hetheridge saw that Emmeline had an unexpectedly robust built, particularly through the upper arms and shoulders.

"Don't call me Emmy! No one calls me Emmy anymore! And I'm done answering questions!"

"Look, love, I know you're knackered, but there's a difference between being firm with these people and behaving like an unreasonable little brat," Oliphant said. Something in his expression—narrowly contained fury—and use of the diminutive "Emmy" made Hetheridge suspect Oliphant was not only her barrister, but a family friend or relative.

"You'd do well to heed your counsel, Ms. Wardle," Hetheridge said, putting all his authority into his voice. "'These people,' as your counsel so elegantly termed New Scotland Yard, have the time, patience and resources to pursue you as long as necessary, and to the fullest extent of the law. We can make your life very unpleasant if you refuse to assist us with our inquiries."

Emmeline uttered a short, incredulous laugh. "Old man. Who do you think you're talking to? I'm not some dozy donkey afraid of the cops. My father can buy and sell you. Tomorrow you'll be begging me for your job back. He'll pull a few strings and you'll find yourself in the dole queue!"

"Emmy." Oliphant closed his eyes.

"Are you threatening me?" Hetheridge asked Emmeline.

"You better believe I'm threatening you."

"Then you're under arrest." Hetheridge gestured to the uniformed PCs watching, expressionless, from the area just outside the formal parlor.

Shrieking in disbelief, Emmeline tried to bolt. The male PC seized her forearms, spinning her around. Planting her feet, Emmeline managed to free herself briefly, only to shriek again as the female officer snapped cuffs around her wrists. Immobilized, Emmeline started calling for Oliphant, pleading until her voice shredded, but the lawyer merely stepped aside, giving the PCs ample room to perform their duties.

"You do not have to say anything," the woman PC recited over Emmeline's halting sobs, "but it may harm your defense if you do not mention when questioned something which you later rely on in court. Anything you do say may be given in evidence ..."

Hetheridge waited silently until Emmeline Wardle had almost been maneuvered out of the room. Just as the PCs hauled her over the threshold he called, "Ms. Wardle! One final question. Do you know who lives next door to you? At number 16?"

"If Sir Duncan did this, it isn't my fault!" Emmeline cried, voice breaking. "I'm not the one who provoked him! I'm innocent!"

It was the perfect declaration for an earthbound angel with crumpled cardboard wings. Still, Hetheridge took those final three sentences more to heart than anything else Emmeline Wardle said, weighing them long after the constables dragged her away.

∽

The body of Trevor Parsons was still being examined by the divisional surgeon when Hetheridge entered the Wardles' vast media room. Judging by the wild disarray, it had been the heart of Emmeline's Halloween party. The vast theater-sized television, taking up an entire wall, had been muted. A zombie film was playing, young women shrieking soundlessly onscreen while SOCOs photographed and videotaped every possible angle. Once Parsons' body was finally removed, the SOCOs would place a robotic camera just inside the taped outline, documenting the crime scene "in the round," from its epicenter. As much as Hetheridge found public worship of the FSS a bit over the top, fueled by television fantasies that distorted their work almost beyond recognition, he had to admit a videotaped record of the scene was helpful. Donning protective gear—booties, paper gown and face shield—Hetheridge approached the divisional surgeon, Peter Garrett, a man he'd known for more than twenty years. Garrett was crouched beside Parsons, examining the body with the aid of a very bright handheld torch.

"Give it to me straight, doc."

"He's a goner," Garrett replied from long habit. It was an old routine, amusing only to cops like Hetheridge who had actually heard defense counselors ask, months after a decapitation or disembowelment, "Did any qualified expert declare the victim to be dead?" So in this modern era, every single murder victim was verified deceased by a qualified expert, even a victim stiff with *rigor mortis*, an axe buried in the back of his skull.

"Have you already examined Clive French?"

"I have. One of the PCs told me you thought the body may have been moved. *Livor mortis* doesn't support that, I fear," Garrett said, referring to the way blood pooled in the lowest part of the body after circulation ceased. "Of course, it's possible the poor young man was moved just after death. Have to wait and see what FSS finds under the remains of that bonfire."

"Were both men killed with the same sort of axe?"

"Precisely the same." Garrett, a thin-faced man with prominent lower teeth, gave Hetheridge his trademark deaths-head smile. "Each was brand new, from the look of it. This one even has its price sticker."

Hetheridge squatted down for a closer look, ignoring the pain in his arthritic left knee. The UPC coded sticker bore a name he didn't recognize: W. C. Marsden's.

"Do I imagine it, or is the blade sunk more deeply into Parson's head than in French's?"

"You do not imagine it," Garrett said, lifting one of Parson's hands, pre-bagged by the scene's first responders to protect potentially vital evidence lodged beneath the fingernails. "The blade is almost three centimeters deeper into Parson's head. It's a clean central blow. As if the killer was trying to separate the right hemisphere of Parson's brain from his left. As for defensive wounds ..." Garrett gently replaced the bagged hand. "I doubt you'll find any. I think this poor boy was taken entirely by surprise."

"It appears both men had their backs to the killer," Hetheridge said. "Might indicate a murderer incapable of facing his victims. Someone physically weaker, like a small male or a female."

"It might," Garrett said, eyes on his work. "Mind you, I can't imagine why a physically weak or intimidated killer would choose a Halloween party to attack. Slaughtering one victim in a Chelsea garden and the other amid a houseful of wild youngsters seems like the height of arrogance to me." He flashed that deaths-head grin again. "But that's why I'm the surgeon and you're the inspector."

After the bodies of Trevor Parsons and Clive French were removed for forensic examination, Hetheridge paced the Wardle house's ground floor, taking it all in—orange and black crepe streamers, abandoned bottles of cider, half-eaten snacks. He'd hoped to meet up with Kate and compare notes—her impressions of Kyla Sloane contrasted with his of Emmeline Wardle—but Kate was gone. She'd accompanied her witness back to New Scotland Yard to log their interview with whichever DI the assistant commissioner had assigned to run the French-Parsons Incident Room. Hetheridge appreciated this diligence on Kate's part, well aware that paperwork was her least favorite part of the job. Given the Met's increasing computerization and reliance on HOLMES—the Home Office Large and Major Enquiry System, an acronym devised purely as an homage to that greatest of British detectives, Sherlock Holmes—timely reports were needed to keep the UK crime database operating at its fullest capacity.

Perhaps I should use HOLMES to run an inquiry on axe murderers? Hetheridge wondered. *On killers enamored with neuroscience—with the notion of separating the right hemisphere from the left?*

He sighed. It was a familiar pitfall of his career, imagining serial killers with bizarre new kinks beneath every shrubbery. Experience had taught him most murders could be traced back to sexual jealousy, financial greed or both. True serial killers were rare.

Rare, yes. If no further than a stone's throw away. At number 16 ...

The Wardles' second floor was unremarkable except for more empties, the sour stink of vomit and the evidence of sexual intercourse in Mr. and Mrs. Wardle's master bedroom. The snowy white sheets were twisted; not one but three used condoms lay discarded on the berber carpet. Apparently the Wardles' king-sized bed had been put to very thorough use. Grateful for the SOCOs who collected all evidence—repulsive as well as benign—Hetheridge exited the master bedroom without touching a thing.

At the end of the hallway a door stood open, revealing another set of stairs. These were short and steep, the risers painted in alternating colors of red and black. At first glance, Hetheridge saw what appeared to be a red paint spatter on the bottom step. He had to get closer to confirm the splotches were actually dried blood.

These must be the attic stairs. Trevor Parsons came down them with the axe in his head.

There were more splotches all the way up. Crime scene booties still covering his Italian loafers, Hetheridge managed to climb the stairs without treading on any but the smallest stains. The Wardles' attic was a claustrophobic, minimally ventilated space. The sharp scent of mildew assaulted him, as well as something chemical—mothballs, perhaps. Cardboard boxes were everywhere, most of them unlabeled, and an unshielded bulb burned only a few inches from the top of Hetheridge's head. Nearby was another spread of blood drops, mingled with the dust on the rough plank floor.

Suppose Trevor Parsons was lured up here, Hetheridge thought. *He's tall, at least six feet, and hunching under the low ceiling. Words are exchanged with the killer. Parsons turns to go. The killer strikes one hard, certain blow. But Parsons is an athlete, a champion. He doesn't faint from shock, or fall writhing on the floor. He tries to seek help. Down the attic stairs ... into the party ... till he can't go any farther. He doesn't leave much blood behind because it's in his hair, it's in his shirt, and the axe blade is staunching the worst of the flow. And what does his killer do, as Trevor tries to save his own life? Slip downstairs. Disappear back into the party ...*

Hetheridge considered that scenario. Of course, it didn't include Clive French's death in the equation, but these things took time.

He crossed to the attic window. Like the boxes and baseboards, the window was coated with dust. Nevertheless, Hetheridge could make out a small light burning in the attic of a neighboring home. It was 16 Burnaby.

Sir Duncan, Hetheridge thought, squinting at the small light as he pondered its meaning. *Have you really come out of retirement?*

CHAPTER SIX

Detective Sergeant Paul Bhar returned to New Scotland Yard in a state of agitation so intense, he fought hard to convince himself it didn't exist. First of all, he was a professional. Second, he had been trained to put aside personal concerns and focus only on the task at hand, especially in a murder case. Third, he'd promised himself if this ever happened —and heaven knew there'd been a time when he fantasized about it almost daily—he would respond as a paragon of cold precision. Not get twitchy. Not feel paranoid. Not spend every second of a rather brief late-night drive rehashing a constellation of past mistakes. Yes, he'd sworn not to indulge in any of those behaviors. Unfortunately, he was guilty of all three.

"Oi! Oi! Oi!" DCI Vic Jackson was shouting at a group of recently processed young male partygoers. "The longer you lot whinge and behave like wee crying girls, the longer this process will take. Buck up, grow a pair and—oi! Don't sit there, son. Do you think an officer wants his desk supporting your doublewide load?"

"You can't talk to me that way! My taxes pay your salary," the offending young man cried.

"Your sweet old mum's taxes pay my salary," Jackson growled, hauling up the party guest by his Che Guevara T-shirt. "Stand up straight and wait like a good little boy or you get a slap, hey?"

Bhar choked back a laugh as the young man did as instructed, at least temporarily cowed by DCI Jackson's slitted eyes and crimson cheeks. The man always looked one powdered doughnut away from a massive coronary, especially when rousted out of bed by the assistant commissioner. Judging by the fine white dust in his whiskers, DCI Jackson had already indulged in his personal drug of choice.

"Speaking of getting a slap," Jackson said. "If it ain't Captain Darkie. Wonder Quim's got three of the girls in a room. Think you can make yourself useful and take three of these shivering poofs off my hands?"

"Of course," Bhar said, not giving Jackson the satisfaction of visibly responding to the slur. As far as DCI Jackson went, "Captain Darkie" was relatively mild. When Bhar joined the Met, his first guv had occasionally amused himself by reciting all the words he could think of that rhymed with "wog."

"Right." DCI Jackson squinted at his tablet computer. Still openly suspicious of digital aids, he tended to use them with excessive care, as if tapping the wrong icon might unleash thermonuclear war. "Quinton Baylor. Jeremy Bentham. Matthew Bice. Follow Detective Sergeant Bhar, he'll interview you together, then separately as the case may be ..."

Because of the sheer number of partygoers due for process, Bhar and his trio had to wait in the hall until one of the interview rooms freed up. Quinton Baylor, tall and broad-shouldered with an athlete's thick neck, seemed to look on the whole experience as a bit of a laugh. He kept nudging Matthew Bice, pointing to a group of girls waiting at the end of the hall and whispering comments. Bice, also thick-necked and overlarge, only nodded and chuckled. Both had hair so closely cropped, they could have been mistaken for skinheads. Jeremy Bentham, only average-sized and apparently not friends with either, kept his hands in his pockets and his eyes on the floor.

"Here we are," Bhar said when the room cleared. It was small, eight by eight, and deliberately stark—nothing but plain white walls, a card table, four folding chairs and a digital recording device. Jeremy Bentham pulled out a chair, sat down, placed his hands on the table and offered Bhar a quick, nervous glance. Had he been crying? Bhar couldn't be sure. All three young men had bloodshot eyes, as likely a consequence of the pre-murder revelry as sadness over Clive French or Trevor Parsons.

Matthew Bice shuffled up to the table, glanced at Quinton Baylor—apparently permission from the alpha male was needed to sit down—and then dropped in the chair. Quinton took the seat beside Jeremy, elbowing him in the ribs and then pretending surprise.

"Sorry, mate! Don't look so scared. My family lawyer's on the way. Should be here any second, officer," Quinton told Bhar. His tone held the casual menace of the habitual bully.

"Detective sergeant," Bhar corrected, grateful that he could proceed without a lawyer present, at least for now. As quickly as possible he ran through the preliminaries, switched on the digital recorder and launched straight into the template for a first round of interviews.

"Did any of you witness the demise of Trevor Parsons and/or Clive French?"

Jeremy and Matthew shook their heads. Quinton grinned.

"Mr. Baylor?"

"Saw Trev right after he bought it. Does that count?"

Matthew chuckled. Jeremy managed what looked like a forced smile.

"No, it does not." Bhar tried to sound as harsh as DCI Jackson. "Did any of you see someone unusual on the Wardle premises? Someone who didn't belong?"

"Oh, aye." Quinton grinned even bigger, revealing a gold

incisor and two golden molars in his upper jaw. "Little bugger's name was *Clive French*."

Matthew chuckled again.

"Yes, thank you. Anyone else?" Bhar asked, fully expecting the answer to be no. Instead, Jeremy opened his mouth to speak. Before he made the first sound, Bhar felt Matthew's leg brush against his as the young man kicked Jeremy beneath the table.

Bhar looked from face to face. "Something the matter?"

Matthew's face went blank. This was no measure of cunning on his part; blank was his natural state. Jeremy shrugged.

"Never mind." He kept his head down, eyes fixed on the scarred tabletop. It was the worst impression of innocence Bhar had ever seen.

"Mr. Bentham. Did you see someone unusual on the Wardle premises? Two men are dead. This information could be vital."

Jeremy lifted his head. "Well, er …" He gave Quinton a weak smile. "What with the murders … the police … it's all a bit confusing, isn't it?"

Quinton's small brown eyes grew even smaller. "Not confused about nothing," he growled, dropping into a fake Cockney, or "Mockney," accent that probably served well to intimidate other rich young uni kids on the rugby field. Matthew and Jeremy looked suitably terrified. Bhar, who'd spent his teenage years ducking and running from actual football hooligans, choked back a laugh.

"What about you, Mr. Bice?" Bhar asked Matthew. "What made you kick Mr. Bentham under the table?"

Matthew's innate stupidity buzzed around him like a force field. "Don't know nothing," he muttered.

Bhar sighed. At this point DCI Jackson would pound the tabletop with his fist, ranting and raving until the prominent vein in his forehead looked ready to burst. Bhar knew he wasn't made for such theatrics. The last time he'd tried it, the interviewees had laughed in his face.

"All right. Let's get back to basics. Clive French. Show of hands — who here was friends with him?"

Matthew, Jeremy and Quinton remained still.

"Trevor Parsons. Same question."

Matthew and Quinton kept their arms folded. Jeremy raised a hesitant hand, looking like he expected one of the other young men to slap it down.

"Close friends?" Bhar asked Jeremy.

"No. But he was dating Emmeline, and I've known Em for a while. That's all." Jeremy shrugged.

Quinton rolled his eyes. Matthew chuckled.

"Were you on the rugby team with Mr. Parsons?" Bhar asked the athletes.

"He was our captain," Matthew said. "*Was.*" He looked at Quinton, clearly expecting an answering chuckle, but got none in return. It seemed the obligation to laugh at jokes was a one-way street.

"Were you ever at odds with Mr. Parsons?" Bhar asked Quinton.

"Every bleeding day of the week. He was a right git." Quinton flashed those golden teeth again.

"Ever feel like harming him?"

"Every one of us on the team did at one time or another. Doesn't mean we whacked him at a party, or Clive either. Some nutter broke in and did them. Serial killer. Google it, mate."

Matthew chuckled again. Jeremy offered the same weak, slightly nauseated smile.

"True," Bhar said calmly. "Mind you, I've investigated a fair few murders in my time. You three are extraordinarily calm to have come fresh from the scene. Especially murders that might have been committed at random. That theory suggests that but for the grace of God, any one of you could have been lying dead beside Mr. Parsons and Mr. French."

He checked for even a flicker of reaction. None. Matthew and

Quinton just sat there, exuding self-confidence. Jeremy continued to look at the table. Either they had already processed the knowledge they could have been victims, or they were in denial, or none of them had ever been afraid at all.

But which? Bhar wondered. Matthew seemed useless to focus on; not only was he transparently thick, he was utterly cowed by Quinton. And whatever Quinton lacked in brains, he more than made up for in testosterone. That left Jeremy.

"Did you ever feel afraid, Mr. Bentham?" Bhar asked, words staccato, stabbing Jeremy with the force of his gaze. As he hoped, the young man blinked.

"No. I mean — it all happened so fast. Trevor was dead, but it didn't seem real. Clive was dead in the back garden, that's what they told me, but I never saw him. Just Kyla Sloane and—" Jeremy stopped, eyes widening. Bhar pounced.

"Who? Who else was in the back garden?"

"An older man." Jeremy sighed. "Thirty-five, maybe even forty. Someone's dad, I thought. I saw him in the back garden near Kyla. But by the time the police arrived, he was gone."

"You saw Em's lawyer, that's all," Quinton snorted. "Elephant, or whatever his name is."

"No, Mr. Oliphant got there later." Jeremy's gaze slid away from Bhar's, focusing on his clasped hands. "This guy was taller."

"Any other details you can think of?" Bhar asked. "What sort of clothes did the man wear?"

"He was too far away. A coat, I think."

"There you have it. Bloke in a coat," Quinton scoffed. "Easy to find."

"Jeremy. To the best of your recollection, can you tell me when you saw this man outside the Wardle house?"

Jeremy looked up. His eyes were more bloodshot than ever — he looked ready to cry right then. "Trev was dead. Everyone was panicking. Trying to get themselves together before the cops arrived. I looked out and saw Kyla and a man in the back garden.

Maybe two minutes after Trev came down the stairs. Maybe a little longer."

"I heard witnesses lie to the police to get attention." Quinton poked a finger in the center of Jeremy's chest. "I heard they make up all sorts of lies to get—"

There was a sharp rap on the door. Before Bhar could respond, an administrative assistant opened it, allowing a white-haired man entry. The man carried a leather briefcase and wore an Armani suit.

"I am William Poul, counsel for Mr. Quinton Baylor," the lawyer announced in withering tones, like an aristocrat announcing himself. "I'll need time to speak with my client before this interview continues."

"Fine," Bhar sighed, and left them to it.

CHAPTER SEVEN

"Deepal!"

Bhar twitched, momentarily wrenched from sleep. But he was an expert in resisting unwanted external stimuli, especially when at rest, and immediately sank into slumber again.

"Deepal!"

A series of rapid metallic clicks followed — his bedroom doorknob being tried with enough force to suggest a house fire or home invasion.

"Deepal, I know you can hear me!"

Jolted back to consciousness, Bhar threw aside his blanket and consulted the bedside clock. 6:02 a.m. He'd been asleep for barely three hours. Had his mother, normally cognizant of everything that transpired in her home — even from the depths of her bedroom, snug under her bloody covers in the middle of the bloody night — failed to notice he'd worked twenty-one hours straight?

Flopping down again, Bhar turned his back on the clock, molding his pillow over his ears.

His mobile shrilled from the nightstand. Groaning, Bhar sat

up. Seizing the phone, he considered hurling it against the wall, then thought better of it. Heaven help the detective who ignored a call while working a high-profile murder case.

"This is Bhar," he muttered.

"Deepal, I am not playing with you. Come downstairs at once."

Giving a mighty, strangled groan — the sound of defeat, not defiance — Bhar threw himself out of bed, bare feet thudding hard enough against the wooden floor to rattle the light fixtures over his mother's head. Pulling on his dressing gown, he yanked the bedroom door open with such force, the knob slammed into the opposite wall. A small crater in the plaster deepened incrementally, as it had been doing for years.

"What?" Bhar bellowed down the stairs. "What in the name of God is so important?"

Sharada Bhar appeared at the foot of the staircase. Short and plump with an impish face, she had a genius for regaining her own tranquility after pushing Bhar over the edge. The look she turned on him now was utterly serene.

"There is no need to shout or be profane."

"I haven't yet begun to be profane," Bhar said in tones of menace. He pounded down the stairs, overlarge robe flapping behind him. It had been a gift from his aunt Dhvani — a towering, robust woman who labored under the delusion he was as big and beefy as those professional wrestlers she adored.

"Deepal. Come and sit with me." Sharada's tone suggested she was at peace with the endless suffering that was her lot. At the same time she widened her eyes, shameless as a greeting card puppy.

He emitted another, weaker groan. In Bhar's experience, the phrase "Come and sit with me" always boded ill. His mother habitually began difficult conversations with those words. Over the years, "Come and sit with me" had preceded everything from "This report from your teacher is unacceptable" to "I do not approve of my only son becoming a uniformed thug" to "Because your father ran off to live with that slut, we may lose the house."

"Come," his mother repeated, still with that unnerving tranquility. She ushered Bhar into the front sitting room, where the large screen telly — his gift to them both last Christmas — hung on the wall. Neither he nor Sharada were Christian — at most, they might be described as unobservant Hindus. But since his early teens, when his mother had dragged a freshly cut fir tree into the house, enlisting Bhar's help to hang ornaments on its fragrant green branches, he and Sharada had celebrated a secular Christmas. His father found the whole thing offensive, even obscurely anti-Indian, especially as the yearly event grew to include stringed lights, inflatable reindeer and hideous Christmas jumpers. But Sharada ignored such criticism. She wasn't one to miss out on a great party just because of a religious technicality.

Stifling a yawn, Bhar dropped onto the sofa — corduroy, over-stuffed and older than he was. The telly was tuned to the local news. Onscreen a pretty blond reporter described the axe murders at 14 Burnaby, then breathlessly recounted the trial and acquittal of Sir Duncan Godington. Blurry crime scene photos from the Godington case — the tamest available — flashed onscreen during her narration.

"Deepal, that man nearly ruined your career. You cannot risk letting him succeed this time. You must recuse yourself from this case." To emphasize the seriousness of her request, Sharada took his hand, her liquid black eyes going still wider.

Bhar, who thought of himself as tough, street-smart and emotionally armored, forgot his irritation. When his mum was worried, his knee-jerk response was to try and make things right.

"I don't think recuse is the word you mean. Maybe resign?"

"Recuse, resign, retreat," Sharada barked, her mask of serenity evaporating. "That man is dangerous. Tell Lord Hetheridge you'd rather work on a different case. He'll understand. I know he will."

Sharada, who'd met Hetheridge exactly twice, considered

herself an authority on his character and behavior. Although on both occasions she'd spent fewer than five minutes with the man, she now seemed to confuse him with her own fictional creation — Lord Kensingbard, hero of a romance novel called *The Lordly Detective.*

As a little boy, Bhar had been thrilled and entertained by his mother's flamboyant imagination. Only when he learned to read did he realize some of his favorite fairy tales existed not in his storybooks, but only in Sharada's head. Although English was her second language, Sharada had never shied away from tasks her husband despised — reading contracts, interpreting financial statements and writing business letters. The year Bhar joined the Met, Sharada decided to finally try her hand at fiction. She enrolled in a creative writing course at the Open University, but gave up after one class.

"Those people. They have spoken English all their lives," she'd told Bhar. "They write prettier sentences than me. But they have no idea how to tell a story."

Despite Sharada's initial disapproval of Bhar's chosen career — in her home village, policemen were just a higher class of criminal — her imagination had been piqued by her son's close association with a baron. Thus Sharada's first novel had featured a fictionalized version of Hetheridge: somewhat younger, considerably taller and in Bhar's opinion, disturbingly randy. He'd read the manuscript in an agony of embarrassment — until then he'd never realized what such books contained, much less that *his mum* was capable of writing it. In the end, Bhar had forced himself to lie, telling Sharada it was brilliant. And so his mother, thrilled, had embarked on the aspiring novelist's time-honored path, querying agents and racking up nothing but denials. Hiding his relief as best he could, Bhar carried home pints of cookie dough ice cream and suggested different hobbies, like needle-point or knitting. Then Sharada discovered e-books and self-publishing.

Her first book, *The Lordly Detective*, sold a surprising number of copies in six months. Emboldened, Sharada wrote another romance. This time around, she sprang for a professional editor and cover artist, reasoning that with better presentation, she might double her sales. They had quadrupled. And to Bhar's private dismay, a career based on smoldering looks, heaving bosoms and bare male chests was born.

Thus far Sharada had written twelve romance novels, all under her Anglicized *nom de plume*, Sharon Lacey. Her income from the novels had saved the house, back when Bhar was a newly made detective constable and his father had withdrawn all financial support. Bhar knew the creative outlet had helped Sharada weather her husband's defection to a much younger mistress. But the fact that she frequently mentioned Hetheridge, and kept a framed cover of *The Lordly Detective* in her bedroom, was a clue to his mother's inner workings that Bhar preferred not to examine.

"This case could be important to my career," he said patiently, hoping to make her understand. "I can't run away from it, especially just because Sir Duncan lives near the murder scene. It might just be a coincidence. In fact, it might be something the killer knew before he or she decided to act. Perhaps they counted on his proximity to confuse the thrust of the investigation."

"But what if Sir Duncan has a new protégé? I saw the footage." Sharada gestured toward the telly. "All those half-dressed tarts remind me of *her*."

Sharada had a habit of refusing to name those females who seriously angered her. Her husband's mistress had long been referred to exclusively as "that slut." And this other woman, whom Sharada despised at least as much as her own rival, was spoken of only as "she" and "her," usually in the sort of withering tones that served as auditory italics.

Bhar rubbed his eyes. They were dry and scratchy after his long night, the lids slightly gummed with interrupted sleep.

"Come on, Mum. You know Tessa wasn't a scrubber. She behaved like any nice girl. You thought she was wonderful."

"I thought she was adequate," Sharada said grudgingly, still holding his hand. "But in the end, she was as evil as Sir Duncan."

Bhar smiled, as grateful for her unstinting devotion as he was suffocated by it. "Mum. Let's be honest among ourselves. Tessa fitted me up royally, but she wasn't evil. And for the mistakes I made, I should've got the sack. The only reason I didn't is because the guv spoke up for me. I can't ask him for another favor. As long as he wants me on the case, I'll be there."

"You were young! Foolish! In love!" Sharada cried.

"Love?" Bhar groaned. "That only exists in your books."

"There is real love between a mother and son," Sharada said. "So I say this with love. If you continue as a part of this investigation, and Sir Duncan proves to be involved, you will be considered a detriment to the case. Can't you see Lord Hetheridge would thank you for requesting a reassignment?"

Bhar stared at his mum, surprised by her acuity in matters he'd assumed beyond her understanding. For all her protests about despising politics and finding the Met's infrastructure impossibly dense, she had checkmated him. If Sir Duncan was even peripherally involved in the murders at 14 Burnaby, Bhar's presence on the investigation team would be a defense counselor's dream.

Playing for time, he sniffed the air. "Is that coffee?"

"I thought you wanted to go back to bed."

"Not anymore. If you'll make me breakfast, I'll tell you what we know so far."

CHAPTER EIGHT

Detective Sergeant Kate Wakefield arrived back at the Yard just before seven the next morning. She was unsurprised to find Hetheridge already at his desk, his neglected breakfast plate pushed away. There'd been some murmurings about Hetheridge's singular habit of bringing in breakfast each morning. A couple of anonymous complainants had suggested *all* officers be required to eat together in the canteen, not merely to cut costs but to promote interdepartmental unity. Hetheridge had responded with a single concession — paying for the catered daily breakfast out of his own pocket. It wasn't that he considered himself or his team above rubbing shoulders with the other detectives. He simply preferred to work while he ate.

That, and he can't abide the canteen's rubbery eggs and cold toast, Kate thought with a smile.

Reading glasses positioned slightly down the bridge of his nose, Hetheridge was intent on his computer monitor. Though his shirt and tie were fresh, that signified nothing. The ghastly Mrs. Snell, revenant of an age when secretaries stood in for wives whenever necessary, might have provided him with that incandescently white shirt and blue striped tie. And if Mrs. Snell somehow failed to fulfill her calling, Hetheridge's devoted valet, Harvey, would have hurried to New Scotland Yard with a mini-wardrobe in tow. What was it about Hetheridge that made people cheerfully, spontaneously want to serve him?

"Work all night, guv?"

Hetheridge smiled. "Why, DS Wakefield. You're quite punctual this morning."

"Tony." Kate enjoyed the way his pale eyes gleamed when she committed the tiny infraction of using his Christian name. "Have you even slept?"

"Sleep when I'm dead. Or this afternoon, whichever comes first. Coffee and breakfast await you, as always," he added, looking mildly surprised that she had not yet loaded up a plate.

"Ate on the run this morning," Kate lied, trying to ignore the aphrodisiac aroma of strong coffee and a wide array of breakfast foods, including sausage, eggs and her childhood favorite, fried bread. Truth was, her favorite slacks were a shade tight, and that was a situation that had to be arrested, post-haste. Especially since the possibility of being seen *au naturel* seemed increasingly likely. When and if she and Hetheridge took their relationship to the next level, Kate was determined to look as good as a stint of short-term starvation could render her.

A second glance at Hetheridge's neglected plate revealed several tempting morsels, including buttered toast, eggs over easy and a wedged orange. Kate tried to ignore each distinct aroma. "You don't seem to have much of an appetite, either, guv."

Hetheridge cast a longing look at the plate. "Last thing I need," he rumbled, tossing his linen napkin over the food and concealing it from view. "Besides, I've been composing my preliminary report."

"I'll have mine for you by noon," Kate said, taking a seat. "But as far as motive, it still boils down to a big question mark. On the face of it, Trevor Parsons and Clive French have nothing in common. They attended the same university but shared no classes. Parsons majored in communications; French had a double major, engineering and maths. This morning I was so wrapped up thinking about them, I nearly struck the boot of some slow plonker ahead of me, trying to imagine how our two victims might be connected."

"Must they be?" Hetheridge leaned back in his chair. From his tone Kate knew it was a genuine query, not a veiled rebuke. And even if it had been a rebuke, Kate would not have been deterred from her opinion. Especially so early in the game, when one point of view was as valid as any other.

"Same mode of death. Same venue," she said, ticking off the points on one hand. "Same time, approximately. Same murder weapon ..."

"Precisely the same murder weapon," Hetheridge said. "I noticed that upon closer inspection. Each axe was previously unused, I think, although we must wait for the FSS to confirm that. One axe still bore a UPC price sticker from W. C. Marsden's. Do you know the company?"

"Never heard of it."

"Nor I. Looked it up. Appears to be a family-run hardware shop in Peckham," Hetheridge said. "I'll send some PCs down there this afternoon to check it out. I suppose it's too much to ask that the owners might have CC surveillance tapes of their customers. Much less some recollection of a young man seeking the best tool for splitting skulls. But you never know."

"A young man, eh?" Kate pounced on the word. "So you've decided our killer is male?"

Hetheridge, who'd apparently used the noun unconsciously, considered for a moment. "For some reason — yes. The crime seems masculine to me — the brutality, the need for a certain degree of upper body strength, the brazen aspect of killing two people during a party. And the choice of weapon — an axe — is plainly masculine."

Kate snorted. "Ever hear of Lizzie Borden?"

"Touché," Hetheridge smiled. "But she was part of a long murderesses' tradition ..."

"... Which consists of slaughtering inconvenient family members behind closed doors." Kate smiled back. She'd heard Hetheridge say that before, when he'd lectured to her class back in her academy days. "True. Whereas Trevor Parsons and Clive French weren't related and had no relatives at the party, at least as far as we yet know. You don't suppose French and Parsons were connected by a mutual partner? A romantic partner, I mean?"

"Perhaps. But tell me this." Hetheridge swiveled his computer monitor to face Kate. She found herself staring at recent photos of Trevor Parsons and Clive French, no doubt provided by the victims' families. Trevor, kitted out in his rugby uniform, grinned at the camera, a golden trophy lifted in triumph. Square-jawed and tanned with sun-bleached hair, he looked like the perfect companion for Emmeline Wardle. Clive, by contrast, was just a disconnected white face staring into a webcam. He kept his mouth shut to conceal his buck teeth and wore a baseball cap to hide his receding hairline, but Kate knew him by his chubby cheeks and weak chin.

"Would you say these young men are likely to be connected by a mutual partner?"

"No." Kate crossed her arms over her chest. "So. Here's what we have so far. Emmeline Wardle, Trevor's girlfriend, screams herself hoarse when she sees him die but doesn't want to be detained under the same roof as his body. What's your opinion, based on her interview? Was Ms. Wardle genuinely distraught?"

Hetheridge shook his head.

"Do you think she may have had a hand in Trevor Parsons' murder?"

"I don't know. I do know she called Clive French a black-mailing little toad," Hetheridge said. "And she was well aware that

Sir Duncan was her neighbor. Yet she told me specifically — so specifically, her barrister now claims it never happened — that if Sir Duncan killed her guests, she did nothing to precipitate it."

"Bizarre."

"Oh, yes. The piss tests are backed up, and we're overloaded with formal complaints, but in a day or two we should have Ms. Wardle's tox screen. Either she's an unusually belligerent young woman, or she was high on stimulants. Meth, or cocaine."

"Kyla Sloane seemed perfectly sober, so I waived the piss test," Kate said. "But overall, her demeanor was much too calm. Answered my questions like a professional witness. Only showed remorse over a broken vase. Think about it, guv. We have two dead males and two very suspicious females. Are you sure you want to hang your hat on the notion of a male killer?"

"Yes." Hetheridge stood up and stretched, fighting back a yawn. "Not merely for the circumstantial reasons I named, but because of Emmeline Wardle's comment. Taken in context with DS Bhar's report, an exploration of Sir Duncan Godington's possible involvement is now inevitable."

"Bhar?" Kate repeated. "What do you mean?"

Hetheridge looked surprised at himself. "Perhaps I'm getting too old for all-nighters. Here. Have a look at this transcript of his interview with three witnesses — Matthew Bice, Jeremy Bentham and Quinton Baylor." Returning to his seat behind the desk, Hetheridge opened the document for Kate to read off his computer monitor.

"That's interesting," Kate said when she'd finished. "A man in the back garden with Kyla?"

"And Clive French's body almost certainly moved from the spot where he died."

"I have to admit, just on the facts alone, it all seems rather cold-blooded," Kate continued. "The murders are committed in a public venue, in close proximity to dozens of potential witnesses …"

"Who must also be considered suspects."

"Exactly. Talk about muddying the waters," Kate said. "Plus, the crime scene included a huge supply of drugs and alcohol. Therefore, most of these witnesses-slash-suspects were in a state of reduced inhibitions during the time of the murders. Who knows whom they argued with, flirted with, even went to bed with? From what I saw, most of the guests acted either terrified or guilty as sin.

"Of course," Kate continued, warming to her subject, "under ordinary circumstances, entering a public place with two axes in hand might be considered bizarre rather than cold-blooded. Except at this one time of year. At a Halloween party complete with rubber rats, joke blood, plastic body parts — and plastic axes, too, right?"

"Right," Hetheridge said. "We'll have to reference the crime scene photos to be absolutely sure, but yes, I seem to recall fake axes. Not to mention the fact virtually every last one of the male party guests had a backpack. Not surprising, since they were all students. And a backpack or large satchel would make it easy to bring real weapons onto the scene."

"So in this scenario, Murder Boy is an invited guest," Kate said. "And at least nominally a friend of Emmeline's …"

"Murder Boy?" Hetheridge raised an eyebrow.

"Have to call him something. Right. Murder Boy does Clive in the back garden. By the time Kyla Sloane finds the body, Murder Boy's upstairs, doing Trevor Parsons in the attic. Probably he means for Trevor to die there. That way Murder Boy can slip back into the party, maybe even hook up with another guest to give himself an alibi. Best-case scenario, neither corpse will be discovered until dawn. MB probably never dreamed Trevor would have the strength to blunder down the stairs with the axe still in his head."

"Wouldn't he? If MB, as you call him, hated Trevor enough to kill him, wouldn't he know Trevor was an athlete in peak condition?"

Kate shrugged. "Statistically, murderers never plan more than five minutes past the act itself."

"Statistically, this case is almost certain to prove an aberration," Hetheridge said. "And Trevor *did* blunder down the stairs to die in front of everyone. Yet there's no evidence MB panicked as a result. Quite the opposite. If your scenario is correct, MB rejoined the party, cool as you please, and accepted his interview along with the rest. Begging the question — did MB betray himself during his initial interview? Can we sift through those statements and find something amiss? Or is MB so calm, so perfectly controlled, he'll always think before he speaks? Even if confronted again and again?"

"You mean the way Sir Duncan Godington did?" Detective Sergeant Paul Bhar asked from the doorway.

"Precisely." Hetheridge leaned further back in his chair. It was clearly such an ingrained habit, especially when his mind was working double-quick, Kate doubted he even realized he was doing it. Listening to the well-worn chair creak in protest, she suspected he might one day lean back a bit too far, and end up landing on his ancestral dignity. God knew Bhar was counting on it.

Except today Bhar looked rather less mischievous than usual. On the way to work he'd purchased a grande drink from Starbucks, doubtless a creamy, sugary latte. In Kate's half-starved state, the mystery beverage's aroma was almost pornographic.

"Composure and affability were Sir Duncan's signatures. Along with his good looks," Bhar added, rolling his eyes.

"Hey! Can't believe I forgot you had a role in the Sir Duncan legend." Kate grinned to let Bhar know that yes, she was unabashedly curious. "The guv hasn't spilled a word, beyond the fact that you were once assigned to the case. So let's hear it."

"Pull the other one," Bhar snapped. "Kate. Please. How can you not know?"

Kate's grin widened. "I have exactly two snouts here at the Yard. Our guv," she gestured to Hetheridge like a spokesmodel showing off a car, "and intrepid young detective Paul Bhar. So if the guv hasn't told me and you haven't told me, I have no way of knowing, now have I?"

"You only have yourself to blame if you have no friends." Bhar sounded uncharacteristically harsh. "So the lads hazed you in the beginning. Get over it. Forget past slights, stop being so prickly and if someone tries to make small talk with you, meet them halfway! Stop bucking like you're under interrogation, for heaven's sake!"

Kate's smile didn't falter. Inside, however, she felt like she'd suffered a hard slap — the kind that didn't ache until the initial numbness wore off. What did Bhar mean by all that?

"Sorry, Kate." Bhar flopped into the chair beside her. "That was out of bounds. When I spend too much time with my mum, I start to sound like her. And God knows she didn't let me get much sleep," he added, taking a sip of his drink.

"No problem." Kate kept her tone light. Had Bhar really just called her prickly? Accused her of holding grudges and refusing olive branches? "Forget I asked."

"No, I'll tell you. But — long story short." Taking a deep breath, Bhar trained his gaze on the corner of Hetheridge's magnificent mahogany desk. "While I was assigned to Sir Duncan's case, I started seeing his ex-girlfriend, Tessa Chilcott. In the course of our relationship," Bhar drew in another deep breath, "I told her things no one outside the investigation should have known. Tessa passed the information on to Sir Duncan. He informed his legal team, and they used that knowledge to get him off. They also ..."

"*Some* of that knowledge," Hetheridge cut across him.

Bhar shrugged.

"Sir Duncan's legal team was excellent," Hetheridge told Kate. "Naturally, they made the most of what they should never have had. But there is no question Sir Duncan was acquitted of triple murder chiefly due to a lack of direct physical evidence. And also, in no small measure, due to his composure and personal charm. The jury liked him. A factor that cannot be underestimated. And like lightning, neither bottled nor bought."

"Sir Duncan's legal team also claimed I had a personal vendetta against their client," Bhar continued, still not looking at Kate. "They argued the obvious point — since the girl in question, Tessa Chilcott, clearly preferred Sir Duncan to me, I responded by manufacturing evidence to fit him up. Of course, by the time this went to trial, I was off the case, and the prosecution downplayed my role in the investigation. They argued that I had no idea Tessa Chilcott was Sir Duncan's ex. They never admitted any wrongdoing on my part at all. But that was for the courtroom. The truth is, I came *this close* to the sack. The only thing that saved me was my good old Asian surname." Bhar managed a transparently false grin. "If I'd been called John Smith, I'd have been chucked into the street."

"You don't know that," Hetheridge said.

"Had to be. The only other thing that could have saved me was if someone up the chain of command intervened. And I had no friends in high places." Lifting his head, Bhar looked Hetheridge in the eye. "Sure couldn't have been my old guv. He refused to work with me afterward. Called me a ruddy idiot."

"I know. I called you the very same thing," Hetheridge said lightly. "Mind you, I say that as a man whose own professional conduct has been damned foolish from time to time. At the end of the day, it no longer matters. Whoever or whatever saved you, Paul, you've proven yourself worthy. This case will resurrect the memory of that bloody mess, but only briefly, I suspect. You've put the ugliest portion of the gossip to rest through your own merits."

High praise indeed, coming from the guv, Kate thought. He wasn't known for spooning honey onto harsh truths — the performance reviews he'd written about previous subordinates were famously unsparing. She should have felt proud for Bhar, but instead she felt a stab of jealousy. Besides — prickly? Grudge-bearing? *Her?*

"So whatever happened to Tessa Chilcott?" Kate asked Bhar, unable to resist poking him in his soft spot. "Did she hook up with Sir Duncan after his acquittal? Or come crawling back to you?"

"Neither. They stayed friends without becoming involved again, from what I could gather," Bhar said coolly. "Tessa lived on his estate for a time, drove his cars, etc. She and I never spoke again."

"Sounds like you kept up with her, though," Kate said. From the corner of her eye, she saw Hetheridge shake his head almost imperceptibly. Why? Did she come off like a prickly, grudge-bearing witch to him, too?

"I mean, if it comes to it," Kate continued, watching Bhar's face, "maybe you should question Ms. Chilcott in regards to this case. If only to show you survived a knife in the back. That your career's still thriving, despite her best efforts?"

"No need," Bhar continued, taking another sip of his drink. "Tessa's renewed friendship with Sir Duncan didn't last long. Then she stabbed a stranger to death and was committed soon after to a psychiatric hospital. There she remains. Probably for life, unless she's improved in the last year or so."

Appalled, Kate glanced at Hetheridge for assistance. His expression was completely inscrutable. Yet something in those ice blue eyes seemed to say, *I did try and warn you. Dig your own self out.*

"I see. Well. Right. Which psych hospital?" Kate asked Bhar.

She expected him to demand how that could possibly be any of her concern, but he didn't. Perhaps something in her crisp, businesslike tone lent the question legitimacy.

"Parkwood."

"I knew it had to be that, or St. Joseph's. My older sister's at Parkwood."

"Is that so?" Bhar feigned interest rather poorly. "Is your sister a doctor or a ward sister?"

"Neither. She's a resident." Kate gave Bhar a moment to absorb her meaning. She'd never told anyone this outside her own meager family, or beyond those who absolutely had to know, like paid carers and social workers. "Maura's a paranoid schizophrenic."

"I'm sorry," Bhar murmured.

Kate risked a quick glance at Hetheridge. He said nothing.

"Well. Yes. Thanks." Kate forced out the words from long habit. "Maura self-medicated her early symptoms with drugs — street drugs, mostly heroin — but eventually no one could cope with her and she had to be committed. It's dreadful, seeing someone you care about disappear into a place like that. Even a decent place, a place where they try to do right by the residents, is still what it is — one of *those* places, if you get me. I'm sure you despised Tessa for what she did to you, Paul. But I know you wouldn't have wished a fate like that on her. Not even if you wanted her dead."

Bhar looked at the floor.

Kate, exhausted by her impromptu speech, had no idea where to go next. She also felt reluctant to turn back and meet Hetheridge's gaze, now that she'd impulsively revealed why she had custody of her eight-year-old nephew, Henry. She didn't want Hetheridge's pity. In fact, she couldn't bear it.

"Well. Thank you both," Hetheridge said in his coolest tones. "Not that all this family background isn't fascinating, but we seem to have wandered far afield. DS Bhar, before you arrived, DS Wakefield and I had gravitated, unbidden, to the notion of a killer who was also an invited guest to Ms. Wardle's party. Someone who saw the event as an opportunity to commit double murder and arrived prepared to do so. But we have yet to seriously discuss the other possibility. That an intruder entered the Wardle property by way of the garden, killed Clive French, slipped into the house, killed Trevor Parsons, then legged it amidst the resulting chaos."

"You mean an intruder other than Sir Duncan?" Kate asked.

"Yes. No. Either," Hetheridge smiled. "The PCs on-scene claimed they caught each and every escapee and dragged them back. Suppose they didn't? Are we remiss in failing to discuss the possibility of an intruder? Especially in a confused scene filled with drugs and alcohol? A setting in which a simple disguise — perhaps just a rubber Halloween mask — might allow a total stranger to pass through?"

CHAPTER NINE

The possibility of an intruder in the French-Parsons case meant New Scotland Yard would muster a more extensive team effort than DS Wakefield had yet participated in. If the inquiry went on long enough, or kept expanding, it was entirely possible that she and DS Bhar might end up supervising ten or twenty subordinates each. The idea made Kate's ambitious side, never dormant for long, perk up. During her first major investigation as a member of Hetheridge's team, she'd distinguished herself by making the intuitive leaps necessary to break the case. She'd also chased after a hunch without proper backup and nearly got herself killed in the bargain. How sweet it would be to fully redeem herself in the course of the French-Parsons investigation. To prove to everyone, including herself, that she hadn't got lucky, that she wasn't just a one-off...

With a start, Kate realized Hetheridge was still speaking. Surprised at herself for losing the thread, Kate sat up straight to listen.

"... anything FSS is prepared to provide. Anything the victims carried on their persons, if they appear to have been robbed by the killer, et cetera," he said. "It may help determine if there actually was some connection between the two men.

"Now. Detective Bhar, I understand Ms. Wardle has been released into the custody of her parents. Given the nature of her arrest and the fact she appears bent on suing the Met as a whole, as well as me personally," Hetheridge permitted himself a small smile, "I shan't be conducting her second interview myself. Read my report and go in my place. See what you can winkle out of her." He glanced from Bhar to Kate. "Questions?"

"Just one. Sir Duncan," Bhar said. "We can't ignore the fact he lives right next door to the crime scene. God knows the media is already in a feeding frenzy. May I assume we'll be questioning him before much longer?"

"Absolutely. Tomorrow night, as a matter of fact, if all goes as planned," Hetheridge said.

"Tomorrow night?" Kate echoed. She could tell how much he relished his subordinates' surprise, even if Bhar could not.

"Indeed. Sir Duncan is to be guest of honor at his sister's Halloween party," Hetheridge continued. "Her home is in Mayfair — a stone's throw from mine, as a matter of fact. My good friend Lady Margaret Knolls, who's invited to every event worth the bother of attending, has managed to secure an invitation for me and a guest. I'd like Kate to accompany me. Together we can ambush Sir Duncan in a venue where his social instincts will require him to answer our questions with all due courtesy."

"What about all due honesty?" Bhar asked.

"No venue on earth can guarantee that. Still, I feel if I speak to Sir Duncan — if I look him in the eye — I can determine if he's a crucial piece of the puzzle, or just another blind alley," Hetheridge said.

Soon after, Bhar left to check on the Incident Room, then re-interview Emmeline Wardle. This left Kate the opportunity to speak to Hetheridge alone — or would have, had Mrs. Snell not chosen that moment to come in. Her pin curls were slightly bluer, Kate noticed, and she wore more makeup than usual. Somehow Mrs. Snell's thin lips looked even smaller when painted with so much red.

"Hot date tonight, Mrs. S?" Kate asked.

The look Mrs. Snell turned on her could have frozen lava. "I beg your pardon, detective sergeant?"

Hetheridge cleared his throat. "I do hate to be a bother, Mrs. Snell, but if you could post this right away, overnight, I'd be ever so grateful. Also — Assistant Commissioner Deaver's birthday approaches. If you could look into something appropriate for him, that would be wonderful."

"Of course, Chief Superintendent." Mrs. Snell smiled her ghastly smile for Hetheridge. Then she swept out of the office without sparing Kate so much as a glance.

"I do wish," Hetheridge sighed as soon as his administrative assistant was gone, "you would reconsider this habit of teasing the poor woman. She's done nothing to deserve it."

"She's the leader of a vast army of the undead," Kate countered. "And she hates me."

"God knows why. May I presume you intend to spend the day in some useful manner? Re-interviewing Kyla Sloane, perhaps, about the phantom man in the Wardles' back garden?"

"Not until I've done all my research. FSS hasn't released any data from the house's CCTV cameras, for one thing. But did I hear you right? Am I accompanying you to some sort of society gala?" Kate asked. Her tone was perfectly professional. Inside, however, she was terrified by the prospect of appearing in "society" — whatever that actually meant — on Hetheridge's arm.

"Yes." Hetheridge used the brisk tone Kate now recognized as one of his absolute commands. "See that you wear something appropriate. Black, body-conscious. Simple. Use a rental agency and put the fee on your expense account. Jewelry should be one piece only, and dramatic. Contact Lady Margaret if you need assistance in that area. She's offered to lend you the right sort of things."

Kate felt her jaw drop. With a supreme effort, she managed to close her mouth. "Well. I see. Any advice on my hair, guv? Or can that be left to my discretion?"

"Up. Elegant. Ask a stylist to give you a French twist."

"Right." To Kate's horror, she felt herself beginning to blush. "Well. Brilliant. I don't know whether I should be relieved by your practicality or insulted by your assumption I don't know how to dress myself."

"Relief is the correct emotion. Believe me. I've suffered through more of these affairs than I can count," Hetheridge said. "If you don't blend with the crowd, you might as well be in sackcloth and ashes. Which would make no difference to me — except a detective in sackcloth and ashes has lost her predatory advantage. Kate — Sir Duncan knows me. He doesn't know you. My plan is for you to slip up on him. If you turn up looking like a copper on the job, he'll be on alert from the start."

"You've forgotten how I speak. My accent isn't exactly Mayfair. Shall I take a gander at *My Fair Lady*? Memorize the best bits of *Pretty Woman*?"

"Nonsense. Kate." Hetheridge rose, crossing to the other side of the desk. A kiss, Kate realized, astonished all over again. The arrogant, blue-blooded son of a gun expected a kiss.

"I hope you'll be moved to consider the occasion something of a date, rather than merely a working assignment," Hetheridge said, leaning closer.

Kate gave an unladylike snort. "Not bloody likely!" Her East End bray, usually under tight control, came through loud and clear as she snatched up her coat and bag. "Sorry, guv, but what you've just described sounds like nothing but a pain in my arse."

And with that Kate strode off, closing Hetheridge's door a bit too hard and ignoring Mrs. Snell's wide smile.

~

No one at Forensic Services seemed inclined to drop what they were doing and answer Kate's questions about initial findings in the French-Parsons case, so Kate had to settle for leaving her name and mobile number. With no desire to turn a corner and run into Hetheridge anytime soon, she wandered down to the third floor, where a bullpen of minimally appointed desks were up for grabs for any officer who needed them. Each desk, as greasy and battle-scarred as a primary school reject, was allotted a telephone, a slow computer, a grotty old mouse and an even grottier old mouse pad.

Settling into a desk near the back corner, Kate found some previous user had replaced the blue Met Police Service mouse pad with a *Hot Jugs* version featuring a bare-breasted cover girl. Even the computer's standard Met wallpaper had been replaced with a new background — a topless woman who was bare south of the border, too. Wearing a constable's hat, she fondled a black police baton as if she might kiss it, or worse. The caption read, RECRUIT ME AND SACK THE SAGGY MAN HATERS.

Kate bit her lip. She didn't mind if her mostly male colleagues enjoyed dirty pictures or an un-PC joke. And when it came to criticizing such behavior, God knew the Met's females had to tread lightly. The old boy crowd drooped like limp fish fingers when confronted, whining to Assistant Commissioner Deaver and anyone else who would listen, "Those birds have no fecking sense of humor!" Topless gals on a mouse pad? Kate didn't care. Officer Sexy as computer wallpaper? She'd seen worse. But that caption? No. That took the joke one step over the line. Why did the old boy crowd always have to drag their adolescent fantasies into the real world?

Why do they pretend they'd rather serve with strippers instead of so-called saggy man-haters like me? Kate, neither overweight nor a man-hater—usually—had given up correcting the assumptions about what sort of woman chose the Met as a career. She no longer cared if her colleagues disapproved of her body type or harbored stereotypical notions about gender roles. What infuriated her was the seemingly indestructible notion that for female officers, sexual availability trumped skill, courage and dedication to duty.

Heaven help these men if they were ever held to the same standard, Kate thought. *Most of them could stand to lose a stone or two. Even then, they'd need new clothes and a celebrity stylist to make them presentable. Lucky me — I work with the only two attractive men at the Yard.*

Of course, that wasn't exactly fair. And since both Hetheridge and Bhar were on her personal no-fly list, Kate pushed the thought away. Glancing around to make certain she was unobserved, Kate logged in with her old super's ID — she'd overheard DCI Vic Jackson boasting about his password, "anaconda" — and spent ten happy minutes selecting new wallpaper. When she was finished, it seemed DCI Jackson had re-adorned the computer with Officer Blow Me. This magnificent male specimen — perfect pecs, six-pack abs and one of the largest male appendages Kate had ever seen — was completely nude except for his unmistakable constable's hat. Another young man, fully uniformed, was waiting open-mouthed to administer the required service. Kate added the caption DCIs DO IT ON THEIR KNEES. She only wished she could be a fly on the wall when her loathsome former guv was confronted, once the IT department fingered him as the culprit.

Buoyed by her bad deed, Kate logged into the main Met database as herself, determined not to stew about Hetheridge, the gala or what his assumptions — much less her reaction to those assumptions — boded for their fledgling relationship. Better to contemplate murder.

And since FSS works slower in real life than on telly, maybe it's time to reacquaint myself with the Sir Duncan Godington case ...

Kate logged into HOLMES for the basics, widening her search via Google as necessary. Once she started reading, it all came back to her, so familiar she was surprised she'd ever forgotten.

The triple murder had been discovered on a Christmas morning, five years past. Sir Raleigh Godington, a baronet as well as an international financier, was found dead in the grand salon of his country estate in Surrey. Also dead: his heir, Eldon Godington, and his butler of twenty-eight years, Philip Jergens. The scene was a bloodbath that seemed to spring from a desperate tabloid editor's fevered psyche; many of the details were too grisly for even the filthiest rag to describe. Of course, HOLMES contained them all, along with the photographic and digitized evidence.

Sir Raleigh had been hacked limb from limb. Eventually the chief medical examiner decided the murder weapon was a machete, though the murder weapon was never recovered, Kate noted. And Sir Raleigh's head had been split down the middle.

But not clean down the midline like French and Parsons, she thought. *Still — is this a coincidence? Or a clue?*

Unlike Clive French and Trevor Parsons, Sir Raleigh had been attacked from the front, by a perpetrator of roughly the same height. According to the chief medical examiner, the blade had been only moderately sharp. The semi-blunt blade had connected with Sir Raleigh's face several times. The damage had been so extensive, Kate stared helplessly at the crime scene photos, unable to discern a face in the ruin that remained.

A personal crime. When the face is destroyed, it's always personal, Kate thought, remembering her training. *With French and Parsons, their faces were left intact.*

Sir Raleigh had also been disemboweled, Kate read. Aware of the effect this news would have on the jury, Sir Duncan's legal team had floated the notion of a sinister intruder. They'd suggested a latter-day Jack the Ripper was responsible, a madman who'd dismantled the corpse with privileged medical knowledge. But one glance at the crime scene photos had put that notion to rest. Sir Raleigh's butcher could only be described as an enthusiastic novice. Bits of organs and entrails were strewn all over the grand salon. Some even decorated the branches of Sir Raleigh's twelve-foot Christmas tree. Among the star-shaped ornaments and silver tinsel, a length of intestine hung, somewhat less than festive.

Sir Raleigh's sexual organs had also been removed. Like the machete, they had never been recovered, prompting the press to screech, "SIR DUNC A CANNIBAL?" in that end-of-the-world-size typeface Kate so despised. But evidence the male organs had actually been eaten was, of course, nonexistent. And as she gazed on the scene with an officer's eye, Kate wouldn't have been surprised if they had simply been misidentified in the overload of bowels, blood and brains.

The crime scene photos of Sir Raleigh's son and heir, Eldon Godington, were equally grim. He'd been sawed in two pieces across the abdomen, like a magician's trick gone awry. His frozen expression, as well as his curled, clawlike hands, suggested Eldon might have survived the process, only to die of shock as he stared at the final result. Kate, whose stomach was reasonably strong, tasted bile at the idea. She was forced to hurry on to the analysis of the last body: the butler, Philip Jergens.

According to the medical examiner, Jergens had been poisoned. He collapsed in the grand salon, prompting the quick attendance of his employers. In the midst of such chaos the murderer had struck, probably first on Jergens — his back bore two enormous stab wounds from the presumptive machete. Then Sir Raleigh and Eldon had faced the blade.

Officers drifted in and out of the bullpen as Kate read, some talking loudly into their phones, others bursting into raucous laughter. Ordinarily she didn't care for such close, overheated quarters, or so much noise pollution. But the Godington case was so compelling, Kate barely smelled the takeaway curry some other detective opened nearby for his lunch.

Fixing an exact time of death was always tricky for medical examiners. In the case of Sir Raleigh, Eldon Godington and Philip Jergens, that difficulty had been compounded by two factors: the grand salon's roaring fire and the great house's excessive gas heat. Someone had cranked the thermostat up to eighty. Therefore, the chief medical examiner's best guess for the time of the murders was anywhere between midnight, December 23, and 6 a.m., December 25. Naturally, Sir Duncan's legal team had made the most of such uncertainty.

"My client arrived in Surrey on December 24 around 9 p.m.," the lead barrister had argued. Did anyone actually believe that after visiting his girlfriend in Paris, Sir Duncan had touched down at the airport, sped home, committed triple murder with a machete and rushed off again to enjoy a round of parties with his old schoolmates? And if he had, where was the physical evidence? Where was the weapon, the bloody clothes, the forensic traces in Sir Duncan's vehicle or his London townhouse?

Where, indeed? Kate thought. Films and books were filled with supernaturally self-assured psychopaths. In the real world, violent personalities usually snapped, acted on impulse and left behind an obvious trail, ineffectually trying to cover up after the fact. Either Sir Duncan was innocent or he was that rarest of creatures — simmering with violence yet controlled enough to plan his triple slaughter to the nth degree.

Often as closing arguments neared, the Crown would catalogue a suspect's damning behavior after the fact — threatening comments, obstructive behavior and self-serving maneuvers. More than once Kate had seen a suspect convicted, not because the physical evidence was unassailable but because his conduct afterward had been so transparently guilty. But as far as the Metropolitan Police Service was concerned, Sir Duncan had been cooperation personified. He submitted to every request for questioning, formal or informal, and allowed his townhouse to be twice searched without a warrant. Even after his arrest, he spoke calmly to the press before his booking, releasing the following statement:

"I am saddened the police mistakenly imagine I had anything to do with the unthinkable murders of my father, brother and family butler. However, I remain convinced the truth will come out, and the real killer will be brought to justice. In the meantime, I will gladly assist the police with their inquiries, as any innocent man or woman would do."

Kate watched that video several times, studying Sir Duncan each time. He was six feet tall and slender, broad-shouldered with a tapering waist. One of those naturally lean men who carried no extra fat, maintaining muscle only with effort. His blond hair was combed straight back from a high forehead; his high cheekbones and square jaw signaled a Teutonic background. Sir Duncan's blue eyes were warm, open, accessible. His mouth was generous — sensuous, even. Never married, he'd been linked to a series of starlets, singers and minor dignitaries. After his arrest he'd nonetheless been the recipient of three marriage proposals and one stalker. The stalker, a sixteen-year-old boy named Ian Burke, had first attempted to gain entry into Sir Duncan's trial by pretending to be a twenty-one-year-old reporter. Phony ID notwithstanding, the teenager had looked perhaps eleven years old in person, putting his masquerade to a swift halt. Later Ian Burke had reappeared on the scene in drag, pretending he was the daughter of a juror, and managed to be seated before a security guard cried foul. Smallish, delicate Ian Burke had been perfectly feminine, it seemed, except for his pesky Adam's apple.

As Kate examined the Crown's prosecution of Sir Duncan, she found it often looked paranoid, if not downright ridiculous. The prosecution had opened by pointing out that Sir Duncan had a chilly relationship with his father.

"What member of the aristocracy does not?" the defense's lead barrister had countered.

Next the Crown had pointed out that Sir Duncan stood to benefit enormously from the death of his brother — a title, ancestral home and considerable wealth.

"What about Sir Duncan's life suggests a love of money?" the defense had countered. "Did he not just spend a year in sub-Saharan Africa, helping to build villages? And another year in Borneo, devoting himself to the Green Party's anti-logging, anti-poaching endeavor? Would a social crusader like Sir Duncan Godington commit unthinkable crimes simply to enrich himself?"

The Crown had been desperate to present another piece of evidence — the unsolved murder of Sir Duncan's nanny when he was only ten years old. But the court had ruled that event inadmissible. Thus the prosecution was reduced to floating a series of unproven scenarios.

Why was there no bloody clothing? Perhaps Sir Duncan had committed the crimes in the nude.

Why had Sir Duncan cooperated with the searches and interrogations? Perhaps he had successfully disposed of the weapon and any other physical evidence.

Why had mates and acquaintances supported Sir Duncan's alibi during the murder timeline? Perhaps they were swayed by his mesmerizing persona. Willing to lie, in other words, for a handsome, charming prince of a man who had a way of making other people feel good about themselves.

Whatever the truth, the jury had finished feeling pretty damned good about themselves, Kate decided. After agonizing behind closed doors for three days, they acquitted Sir Duncan of all charges. Post-trial interviews told the tale as effectively as any crime writer's analysis.

"Sort of bloke all aristocrats should be," said the jury's foreman. "Regular, but gracious. Quality is the word I mean."

"Dead handsome but dead sweet, too." This from the jury's oldest member, a grandmother with sparkling eyes and an enormous vinyl handbag.

"Fitted up by the plods, he were, simple as that," said the man on the street, who favored acquittal by a two-to-one margin.

After the trial, Sir Duncan had expressed gratitude to the jury for perceiving his innocence, and to the nation for rallying behind him. His prepared statement read in part:

"This ordeal has been painful. But not as painful, I must say, as the fate suffered by my beloved father, brother and family butler. My hope is that my trial will be swiftly forgotten, as mistakes should be. And our collective hearts and minds shall be fixed, henceforth, on honoring the true victims in this tragedy."

Oh! Kate was startled by a post-acquittal photograph of Sir Duncan. *Kyla Sloane! So that's where I know her from!*

But no. According to her ID, Kyla Sloane was twenty-one years old. This picture had been snapped by a tabloid photographer just three days after Sir Duncan's acquittal, when Kyla would have been barely sixteen. In the photo, Sir Duncan presided over the opening of an exclusive West End restaurant. A beautiful brunette sat at the table beside him, her thick, wavy hair cascading over her shoulders. Slim and small-breasted, she wore a red gown with spaghetti straps that highlighted her prominent collarbone. Borderline anorexic the girl was, or an aspiring model who lived on sparkling water and no-dressing salads. And a dead ringer for Kyla Sloane, too. Except for a small difference around the nose and upper lip, the resemblance was breathtaking.

The photo's caption named the brunette only as Sir Duncan's friend. It took a photographic reverse-search engine to confirm Sir Duncan's companion was none other than Tessa Chilcott.

No way, Kate thought, even as she knew it was true. Tessa had no breast implants, no Botoxed forehead or veneered front teeth.

The young woman looked starkly real, not to mention fragile, compared to DS Bhar's usual type …

Kate's mobile vibrated from inside her bag. Irritated by the interruption, she snatched it up. "Hey?"

"This is Dennis Chen, calling from Forensic Services," the caller stated in a flat, robotic monotone. "Is that Detective Sergeant Kate Wakefield?"

"It is." Kate added the requisite identifiers needed to retrieve privileged data. Then she listened carefully to what Dennis Chen had to tell her about the ongoing analysis of Clive French and Trevor Parsons.

CHAPTER TEN

D S Paul Bhar decided to tackle Hetheridge's orders right away. He felt jittery and hostile after his all-too-brief sleep, not to mention his mum's concerns and the necessity of confessing his professional sins to Kate. Now he was spoiling for a fight. Re-interviewing Emmeline Wardle in the presence of her parents would probably guarantee it.

From behind the wheel of his car, a dark blue Astra Elegance with a recent wax job, Bhar pulled out his iPhone and rang the Wardles' primary number. A woman answered on the second ring. Mrs. Wardle, who along with her husband had been back in London less than a day, barely listened to his name and request before launching into what sounded like a rehearsed reply.

"I consider it outrageous that Scotland Yard has decided to waste their resources and intelligence — *presumptive* intelligence — harassing a blameless young girl. For the second time in forty-eight hours, I might add." Mrs. Wardle's chirpy voice, not designed for ranting, grated in Bhar's ear. "On the other hand, perhaps I shouldn't argue. Perhaps it would be best if you turned up and let me sort you out. My husband and I have spent thousands of pounds in taxes to provide your salary. Perhaps it's time we looked our employee in the eye and explained that victims have rights, too."

"With all due respect," Bhar ground out, employing a phrase he reserved for those he respected not at all, "the victims in this case were Clive French and Trevor Parsons. Let me assure you, securing justice for Mr. French and Mr. Parsons is uppermost in my mind."

"Is that so?" Mrs. Wardle snapped. "Your supervisors, including *Baron* Hetheridge — yes, I know who he is — have been dreadfully remiss if they haven't advised you about the matter of a certain Greek amphora vase appraised at over two million pounds."

Startled — he'd only just rechecked the list of principal physical evidence — Bhar withdrew his notebook, thumbing through his own neat, closely written notes. "What vase?"

"The vase the Met destroyed when it crashed through my home, violating my privacy and my basic human rights! The vase for which we expect full compensation, or you can be sure the civil suit against Baron Hetheridge will go forward without delay!"

Bhar resisted the temptation to ask, "Are you threatening me?" It had been all over the Yard the next morning — Hetheridge putting the question to Emmeline Wardle, cool as only their guv could be, before ordering her taken into custody. Having spent two minutes talking to Mrs. Wardle, Bhar reckoned that when it came to Emmeline, the acorn hadn't fallen far from the tree. Or his mum's slightly skewed version, "When you are a nutter, your children are nuts, too."

Bhar smiled. Just once he wished he could bring Sharada along during an investigation. Watching her lecture the suspects with bits of mangled folk wisdom would alone be worth the price of admission.

"Mrs. Wardle," Bhar said with all the phony warmth he could muster, "I am shocked to hear about the loss of your priceless family asset. In addition to speaking to your daughter — our most important witness, as I'm sure you're aware — I'd like to discuss the vase. Are you at 14 Burnaby?"

"Of course not." Mrs. Wardle sounded somewhat mollified, as if Bhar had finally pushed the right button. "We just flew back from the French Riviera. The last thing we wanted after a perfectly idyllic holiday was to enter a murder house. We're in Holland Park at present." She rattled off the address, adding, "Be so good as to give us an hour."

"My pleasure." As Bhar started the Astra's engine, a gleam of gold on the passenger seat caught his eye. Ah, yes. A long, blond hair. Closer examination of the passenger side's floorboards revealed a crumpled leaf. This was what came of giving the likes of Kate Wakefield a ride in his usually immaculate car.

Taking an evidence bag from the glove box, Bhar sealed the blond strand and bits of leaf inside. Later, he would confront Kate with proof that she'd broken the rules regarding his beloved Astra. Bhar felt terribly guilty about telling her off, especially in front of the guv. Leaving aside the added dimension of Kate and Hetheridge's extracurricular relationship, to embarrass a colleague in front of her superior was out of line. And saying sorry afterward had been meaningless. How could Kate do anything but accept his apology with the guv sitting right there? Of course, a second *private* apology would be excruciating for them both. Instead he would spring his evidence on Kate and accuse her of deliberately befouling his still-new car. And after they'd had a laugh together, a real laugh, maybe he wouldn't feel like rubbish anymore.

Bhar had been trapped in the creep-and-crawl of midmorning London traffic for more than half an hour when his mobile rang. It was Kate.

"Have you re-interviewed Emmeline Wardle yet?"

"Of course. Popped round by helicopter and videotaped her confession. Wrapping the case in time for tea." Bhar sighed. "Or I'm trapped behind the boot of a very dirty Ford Anglia. Guess which."

"I have some data from FSS. Not official, mind you—just a courtesy report because we're working such a high-profile case. Ready?"

"God, yes." Bhar hoped the fervency of his reply conveyed his real meaning—gratitude that Kate always played fair, even when cheesed off at him. Was Kate prickly and prone to holding a grudge? Yes, and everyone in the Yard knew it, except possibly Kate herself. But her first priority was always solving the case, no matter whom she had to work with or what personal indignities she had to swallow. And such dedication to duty was far rarer than it ought to be.

"First—Clive French always earned top marks at uni," Kate said. "But he was recently placed on academic probation."

"Why?"

"He was accused of helping other students cheat. Providing them with term papers and finished science projects. The investigation was still open when he died," Kate said. "Second, according to his professors and his dorm mate, he was gay."

"So?"

"So he was bullied for it. Even in this day and age, he had to register two formal complaints with the dean's office. That's a motive for murder, isn't it? Suppose Clive came on to the wrong guy. A bloke so insecure in his sexuality, he decided to prove he wasn't gay? As in, with an axe?"

"True. Then again, maybe Clive insulted a bird?" Bhar suggested. "Said no thanks, you're not my type, and wound up paying the price?" Traffic was so slow, Bhar had no difficulty jotting in his notebook and steering simultaneously.

"Not bloody likely," Kate snorted. "You saw Clive. He looked as bad in his family photo as he looked in a body bag. That poor kid couldn't have got lucky in the women's nick with a fifty pound note taped to his willy."

Bhar laughed. "Oh, really? If I'd made the same comment about a female vic, you'd be tutting at me." He imitated the sound, a prissy *tch-tch-tch*, until she laughed.

"Fair enough," Kate agreed. "One more thing about Clive French. Speaking of money, he was packing more than a fifty pound note. He died with nine hundred pounds tucked in the front pocket of his jeans."

Bhar gave a low whistle. "How about that. And didn't Emmeline Wardle call him a blackmailing little git, or thereabouts? I don't suppose there are any useable prints on the money?"

"Of course not. FSS tested them and found all the usual stuff —a million partials, a bunch of random skin cells and a whiff of cocaine. But that last ..." Kate trailed off in a teasing little sing-song.

Bhar grinned. Kate always went a bit giddy when dishing up clues. "By all means, keep torturing me. I have it coming. I was a prat to you this morning. In the guv's office," he admitted, surprising himself.

"Think nothing of it. But be advised, I'll bear a grudge." Kate's tone was featherlight. "Now—would you care to guess what Trevor Parsons had on his person when he died? Also stuffed in the pocket of his y-front. I'll give you a hint: it wasn't cash."

"Let me guess. Cocaine?"

"Brill! And one more thing about our victims," Kate said. "Trevor had sexual intercourse sometime that day, either in the late afternoon or early evening. Probably it doesn't signify—I'll bet the same can be said of at least half the guest list—but there it is. Since Trevor was Emmeline Wardle's one and only, presumably the deed in question was done with her. Because if not ..."

"We have another motive for murder. Now I can't wait to get to Holland Park." Bhar clutched the wheel with both hands. "Mr.

and Mrs. Wardle will be present, you know. Coming off a posh holiday ..."

"Posh?" Kate laughed. "Paul, I know you're hard up for a break, but would you really call Arkansas posh?"

"Arkansas? As in—the United States?" Bhar laughed. "Are you telling me the Wardles were in *Arkansas* when the murders happened?" He had only a vague idea of the place—somewhere in the American South, presumably where chickens roamed dirt roads and buttered grits were served with every meal.

"Confirmed this morning," Kate said. "You know the guv. He has the juniors verify every possible detail that might bear on the case. Especially since the Wardles are threatening to sue him on their daughter's behalf."

"Mrs. Wardle told me they'd just returned from the French Riviera. What were they doing in Arkansas?"

"You'll have to ask them. We should be able to trace some of their movements by requisitioning credit card statements and mobile phone records. But only if we get a warrant," Kate said. "Otherwise, digging any deeper into Mr. and Mrs. Wardle's private life would just make the guv look like he truly is harassing them."

"Oh, I'll ask them, unless they pass a much shinier object in front of my face," Bhar said. "Why should the guv get all the drama? Civil lawsuit, here I come."

The house on Addison Road was, for want of a better word, a mansion. Bhar had expected a detached three- or four-story home with a gated driveway and an enormous back garden. He had not expected a vision in pure white, peaked and gabled like a fairy tale castle. The lawn was still as green as Astroturf; the maple trees had turned red and gold. Even as the security guard buzzed him through the gate, Bhar saw a gardener patrolling the front garden with a rake, clearing up leaves the moment they drifted to earth.

As Bhar emerged from his Astra, the front door opened and a fortyish woman stepped out. He required no introduction to recognize her as Mrs. Wardle—the resemblance was so startling, she could almost have been Emmeline's elder sister. Like her daughter, Mrs. Wardle's hair was straight and blond, falling several inches past her shoulders. Only a little larger than Emmeline—size 10, perhaps, rather than 8—Mrs. Wardle wore a tight T-shirt and black stovepipe jeans. Clearly, mother and daughter frequented the same shops.

"Where's the man I spoke to on the phone? He was English," Mrs. Wardle asked as Bhar climbed the white marble steps. "Name of Barr, I think."

"That was me." He put out his hand, which she ignored. "Paul Bhar, B-h-a-r. And I *am* English. Born in Clerkenwell," he added, unable to resist the chance to irritate her even more.

For a moment Mrs. Wardle looked thwarted, but rallied with admirable speed. "Yes, well, have it your own way. But before you set foot over this threshold, let me make one thing perfectly clear. My daughter is the true victim in this travesty. She's never been in trouble a day in her life. Never been anything but a joy to Mr. Wardle and me. I'm sorry some homicidal maniac killed those boys, but there it is. They're at peace now. My daughter cannot say the same. She has to live with the memory of poor Trevor falling down dead in her home—before her very eyes, Constable."

"Detective sergeant," Bhar murmured, but she took no notice.

"And before you see Emmeline, there's the matter of my amphora vase. Come along! No time to waste!" Closing the door behind him, Mrs. Wardle waved Bhar through the foyer. "Our family barrister is waiting with all the necessary documentation. Lionel! The detective is here to discuss our damages!"

"Well, strictly speaking, I'm here to re-interview Ms. Wardle," Bhar objected, finding himself herded into an airy front parlor larger than the ground floor of his mum's house. He had only a moment to register the basics—parquet floor, vaulted ceiling and a grand piano positioned before the picture window. Then a harried-looking man in a rumpled suit came at Bhar with an armful of papers.

"I'm Lionel Oliphant, family counsel for the Wardles. If Scotland Yard is prepared to take responsibility for the loss of the amphora vase, we should be able to get all the details sorted in less than an hour. Here's the most recent appraisal. And here's a photograph," Oliphant added, showing Bhar a faded snapshot of something that resembled a Victorian chamber pot. "Magnificent, wasn't it? As the appraisal indicates, Lloyd's of London valued the item at 2.1 million pounds ..."

"In 1990," Bhar burst out, pushing aside Oliphant's thumb to see the date at the appraisal's upper left-hand corner. "Mate! You do realize what year this is?"

Mrs. Wardle clapped a hand to her throat, pink lips forming an "O" of disbelief. Mr. Wardle, whiskey in hand, stood up. Judging by the deep red blossoms on his nose and throat, this wasn't his first drink of the day. Oliphant only coughed.

"Timeless items need not be reevaluated every year, Constable."

"*Sergeant*. And be that as it may," Bhar dodged the fountain pen Oliphant tried to thrust into his hand, "I am not here to discuss damages the Wardles believe they sustained during the police investigation. I am certainly not here to sign anything or—"

"Do you lack the authority to handle this, Detective?" Mrs. Wardle snapped. It was necessary for her to take the lead—whiskey had apparently rendered her husband mute. "Shall I ring your superiors and demand an officer with greater powers?"

Bhar took another deep breath. Then he put on his most charming smile, wishing his guv was present to see him gamely swallow the insult.

"Mrs. Wardle, I have sufficient authority to ensure your daughter's interests are correctly represented. I realize that on the night of the murders, there was a misunderstanding with another officer. I would like to take this opportunity to sit down with your daughter and re-interview her from scratch, to be certain no details were taken out of context or overlooked."

"The amphora vase comes first! Nothing is more important!" Mrs. Wardle cried, jerking the papers out of Oliphant's hands and trying to force them into Bhar's. "I have lost a priceless family heirloom and no one will speak with Emmeline until someone from Scotland Yard accepts responsibility!"

"Candace, you cannot issue that sort of condition to the police," Oliphant murmured, lips barely moving. "Emmeline is an adult. She is therefore obligated to assist with their inquiries. To submit to any and all reasonable requests by—"

"Submit?" a voice said from behind them. Bhar turned first.

Emmeline Wardle had been working out. She wore a pink sleeveless T-shirt over a sports bra. Her shorts were the same color pink, matching the "swoosh" on her Nikes. Bhar was surprised by how robust Emmeline looked compared to her mother's prematurely brittle pallor—perhaps they weren't so sisterly after all. Emmeline's blond hair was pulled back in a long braid. She wore no makeup Bhar could detect, nor did she need it.

"Ms. Wardle. Please forgive the intrusion. And accept my condolences on your loss," Bhar said, smiling at Emmeline. It wasn't difficult. She was pretty, haughty, posh and, fortunately, legal. Just his type.

"I'm not into submission." Emmeline met his gaze and held it.

"Well, I don't expect for you to go for my first suggestion. We can negotiate," he replied, captivated, before remembering her parents and lawyer were still present in the room.

"This is unacceptable," Mrs. Wardle snapped. "Mr. Bhar, I want you out of the house this moment!"

"Oh, Mum, do go upstairs and take one of your pills. Take Daddy along, too." Folding her arms across her chest, Emmeline gave Mrs. Wardle an implacable stare.

"We won't be spoken to this way," Mrs. Wardle hissed. Mr. Wardle, Bhar noticed, was already moving toward the distant stairs and Oliphant was gathering up his papers.

"Mum! I witnessed the murder. Not you. Now go upstairs."

"At least allow Lionel to—"

"Lionel didn't stop me from getting arrested, now, did he?"

"I have a prior engagement," Oliphant muttered, exiting without a backward look. Mr. Wardle was halfway to the stairs, ice cubes clinking, having never said a word.

Left alone, Mrs. Wardle blew out her breath in frustration. Her immobile forehead never creased, but tiny lines appeared at the corner of each eye, revealing who was the mother and who was the daughter.

"Very well. Call for us if you need us," Mrs. Wardle told Emmeline, and followed her husband upstairs.

CHAPTER ELEVEN

"Thank God." Emmeline shot Bhar a conspiratorial look. "I swear, if I wasn't moving out in six months, I'd top myself. Now." She tossed herself down on the sofa. "Sorry to turn up in spandex, but I've been working out like a fiend since the murders. It's the only thing that keeps me from going crazy."

"You seem fit," Bhar said, trying to keep his eyes trained on Emmeline's. If he raked his gaze over her well-toned body again, he would cross the line from human male to overreaching authority figure.

"Swim team. Gymnastics. Archery," Emmeline smiled. "Me and Kyla Sloane, since we were both eight years old. Always trying to outdo each other."

"Who's better?"

"I'm a much better swimmer," Emmeline said. "You should see my breast stroke. Better at gymnastics, too. But I can't touch Kyla when it comes to archery."

"Lots of upper body strength needed for archery."

"You'd better believe it." She smiled at Bhar. "So. Are you here to beg my forgiveness for your boss's behavior?"

"Not exactly." Bhar couldn't help grinning at her cheekiness, not to mention the unapologetic sparkle in her blue eyes. "But you're being so reasonable compared to—well, certain others—I'm tempted to give it a go."

"Smart man. I don't suppose you have any ciggies, do you?"

"Actually …" Bhar felt in his jacket's inner pocket. He didn't smoke, not really—if he made it a habit, Sharada would have his head—but he kept cigarettes with him most of the time. Not just for interviewees, but for bar girls. Nothing worse than chatting up a bird in search of a fag and finding oneself empty-handed.

"Thanks." Emmeline held the cigarette between her lips as he lit it. Yes, he had been right—no makeup of any kind. Those flawless pink lips and blooming cheeks were perfectly natural.

Taking a long, satisfied drag, Emmeline smiled at Bhar. "So. What do you want to know?"

Some detectives would use such an opening to cut right to the meat of the interview. If things turned hostile, they'd pivot back to minor details, circling back to the meat as soon as possible. It was a legitimate strategy, one Paul often used for antagonistic or transparently stupid witnesses. But Emmeline didn't strike him as either, so a more linear approach seemed best.

"What made you decide to throw a Halloween party?" Bhar opened his notebook and waited, pen poised.

"I've thrown one every year since I was fifteen." Locating an ashtray, Emmeline balanced it on her lap as she smoked. "People expect great parties from me. The secret to staying popular is giving the people what they want. Half the time, anyway."

"And the other half?"

Emmeline blew out a plume of smoke. "Mess with their minds and keep them guessing."

"Fair enough." Bhar smiled. "According to public records, Sir Duncan Godington bought 16 Burnaby less than a year ago. Did throwing a Halloween party next door to a man acquitted for triple murder make your friends and schoolmates more eager to attend?"

A pause, and a flick of the eyelashes. What came next from Emmeline was probably a lie. "None of them knew."

"Oh, really?" Bhar did his best to sound neutral. "You had a piece of gossip that choice and shared it with no one?"

Emmeline took another deep drag. "How do you think Mummy and Daddy took the news we lived next door to a serial —excuse me, *alleged* serial killer? They wanted to sue him for bringing down property values." She smiled. "Of course, that went up in smoke, so all the families on Burnaby got together and made everyone swear we wouldn't spread the news around. You can see we went ten months before the story went global. Better than I expected, given Mum's big mouth."

"I understand. My mum gets on my nerves sometimes, too," Bhar said. "But yours is very protective, you must admit. Threatening a civil suit in defense of her daughter."

Emmeline tossed her head. "That's all for Mum, not me. You won't see me getting any of the money. I've half a mind not to testify, if it comes to it. Just to see her face when I take the mickey."

"So absolutely none of your friends knew that Sir Duncan lived next door?"

Folding her arms across her chest, Emmeline tapped her cigarette against the ashtray, watching Bhar with narrowed eyes. "Kyla Sloane knew. She knows everything about me. But she never would have said anything."

"What about your boyfriend, Trevor Parsons?"

"No."

"Clive French?"

Emmeline gave a huff. "Of course not. If I've said it once, I've said it a hundred times. Clive wasn't a friend. He wasn't invited. I don't know why he so much as set foot on my property." She stabbed the cigarette toward his notebook. "Write that down!"

Bhar jotted, *More emotional re: French than boyfriend Parsons.*

"Noted. So it is fair to say you disliked him?" Bhar deadpanned. When Emmeline's eyes widened, he grinned. To his pleasure, she grinned back, the tension across her shoulders disappearing.

"You're nothing like that old man. What made you decide to join the filth?" Issuing from her pink lips, the old-fashioned slang sounded sweetly ironic.

The doorbell rang. Emmeline ignored it. By the second ring, Mrs. Wardle was already hurrying down the grand staircase. Emmeline still paid no attention, so Bhar decided to answer her.

"I knew the filth didn't want me, so what can I say? I barged in. Do you think that's what Clive was about? Crashing your party because he knew he wasn't welcome?"

Emmeline frowned.

"Seriously," Bhar urged. "I'll never put all this together if people like you don't give me your ideas—good, bad or indifferent."

"Em," Mrs. Wardle sang out from the foyer. Her heels clicked across the marble as she appeared with a hulking figure behind her. Bhar, rising automatically—his mother had taught him well —was dismayed to see one of the athletes he'd interviewed at Scotland Yard, Quinton Baylor.

"Thank you for coming over so quickly," Mrs. Wardle told Quinton with a hammy emphasis surely intended to ruffle Bhar. "I fret about Em so, I feel better with you around."

"Not a problem, Mrs. W., glad to help," Quinton said crisply, forgetting his Mockney altogether. Clearly when it came to the Wardles, he embraced the Received Pronunciation he'd known since his first words. Then he saw Bhar and the Mockney was back, as if they were meeting one another on the rugby pitch. "Oi! Don't I know you?"

"DS Paul Bhar." Removing his warrant card from his inner

jacket pocket, he held it out for Quinton's perusal, silently wondering if the giant could read.

"Fair enough," Quinton said, frowning as if the effort of taking in so many words had indeed been a bit too much. "Wotcha? Didn't you lot already grill Em on the night of the party?"

"Just a follow-up interview," Bhar said serenely. "I should be done in a quarter hour, if you'd like to wait ..."

Quinton dropped onto the sofa beside Emmeline. "I'll wait right here, thank you." Pulling Emmeline into an embrace, he kissed her full on the lips, turning back to Bhar and grinning for emphasis. "Anything you say to Em, you say to me."

Bhar bit back a sigh. Emmeline, at least, had the grace to appear mildly embarrassed. Quinton was all muscle-bound smugness and Mrs. Wardle looked ready to play the wedding march, if she only had an organ.

"You're not wanted here, Mum," Emmeline said at last, when Mrs. Wardle showed every sign of hovering throughout the end of the interview.

"Shall I send Lionel back in, or—"

"I have this *quite under control*," Emmeline snapped. Biting her lip, Mrs. Wardle stalked back upstairs again.

"Now. Where were we?" Emmeline asked Bhar, as if Quinton hadn't slid a possessive arm around her waist.

"I was given to understand you were dating Trevor Parsons," Bhar said, trying not to sound as inexplicably irritated as he felt.

"She was. Planned to split up with him before he got himself —*deceased*," Quinton said, transparently choosing a new word when Emmeline narrowed her eyes at him. "Now Em's with me. Like it should be. Got a problem with it, officer?"

"No problem. Now. As to where we were," Bhar said, pretending to consult his notes. It would never do to let a Neanderthal like Quinton know he was having an effect. "Ms. Wardle, do you think Clive deliberately crashed your party?"

"Oh, wow. Perfect," Emmeline sighed. "I'm not a grass, I've never been a grass, but the little tosser is dead. Did you know he was in trouble at uni? Being investigated for selling research papers and test answers?"

Bhar nodded.

"Well, Clive had started harassing Trevor for money. Blackmailing him, really. Saying he'd confess to the dean and name Trevor as one of his customers. That would have bounced Trevor off the rugby team, at least temporarily."

"About the team," Bhar said, trying to sound completely offhand, "who stands to be captain now?"

"It's not official yet. But me," Quinton said.

Bhar let that revelation hang in the air, flicking his eyes once to Emmeline.

"That's right. The team traded up. Em traded up, too," Quinton said, giving her a squeeze.

"Get off," she snapped, pulling out of his grasp. When he reached for her again, Emmeline transferred to an overstuffed armchair. "You're lucky I let you get within a meter."

"Spirited. Sort of sweaty after the workout, too. I like it," Quinton leered before turning back to Bhar. "As far as Clive goes, write this down in your little book. The dirty yob probably thought crashing the party was a safe bet with so many witnesses around," Quinton volunteered. "That instead of beating him bloody, Trevor would pay up."

"Yob?" Bhar asked.

"Yeah. Not our sort," Quinton said, which sounded all the more ridiculous when spoken in Mockney. "On scholarships and whatnot for being an egghead. Lives in a council flat, or close enough."

"I see," Bhar said, careful not to let his rising disgust show in his tone. "I'm still unclear about why Clive would be willing to risk collecting on debts in the middle of an investigation. What if Trevor had turned the tables and just come clean? He might have lost his position on the team, but Clive would have been expelled."

"What? Grass on another student and himself, too?" Emmeline looked shocked. "Trevor always settled things privately, like a man."

"Do you know how much money Trevor owed Clive?"

She shook her head. "Once he said it over a thousand pounds. Then he said he was joking. Surely it wasn't that much."

Parsons may have owed French over 1000 pounds. 900 found on French's body, Bhar wrote in his notebook.

"As far as you know, Ms. Wardle, is this all that ties Clive French and Trevor Parsons together? The uni work Clive sold Trevor?"

"Of course." Emmeline stubbed out her cigarette fiercely, as if grinding it into Clive French's corpse.

"No mutual enemies at uni? No old girlfriends in common?"

Emmeline let out a bark of laughter. "Do you really think Trevor and Clive were in the same weight class when it came to girlfriends? Trevor and I were together for six months. Before that, he was with Kelsey Hoskins. As for Clive …" She waved a hand. "I always reckoned he was a poof. Or asexual, like one of those mollusks."

"Hermaphrodites."

"Beg pardon?" Emmeline gazed at him, eyes wide.

"Mollusks aren't asexual. They're hermaphrodites—both male and female." Bhar smiled, wondering how he ever managed to date at all, given how often his mouth functioned independently of his brain. "Sorry about that. At uni I was a good deal closer to a Clive French than a Trevor Parsons, I fear."

"No need to state the obvious, mate," Quinton said.

"Shut it." Emmeline scowled at Quinton. "He's being modest, something you wouldn't understand. As for Clive," she added, turning back to Bhar, "I hope he was a hermaphrodite, because it's the only way he ever got laid. He had the *personality* of a mollusk, detective sergeant, and I'll stand by that no matter what additional nuggets of genius you manage to vomit up."

They were grinning at each other. Quinton made a displeased noise, but they both ignored him.

"What about the girl who discovered Clive—Kyla Sloane. She was the only one of your guests outside when the bodies were discovered," Bhar said. "Did something go wrong for her during the party? Did she become upset or have a row with someone?"

Emmeline's grin didn't precisely disappear so much as lose all warmth. "Not as far as I knew. We hung out with different people that night. I suppose you'd have to ask her."

"I will, of course," Bhar said mildly, wondering what in that question had triggered the shutdown. "But now I'm asking you. Is there any particular reason Ms. Sloane was in your back garden alone? Or why she might have moved Clive's body or delayed reporting its discovery?"

"Oi! Em already told you, you'll have to ask—"

"Shut it!" Emmeline cried. "Just bugger off, Quinton, please! Go upstairs and flirt with Mum. Have a drink with my dad. Anything!"

When it came to Emmeline, at least, Quinton was clearly all bark. Muttering, he rose, glared at Bhar and then launched himself up the stairs two at a time.

"Amazing specimen," Bhar said.

"Amazing he had the brains to make it here alone, you mean." Emmeline laughed. "Anyhow, about Kyla—I'm sorry. You'll just have to ask her."

"Very well. One more thing. On the night of the murders, DS Wakefield noticed what looked like the remnants of a broken sculpture or vase. On questioning, Ms. Sloane became quite agitated and said …" Bhar flipped to the relevant page in his notebook. "I quote: 'It was an accident. But it's gone now and Em and I might as well be dead. Because her parents are going to kill us.' End quote." He met Emmeline's eyes. "What do you think she meant by that?"

"It's obvious. My parents weren't home when the Met burst in. Kyla's been a friend of the family for years. She thought we'd be blamed because a policeman broke the vase."

"Yet the quote almost sounds like she felt personally responsible. Is that possible?" Bhar tried to look and sound neutral, like someone in whom Emmeline could confide. "Did she break it, then go outside to gather her wits?"

"The vase was in perfect condition before the police entered my house," Emmeline insisted.

"You noticed the vase's condition? Even with Trevor dead? I was given to understand you spent quite some time … screaming."

Emmeline drew in a breath. "Have you ever seen someone die right in front of you?"

"Not anyone I was personally acquainted with," Bhar said truthfully.

"Look. I wasn't in love with Trevor. I wasn't going to marry him and change his babies' nappies. Half the time he was no better than Quinton." Emmeline's gaze slid away. "But watching him die was awful. His eyes rolled up. His heels drummed the floor. You would've screamed, too, if you'd seen one of your girl-friends die that way."

Bhar thought of Tessa Chilcott. Watching her return to Sir Duncan, unraveling mentally until she became a murderer in her own right, had been close enough. "I didn't mean to be insensitive about the screaming," he said gently. "It's just … I'm a detective. It's my job to notice when details don't add up. The idea you could be sure the vase was intact after the shock of watching Trevor die is … problematic."

Emmeline studied Bhar for a moment. Then her blue eyes flicked once, pointedly, toward the stairs by which Quinton and her parents had exited.

He nodded to show he understood. "Thank you, Ms. Wardle. I'm quite likely to have more questions, so please stay in touch. Don't leave the country. And if you change residences again, let us know in advance." He passed her his card. "If you remember any additional details—someone who might have wished Clive or Trevor ill, for example, please call me directly."

"Of course. Let me see you to the door." Hooking her arm in his, Emmeline steered him toward the foyer. "It's true, someone I know was obsessed with my neighbor—Sir Duncan—for a time."

"Oh, yeah?" Bhar strove to remain composed, but the hairs on the back of his neck rose.

Emmeline nodded. "My friend Kyla. Why do you think she dressed like a monster—Frankenstein's monster—at my party? She felt guilty about it. Don't tell her I said anything." Just as Bhar stepped over the threshold, Emmeline leaned close to his ear and added, "Here's what matters. Everyone hated Clive. But only Phoebe Paquette hated Trevor. Want to know why? Go and see her."

CHAPTER TWELVE

By the end of the next day, DS Kate Wakefield had little additional progress to show for her efforts. Clive French had no siblings or significant other that anyone knew of; his father had been dead for years. Kate rang Mrs. French's number to request an interview, only to have the landlord explain Mrs. French was "in temporary residential care." In other words, news that her son had been found dead with an axe buried in his skull had resulted in his mother's short-term committal. Kate wasn't surprised—in fact, she was only surprised such reactions didn't occur more frequently.

Trevor Parsons' family was readily available, but had nothing of substance to offer. Kate interviewed them all by phone—father, mother and three younger brothers—without hearing a single detail that warranted a personal interview. According to the Parsons family, their eldest son was more than an athletic star. He was a golden child.

"Apparently, to know Trevor was to love him," Kate told DS Bhar, who had called to pass on the salient details of his meeting with Emmeline Wardle. "The only possible motive for murder the family could offer was jealousy."

"Which is valid. But maybe he was into something top secret —he and Clive French. Something his family knew nothing about," Bhar said. "Tomorrow I'll look up Phoebe Paquette. A standard background check turned up nothing except she's a student at University College, just like all the rest. Ms. Paquette has no unpaid debts, no arrest record, no traffic warrants."

"I'll bet it's just a prank on one of little Miss Emmy's school enemies," Kate said. "That girl strikes me as a right spiteful cow."

Bhar laughed. "Now, now. You're just upset because she insulted the guv. Emmeline's not so bad. Her mum's a real grasper, though. And her new boyfriend, Quinton Baylor, stands to make rugby team captain now that Parsons is out of the way."

"'Emmeline,' eh? Don't you sound chummy."

"Oh, excuse me, *Ms. Wardle*. And speaking of Ms. Wardle, she fed me an interesting nibble about Kyla Sloane. Apparently Kyla was the only party guest who knew Sir Duncan lived at 16 Burnaby. And she was very interested in him. Obsessed is the word Emmeline used."

"Obsessed?"

"Right. Claims Kyla felt bad about it. Came to the party dressed like a monster."

"A sexy monster," Kate said, unable to keep the knee-jerk skepticism from her voice. "I had the impression Ms. Sloane and Ms. Wardle were lifelong friends. Why toss her under the lorry?"

"Why do women do anything?" Bhar sighed. "I read your report on Kyla and listened to the formal interview taped at the Yard. Both times she claimed she went outside due to cigarette smoke aggravating her asthma. I happen to have her uni student health file here ..." Movement transmitted over the connection as Bhar shifted papers around. "Right. Kyla Sloane. No drug allergies, no medical diagnoses. Acknowledges alcohol use. Acknowledges tobacco use, a half pack a day."

"So she lied about why she went outside."

"And not that convincingly," Bhar said. "Just keep it in mind. I have a feeling we'll be re-interviewing her soon … her and Quinton both. So—how else have you occupied yourself all day? Full treatment at the salon? A dress fitting with Lady Margaret, so you won't embarrass the guv to death? Remember that scene in *Bridget Jones's Diary*? When she turns up at the garden party in a Playboy bunny costume because she thought the theme was tarts and vicars?" Bhar hooted. "If I bring you the bunny costume, will you wear it?"

"If it fits you, it'll be three sizes too big for me," Kate said sweetly. "But you're such a clever little git. When I think of you and your mum eating supper together every night, I can't imagine why you don't have a partner."

"How do you know I don't? Maybe I just don't kiss and tell. *Or* make sheep's eyes at the guv. Anyhow, lovely to chat with you, Kate, I know you're hard up for basic human contact, but now I must dash …"

"Hurry home or Mummy will fret!"

"Hilarious. Tears in my eyes. Really." Bhar rang off.

Hetheridge was due to pick her up at eight; when Kate glanced at the clock, she saw it was barely six. Her hair was already salon-perfect—accustomed to styling her unruly blond hair herself, the cost of a trim and an updo had shocked her, though she'd grudgingly paid. Taking her time with her makeup, she decided to stick to the classic: no foundation on her fair skin, just jet-black mascara and deep red lipstick. Once that was done, there was nothing left but to wriggle into her rented gown, enlisting the help of her nephew, Henry, with the zip.

"It's awfully tight," he said doubtfully.

"It's supposed to be. I'm part of an undercover operation," she said, enjoying how the eight-year-old boy's eyes widened. "I have to blend in with all the poshies, don't I?"

"Shouldn't be hard. You look good. And Tony will be there," Henry said wisely. Highly verbal and already reading at an advanced level, he frequently spoke like an adult, although he lagged behind developmentally in almost everything else. "Do you think he'll have time to read my school essay? I want him to—"

"Lego," Ritchie called from the front room, revealing he wasn't as mesmerized by BBC World News as he appeared. "I have a new Lego."

Her brother had been saying that for two days; when he stumbled upon a phrase he liked, he tended to stick with it as long as possible. "I have a new Lego" referred to the latest project on his bedroom floor—asymmetric yet oddly compelling, like most of his nameless creations. Tall and slender, with curly brown hair and a perpetually spotty face, Ritchie was three years Kate's senior and resembled her not in the least. Then again, it was highly unlikely they had the same father. Kate's mum wasn't around to ask. Mrs. Wakefield had spent most of Kate's formative years either on the game or serving time, either for petty theft or prostitution. Now her whereabouts were unknown, a circumstance Kate occasionally paused to give thanks for.

At least I don't have to worry about Mum turning up and demanding to have Ritchie back, Kate thought. *She'd sell his organs on the black market before she'd take charge of him again. Assuming she's still alive ...*

"I have a new Lego," Ritchie repeated, louder.

"And I adore it," Kate called back, sucking herself in as Henry, short and pudgy for his age, strained to zip her all the way up. "But Tony's on a tight schedule, luv. I don't think he'll come up to the flat to hobnob with you lot tonight. More like, I'll walk down and meet him at the curb."

"Balls," Henry said, deflating.

Kate gave him a quick consoling hug. Henry and Ritchie's transparent starvation for male attention was something she preferred not to dwell on. Not long ago she'd made the mistake of letting them get too close to her ex-boyfriend, Dylan. And his sudden disappearance from their lives had hurt Henry and Ritchie far more than it hurt her.

No more male bonding. Not till I'm sure where Tony and I stand.

With almost an hour left to kill, Kate stood in the living room —her dress was too snug for extended sitting—and watched the news over Ritchie's shoulder. Often her mind wandered to the case, to the physical similarities between Kyla Sloane and Tessa Chilcott.

Could they be related somehow? Kate wondered. *Has anyone checked?*

"… with Roderick Hetheridge, spokesman of the Foxhound Fanciers," a TV voice said, rousing Kate from her thoughts. Onscreen, a reporter for the Beeb thrust his microphone toward a dour man with the high forehead and jutting chin of an aristocrat. "Mr. Hetheridge, why do you believe so passionately that the national ban on foxhunting should be lifted?"

"Well, it isn't quite fair, is it?" Roderick Hetheridge flashed a toothy smile. "Foxhunting isn't banned in Northern Ireland. Yet all the rest of us are made to suffer. And moreover, it isn't fair to rural culture. This country is already going to the dogs. Do we really want to stand by and give up every last thing that makes us British?"

"Wanker," Henry groaned. He couldn't bear stories of animal cruelty in the news. When a cat was flattened by a lorry just outside their building, he'd cried for hours.

"Gone to the dogs?" the reporter repeated. "But Mr. Hetheridge, critics of the Foxhound Fanciers would say that's just the problem. The fox is beset by hounds and killed, they would argue, quite inhumanely …"

"I don't agree. Foxhunting began as a vital form of pest control and grew into a highly disciplined sport. All this handwringing about kindness to animals is pure emotion," Roderick

Hetheridge said. "And propagated, I might add, by those who came to this country as immigrants and now seek to replace our historic way of life with their own."

When the segment wrapped, the studio newsreader added, "That was Roderick Hetheridge, first in line for the barony of Wellegrave and founder of Foxhound Fanciers, a pro-hunting activist organization."

"But Tony's the baron of Wellegrave," Henry said. "How can that prat be first in line?"

"First in line when Tony dies," Kate said. She narrowly resisted the temptation to rush to her computer, Google that video snippet and replay it in all its horror. Once or twice she'd imagined Hetheridge's relatives, envisioning them as cold, arrogant and out of touch. How bracing to discover the reality was, quite possibly, even worse.

"Dies?" Henry's eyes widened behind his round specs. "Tony's not that old, is he?"

"Nope. Just turned two hundred last week," Kate laughed, mussing Henry's hair. He still looked worried, so she started to tickle him, keeping up the assault until he darted away.

"I've got it!" Henry called from the safety of his bedroom. "You can marry Tony and have his baby. Then the baby will be the next baron and Mr. Fox-killer can shut his cake-hole!" Giggling madly, the boy shut his door and locked it before Kate, hampered by her gown, could follow.

At eight o'clock Kate exited her flat. Four-inch heels in hand, she boarded the lift barefoot, sharing it with a greasy-haired delivery boy. All the way down she pretended not to notice his lascivious gaze, despite the fact it never left her breasts.

"Dead sexy," he announced as the jerky old lift finally shuddered to halt. "What you charging, luv?"

"Night in the nick." Kate wished she had her warrant card to wave under his nose. "Care to get banged up?"

"Blimey. Just joking. Wouldn't poke you with a borrowed stick." Tossing an unimaginative curse over his shoulder, the delivery boy hurried away.

It was a cool night, too breezy to stand outside for long, at least without a wrap. Unwilling to spoil the effect of her gown with her grotty old trench coat, Kate elected to wait in her building's glass-fronted lobby. After three minutes barefoot on the linoleum—originally white, but now a sludgy gray—she imagined she could feel fungus creeping in, so she set about putting on her shoes. Brand new and a wee bit too small, they had delicate ankle straps that were so difficult to fasten, she didn't notice as Hetheridge's silver Lexus appeared in front of her building. By the time Kate straightened, Hetheridge was emerging from the sleek sedan.

The man had been made for evening dress. Despite her awareness of that fact, Kate still caught her breath when she saw Hetheridge. His dinner jacket was no rental—she happened to know he owned three. Its precise fit, along with his steel gray hair and ice blue eyes, combined to make the man ludicrously handsome. Which explained the nervous thumping inside her chest.

"Kate." Hetheridge stopped dead, staring.

Determined not to mince or teeter, she strode toward him. Her long black gown was couture, or so the shop girl claimed. It had a V-shaped neckline, revealing the cleavage that had so mesmerized the delivery boy, then nipped in at the waist, emphasizing Kate's curves. It fell to her ankles, except on the left side, where a deep slit exposed her leg to midthigh. She wore only one piece of jewelry—a necklace Lady Margaret Knolls had lent her from her own collection. Fashioned in the shape of a golden serpent with jeweled eyes and stylized scales, the necklace hung heavily against Kate's flesh. And those heels, the highest she'd ever attempted, gave her the very boost she'd aimed for. For her evening on Hetheridge's arm, she'd be the taller of the pair by at least three inches.

"What do you think?" Kate hadn't meant to ask—nothing made her hate herself more than whinging for approval—but the words were out before she could stop them.

"I think what every man thinks in the presence of such a beautiful woman." Taking her right hand, Hetheridge brushed his lips against her knuckles. "That I am undeserving, but not unwilling."

He helped her into the Lexus. Kate climbed into the bucket seat with care, mindful of her gown, which pulled snug across her backside. Hetheridge, clearly at home in evening dress, dropped behind the wheel as if wearing a track suit. Was he slimmer? Kate decided he was, and after only few days' abstinence from the team's usual rich breakfast. She'd barely eaten for almost two weeks, yet the scale refused to budge. Typical.

As the Lexus pulled away from the building, Kate glimpsed movement at her front window. No doubt it was Henry who watched them go, still disappointed that Hetheridge hadn't come up to critique his school essay. Ritchie loved TV more than anything; when immersed in one of his many programs, he required little else. But Henry needed more attention than Kate alone could give him.

"There's something I've been meaning to mention." Kate took a deep breath. Keeping family matters private was an ingrained survival strategy, despite the fact she pried into other people's lives—and deaths—for a living.

Hetheridge muted the Lexus's stereo. "Yes?"

"Next time I drop off Henry for his fencing lesson, I'd appreciate it if you don't reference his mother. I never meant to spring it on you, about Maura residing in a mental hospital. It just popped out when Paul explained about Tessa Chilcott," Kate said. "Henry's delicate when it comes to his mum. He says he wants to visit her, but he always comes back from Parkwood depressed and anxious. He really enjoys his time with you, Tony. I'm sure if you brought up his mum, it would only be out of kindness. But I don't want to risk upsetting him."

"Of course." Slowing for a traffic light, Hetheridge added, "Mind you, I already knew. About Maura being a resident at Parkwood."

"What?" Kate's voice sounded strange to her own ears. "You ordered a full intelligence report on me?"

Hetheridge shot her a startled glance. "Of course not. It was Henry who told me about his mother. Sometime around the third or fourth lesson, while you were still in the hospital."

"But he ..." Kate started to say, "wouldn't do that," and realized she wasn't sure. Just because she preferred secrecy over confession didn't mean her nephew felt the same way. "He's usually close-mouthed about family problems."

Hetheridge nodded.

Kate, who for some reason had expected Hetheridge to keep talking—to pass on everything Henry had said—realized he had no intention of doing so. Just as Bhar's professional missteps had been safe with him, so were a young man's secrets.

"I notice Henry's lost a smidge of weight," Kate said at last. "He was getting too big for an eight-year-old, so fencing must be giving him a good workout. And his school hasn't called about him being bullied lately, either."

"That's all well and good, but those bullies aren't done with Henry. These things always get worse before they get better," Hetheridge said. "I think Henry understands that now. He's resolved to hold his head up and ignore as much as he can. Then, when the time comes, he'll have to fight."

Kate's jaw dropped, but with effort she bit back her initial response. What would a sixty-year-old bachelor know of modern schools, zero tolerance and student behavior contracts?

"Henry can't actually fight the kids who are bullying him," she explained gently. "That's against every rule under the sun. He'd get detention, maybe even expulsion. And if he managed to actually hurt one of the bullies, their parents would have me up on charges."

Hetheridge kept his eyes on the road. His expression, illuminated by passing streetlights, was serene.

"Did Henry already tell you that?" Kate asked.

"He did."

This time Kate couldn't stifle a huff of frustration. "Knowing all that, you still advised him to fight back?"

"I told Henry it's very simple. If they call you names, ignore them. If they get in your way, step around them. Face blank, head high. But if they touch you, if they place so much as a finger on you ..." Hetheridge's gaze flickered toward Kate, then back to the road. "Issue one warning. Then attack. If your opponent is your size or smaller, punch him in the face. If your opponent is bigger and stronger, go for the bollocks. Strike as if you have only one chance to make your point."

Kate stared at Hetheridge. "I see. And did you advise Henry on what do when the teacher hauls him off for punishment?"

"I did. Take it like a man and have done with it."

"But suppose he follows your advice and gets expelled?"

"Then when he's permitted to return, he won't have as many bullies waiting for him."

Kate, who'd survived her middle school years by repelling her tormenters with her fists, gave a little laugh. "Well, Tony, I must say I'm surprised at you. I wouldn't expect a high-ranking Scotland Yard official to recommend breaking dozens of rules to settle a score violently. As opposed to the proper nonviolent channels."

"Henry raised the very same objection. He just used smaller words," Hetheridge grinned. "I told him there's a time in your life for following the rules. Ninety-five percent of the time, truth be told. But when the price of following the rules is being afraid to go to class, or even to use the boys' toilets, then it's time for a cost-benefit analysis. Sometimes improving your lot in life means breaking a rule and accepting the punishment. The key is, don't whine about the consequences. Just take them and move on."

Kate recalled something Hetheridge had once told her about his childhood. "I suppose this method worked well for you?"

"It did."

"You're such a dinosaur. You do realize that, don't you?" A fond note crept into her voice.

"Dinosaurs ruled this planet for well over a hundred million years." Hetheridge sounded pleased with himself. "Many are still running the Met. I consider myself in good company."

After that, they traveled in companionable silence. And despite Kate's declaration that the evening would be purely business, she liked it when Hetheridge took her hand, holding it as they drove the rest of the way to Mayfair.

CHAPTER THIRTEEN

The home of Lady Isabel Bartlow, half-sister of Sir Duncan Godington, came as a minor disappointment to Kate Wakefield, who had expected something akin to Kensington Palace in scope and grandeur. But the exterior of Lady Isabel's home was exactly what the name Mayfair brought to mind: stuccoed, terraced and five stories tall. Its brilliant floodlights shone across the façade at various angles, creating odd pockets of gloom. All in all, the house hunched over the street, less a gracious Georgian lady than a craggy-faced earl, squinting at visitors he neither knew nor trusted.

The line for valet parking was long and slow. When it was finally their turn, Hetheridge handed his keys to the uniformed man at the podium. As he made for the passenger door, Kate— not realizing he intended to open it for her—opened it herself, smacking him right in the midsection.

Someone laughed. Startled by her gaffe, Kate stumbled out of the bucket seat, hobbled by her tight-fitting gown. As she rocked on her heels, turning an ankle, Hetheridge caught her with both hands. With his help Kate managed to keep from falling, but her black clutch flew into the street.

The valet drivers were watching. The guests milling about near the entrance were watching. The doormen, top-hatted and tailed, watched. Kate froze.

"Allow me." Hetheridge bent to retrieve the clutch before Kate could thoughtlessly lunge for it herself, probably ripping her gown in the process. As he handed it back to her, his eyes gleamed with amusement.

"They think I don't belong here," she whispered.

"Nonsense," Hetheridge said soothingly. "They think you're drunk."

He offered his arm, which Kate hooked onto gratefully. She wanted to dart inside and search for a place to hide, but Hetheridge set a measured pace toward the grand, gaslit entrance. Everyone was still watching, silent, unsmiling. Kate decided to pretend all those pairs of eyes were overcome with envy. She *was* on the arm of the Peerage's most eligible bachelor, after all.

Lady Isabel's foyer reminded Kate of a posh hotel with its gilt-edged mirrors, exotic flower arrangements and glittering crystal chandeliers. But even the best hotels permitted anonymous entry, a quick dash to the ladies' or the bar. This party had a receiving line.

"Oh, Lord," Kate whispered. "You never mentioned I'd have to run the gauntlet."

"Courage," Hetheridge said in her ear. "The first woman on the left is Lady Isabel."

Lady Isabel was tall, willowy brunette with bobbed hair and a square jaw line. Her cream-colored gown had a high neck, no sleeves and a drop waist. Most females, including Kate, would have looked better in a flour sack. But Lady Isabel looked elegant and timeless, like a throwback to the age of jazz.

Beside Lady Isabel stood two women of mid-to-late middle age, well coiffed and stylishly attired. One wore beige; the other, dove gray. They were Lady Isabel's relatives, Kate decided, enlisted to help greet the guests and ensure everyone received equal attention. And at the end of the receiving line hovered a fourth woman, an almost-empty whiskey glass in hand. If this woman was meant to help issue compliments and air-kisses, she was falling down on the job. The most any guest got from her was a curt nod.

"Lady Margaret!" Kate cried, so relieved to see that androgynous, rather bad-tempered face, she tried to steer Hetheridge in Lady Margaret's direction. He tightened his grip, holding her back.

"Our hostess first," he chided, propelling Kate toward Lady Isabel instead. The young woman turned such a warm, winning smile on them that for a moment, Kate believed Lady Isabel and Hetheridge were actually friends. Then Hetheridge cleared his throat in his usual highbrow manner and said, "We last spoke so long ago, my dear, I can't expect you to remember. It's Tony Hetheridge. Leo and Patricia's son."

"My goodness! It is you," Lady Isabel cried with such sincerity, Kate had no idea whether she truly recognized Hetheridge or not.

"Lord Hetheridge, Baron of Wellegrave," the lady in beige intoned.

"Thank you, Aunt Fiona, but I quite remember." Lady Isabel air-kissed Hetheridge on both cheeks. "He's the one with the extraordinary career! Oh, Fee, wait till Duncan sees I've invited a policeman! Won't he just choke?

"Of course," Lady Isabel continued, still with that winning smile, "you mustn't worry, Tony. Duncan isn't really frightened by the police. It's only that he had *such* famous troubles with Scotland Yard—that's your branch, is it not?—that you may find yourself the center of attention. Thank you so very much, Margaret, for remembering Tony to us!"

"I render such small services as I may," Lady Margaret said. Unlike the ladies in brown and gray, Lady Margaret wore metallic sapphire, a color that emphasized her blue eyes and close-cropped gray hair. Her ensemble—slacks, tank and billowing overshirt—looked jarring among a sea of gowns. Kate thought it was marvelous.

"And who might this be?" Lady Isabel turned the same wide-eyed friendliness on Kate, who found herself suddenly mute. To her relief, Hetheridge answered for her.

"Lady Isabel Bartlow, may I present my good friend, Kate Wakefield." The note of pride in his voice made Kate's face grow even warmer.

"Hallo, Kate." Isabel gave her a brief, limp handshake. "I hope we manage to entertain you. The halls are decked for All Hallows' Eve. Though I can't help but wonder if Duncan and I shouldn't have gone for costumes instead of fancy dress."

"For some of us, fancy dress is costume enough," Lady Margaret said. Hooking her arm through Kate's, she began steering her toward a wide archway.

"Don't worry, Izzie, I'll make these two comfortable," Lady Margaret called over her shoulder. "Come along, Tony. Try and keep up."

Beyond the archway was a ballroom larger than any Kate had ever seen. The walls were draped in black velvet except for a row of tall, floor-to-ceiling windows. Before those windows stood a nine-foot wicker man. Dozens of glass spheres and votive holders were embedded among his bound willow strips. The flickering candles inside that multitude of glass made the wicker man seem perpetually alight, burning for the pleasure of Sir Duncan and Lady Isabel's guests.

"So the party's theme is human sacrifice?" Kate asked Lady Margaret.

"My dear child, the *family's* theme is human sacrifice. Society as a whole continues to embrace those two because the vast majority of its members cannot discern a terrier from a wolverine. And someday one of them will pay the price."

Kate must have seemed overeager, because Lady Margaret glanced about suspiciously, as if they might be under surveillance. "Do try and stop looking like a copper. What's wanted next is a drink to occupy those nervous hands of yours. Then I'll tell you all I know."

At the ballroom's far end, a life-sized triple tableau had been erected. On the left Kate saw a gallows. From its rope a male mannequin hung head-down, arms tied behind his back and one foot in the noose. In the tableau's center stood a perfectly realistic guillotine. The executioner, a female mannequin, seemed ready to release the blade; a naked baby doll lay on the block, awaiting the blow that would chop it in two. And on the tableau's right, Kate saw a tall wooden stake surrounded by stacked cords of wood. A male mannequin with silver hair was tied to the stake. Like the party's male guests, it was attired in standard evening dress—black coat, white shirt, black tie. But even from several meters away, Kate recognized the oversized faux warrant card pinned to its lapel.

"They knew you were coming," she whispered to Hetheridge, shocked by the insult's sheer audacity.

"When it comes to these people, assume they know all." Lady Margaret led Kate and Hetheridge toward one of three open bars. "Glenfiddich," she barked at the bartender, a short black man with a face so carefully blank, Kate doubted any demand could have fazed him.

Silently the bartender opened a bottle of Scotch as a woman unloaded a tray of premade martinis. Each had a slice of red apple on the rim and a piece of candy floating inside.

"Toffee appletini?" the woman asked, smiling at Hetheridge.

"Good God, no. Scotch and soda, please." He glanced at Kate.

"Nothing for me." She could hardly tear her eyes away from

that detective effigy. Would Sir Duncan and Lady Isabel actually contrive to burn it before the evening was out?

"Prosecco for the lady," Hetheridge told the bartender. "With a strawberry."

Within moments they all had their drinks. Hetheridge passed the bartender a folded note. Kate, glimpsing the denomination, almost dropped her glass.

"Oi!" She poked Hetheridge in the arm. "Did you mean to tip him that much?"

He winked. "Drink up."

As a trio, they worked their way through the crowd, Hetheridge nodding and greeting guests by name until they found a suitable place to hover—one of the many chairless round tables dotting the ballroom. As Kate tasted the sparkling Italian wine, Lady Margaret appraised her through slitted eyes.

"Very nice. That serpent choker looks better on you than it ever did on me."

"I like what you're wearing, too," Kate said.

Lady Margaret's smile was impish. "Take note: there's an upside to being the rich old bat everyone fears. Wearing what I choose, when I choose, is just the tip of the iceberg. Now, you wanted to know about our guest of honor and his half-sister." Lady Margaret's sharp gaze raked the room once more. "I haven't seen him yet, and Izzie's probably still up front, receiving. Here's what I can tell you.

"Duncan's father, Raleigh, was a bit of a bastard. Used to be a rumor going round that he beat his wife, Opal—Duncan and Eldon's mother." Lady Margaret shrugged. "I never did see any bruises on her, but who knows what happens behind closed doors. I will say, she was always a timid little thing. Loved her boys and talked about nothing else. Then one day she was dead. Raleigh said it was brain aneurysm. He made the most of his situation, playing it for all the sympathy he could get, nattering on about his poor, motherless boys. Eldon was about twelve then, I think. Which would have made Duncan about ten.

"Next I heard of the family, the boys' nanny was found dead. Smothered in her bed, right inside the Godington house. Of course there was a police inquiry and requests for anyone with information to come forward, but nothing came of it. Eventually the case was closed. But you know gossip." Lady Margaret smiled, but her sharp eyes remained humorless. "People began to talk of Raleigh as if he were Bluebeard. The nanny had been young and pretty. Rumor had it, he killed his wife, had it on with the nanny for a time and killed her, too.

"Eventually, it died down, or some better scandal took its place." Lady Margaret took a sip of Glenfiddich. "Raleigh remarried Helen Parry. You saw her in the foyer. The lady in gray. Helen had two girls, Izzie and …" Lady Margaret paused. "Oh, I can't believe it, I've forgotten that second child's name. She died before she was a year old. In those days we called it cot death. Not too long after that, Raleigh and Helen separated. They never actually divorced—technically, she's his widow, though he left her nothing."

"So why is Lady Isabel called Bartlow?" Kate asked. "Is she married? I didn't see a ring."

"Do let me continue," Lady Margaret said, pale eyes gleaming. "Despite their parents' separation, Duncan and Izzie were always close. They grew up summering together, going on holiday together. And Duncan was never hard up for companionship. Even before his trial, he had a crowd of followers and devotees. He was one of those boys who never had to do his own school-work—there was always a line of would-be mates to do it for him. Have you noticed all the young people here tonight?"

Kate was startled to realize she hadn't, not until Lady Margaret pointed it out. Clearly the necessity of dressing up and running the genteel gauntlet had short-circuited her detective instincts. Looking around the ballroom with fresh eyes, Kate realized that more than a third of the guests were in their early twenties. Many of the faces looked familiar, like guests from Emmeline's party.

"I've never seen so many past interviewees in one place," she laughed. "Well, except for a courtroom. Are they all personal friends of Sir Duncan and Lady Isabel?"

"Friends, friends of friends, or ambitious hangers-on, eager to befriend the beast. The man has charisma a movie star would kill for," Lady Margaret said. "He's a woman magnet, too, if you didn't know. But he never married. Izzie is his one constant. Even when her husband, Mike Bartlow, walked out on her, Izzie hardly seemed to notice. I shouldn't have to tell you what sort of rumors all this coziness between siblings has given rise to."

"Are the rumors true?" Hetheridge asked.

Lady Margaret considered. "Izzie has a certain charm about her. I'd like to say, no. But I can't. Not after all the odd behavior I've witnessed between those two over the years. So the jury is still out."

"Three deaths in one family is excessive as far as coincidences go," Kate said to Hetheridge. "And that's not even counting the triple-murder trial. Do you think Sir Duncan was responsible for any of them? His mum? The nanny? His little sister?"

"Never made my mind up." Hetheridge took a sip of his drink. "But if I were to place a wager, I'd say yes to the nanny and the youngest sibling. No to his mother."

"Why?"

Hetheridge shrugged. "Instinct. Nothing more."

The band, apparently on break when Kate and Hetheridge arrived, chose that moment to resume playing. Joining synthesizer, drums, bass and electric guitar, they produced a slow, excruciating instrumental Kate finally recognized as the Beatles' "Yesterday."

"Crikey. A slow dance."

"Tony, that's your cue," Lady Margaret said with an evil grin.

"No, truly, this isn't my sort of dancing," Kate protested as several couples took to the floor.

"Of course it is." Lady Margaret's tone was breezy. "Haven't you read Austen? At parties, the only worthwhile conversations happen whilst dancing."

Placing his glass on the tabletop, Hetheridge extended a hand to Kate. "Will you do me the honor?"

"Bleeding buggery bollocks," Kate groaned. She knocked back the rest of the sparkling wine like it was soda, dropping the strawberry next to Hetheridge's Scotch. "I mean—sorry. Yes, of course."

She allowed Hetheridge to lead her onto the dance floor, wondering how embarrassing this would be. A good dancer, Kate had long ago made peace with the fact she never chose males who could keep up with her on the dance floor. They always seemed to rely on one of two approaches. There was the full body clutch, refuge of non-dancers the world over. Or there was the "man dance," an arrhythmic bob and weave, performed whenever the music ran faster than a funeral march …

Smiling, Hetheridge positioned Kate's hands traditionally. Taking a step backward, he began leading her along with the music. Assessing his movements, Kate followed them easily, matching each step and turn. Among the small crowd they soon drifted into the center, other couples moving aside for the pair that was actually dancing.

"You've had lessons," Kate accused.

"At school. It was considered part of our education, if you can believe that," Hetheridge said.

Kate thought of all the subjects—including higher maths, computer science and world politics—children as young as Henry were expected to learn. Where on earth would dancing fit in?

"That's a bit dodgy. What sort of schools did you attend?"

"Eton. Then Oxford. Now—look." Hetheridge twirled Kate in

the opposite direction. "There's Sir Duncan at last. See him, close to the wicker man?"

Kate looked, but the selection of tall, distinguished men in evening dress was too plentiful for her to make a positive ID.

"Perfect timing," Hetheridge said when the music ceased. "I hope he didn't see you with me. We should part ways for a time. I'd like you to chat him up. Mention the French-Parsons case if you can."

"Just ask him if he did it? And if so, how and why?" Kate felt nervous all over again. Yet she suspected if she were dressed in her daily work garb, she would see Hetheridge's request as an exciting opportunity, not a potentially humiliating encounter. "Can't you just send Lady Margaret? I'll bet she could force a confession in five minutes, guilty or not."

"I fear you're more to his taste. And mine, too, lest you forget," Hetheridge said. "Take care. I'll keep an eye out for you."

"Fine." Squaring her shoulders, Kate made her way toward Sir Duncan and the towering, candlelit wicker man.

CHAPTER FOURTEEN

A s Kate elbowed her way into the thick of the guests, earning a sharp "I say!" from a stooped man with a red nose, she at last caught sight of Sir Duncan Godington —blond hair, high cheekbones and sensuous mouth. He looked like a fairer, masculine edition of his lovely half-sister—and, yes, a bit like James Bond, especially in evening dress. But Bond, at least in Kate's imagination, possessed the dispassionate stare of a professional killer. Sir Duncan, caught in a knot of stylishly disheveled young people, had gentle, even humorous eyes. As Kate watched, Sir Duncan smiled at the slender brunette before him.

Oh, yes. Sir Duncan had two smiles, Kate knew. One was famous—that sharklike grin that bared every possible tooth. The tabloids loved to pair that grin with captions like, "Sir Dunc Shows His Fangs!" But Sir Duncan's other smile was tender, both masculine and sweetly sympathetic. A smile that made many women think of a frilly white wedding dress and a crotchless black teddy, both at the same time.

But not me, Kate told herself. *Never fancied the rich blokes.*

Cinderella snags a toff with hands softer than hers? That story always made me want to puke ...

Suddenly, she cut off that line of thought, no longer certain it was true. Discovering Hetheridge could dance had been such a welcome surprise. And hearing him introduce her with obvious pride had made her blush like a schoolgirl.

Kate glanced back the way she'd come, but Hetheridge wasn't there. He'd faded away from the dance floor, no doubt to avoid Sir Duncan's line of sight.

It's not like Tony lives off his cash, hunting foxes all day like skeevy old Roderick, Kate told herself. *And as for his hands, they certainly aren't softer than ...*

A familiar voice cut through her reverie. "Of course I don't mind if a police officer is here. I'm having a lovely time. Perfectly at ease."

Elbowing past another knot of guests, Kate pushed forward until she saw the face of the slender brunette in that shimmering white gown. Yes. It was Kyla Sloane.

She looked beautiful, and even more like Tessa Chilcott than Kate remembered. Kyla's long, dark hair was sleek and perfect. Like Tessa, Kyla was fragile-looking, almost too thin in her glittery sheath. Though she sounded cool and intelligent, there was something brittle about the girl, especially with Sir Duncan towering over her.

"It means a great deal to Izzie and I, having you here," Sir Duncan was saying. "Don't feel obliged to hide yourself away. You've done nothing wrong."

"I know. But sometimes I feel like the perception of guilt is as damning as the reality," Kyla said. She held a toffee appletini in her hands. The glass looked sweaty, its contents untouched.

"Only to the rabbit-hearted." Sir Duncan's smile reappeared. "You are made of sterner stuff, my girl."

"Does the way he fawns over her make you want to puke?" someone asked near Kate's ear.

Kate turned, surprised to see a male after hearing those chirpish tones. A young man of about Kyla's age stood beside her. Attired in evening dress, he had straight hair, a good smile and the sort of wide-cheeked, pleasant face universally thought of as cute.

"Sorry, you may not remember me. Jeremy Bentham." He offered a small, delicate hand, which Kate shook. "I was a guest at Emmeline Wardle's on the night of the murders. I saw you at Scotland Yard while I waited to be processed with all the rest." Jeremy gave her a self-deprecating grin. "DS Bhar talked to me and a couple of other blokes at the same time, then let us all go. I reckon we didn't seem guilty enough to be interesting."

"Bentham?" Kate thought for a moment, mentally rifling through the many reports gathered the case's Action Book. "I remember. You saw someone in the back garden."

"I suppose," Jeremy said. "Now when I look back, I'm not sure. It was all so confusing. I'd hate to be on record for saying something that wasn't perfectly accurate. Not when it might lead to—I don't know. Somewhere it shouldn't." He shrugged, shifting from foot to foot.

"Of course not." Kate lowered her voice. "Mr. Bentham—Jeremy. I know Mr. Parsons was a star athlete. I'm sure he had some intimidating mates. Has one of them approached you? Asked you to retract some part of your testimony?"

Jeremy shook his head.

"You're quite certain?" Kate asked gently, thinking of all the times Henry had slunk home, miserable, after a bad day at school and then tried to deny it.

"If someone did try and intimidate me, it wouldn't be one of Trev's friends," Jeremy whispered. "It would be one of his."

Kate glanced in the direction Jeremy was looking. Sir Duncan had just finished chatting with Kyla. Now his gaze shifted to Kate, smiling that easy, charming smile.

No, not at me, Kate realized with a strange burst of relief and disappointment. Sir Duncan was looking at Jeremy. In response, Jeremy grinned and waved. For a moment, it looked as if Sir Duncan would respond by joining them. Then another guest, a horse-faced woman with a loud, braying laugh, accosted him.

"A friend of yours?" Kate asked.

"I wish," Jeremy sighed. "A friend of a friend, actually. I've only met Sir Duncan twice. He's cordial to everyone, but to really run with his crowd you have to be one of the chosen people. I grew up in Peterborough. My dad sells shoes."

"Came to uni on scholarship, then? Like Clive French?"

Jeremy nodded. "We took a lot of the same courses, but we weren't friends. Acquaintances, really. As for Trevor ... well. Mustn't speak ill of the dead."

"Of course." Kate tried not to look disappointed. Of course, there were three open bars. Would Jeremy Bentham be more forthcoming on the topic of Trevor's character if he had some alcohol in him? "No toffee appletini for you?"

"Afraid not. Just soda or water. Like Phoebe." Jeremy pointed out a young woman not far away. She was chatting with a large group of girls, most in stylish red or black. Phoebe, dressed in pink silk, was the blondest and prettiest. She was also the widest, her A-line dress flapping with every movement.

"Isn't she perfect?" Jeremy turned a goofy grin on Kate, who couldn't resist grinning back. The kid was about as subtle as Tom Cruise jumping up and down on Oprah's sofa. He was in love.

In the course of her animated conversation, Phoebe pivoted, revealing toned arms, a slender neck, and shapely legs. Suddenly, the reason for her expanded midsection was obvious. Phoebe was at least eight months pregnant.

"I'm laying off the booze to be supportive," Jeremy confided to Kate. "Pheebs hasn't had a drink since she found out, and neither have I. It's a little weird, being sober all the time. Makes you feel like a grown-up. Oh—and it's not my baby, if you want to know."

"No?" Kate felt awkward. Rarely did conversations take this turn. Especially at a party full of strangers.

"Nope. Just a friend," Jeremy said. "But that's okay. It's not like being a friend is unimportant. Pheebs really needs her friends right now."

As if hearing her name, Phoebe turned, catching sight of Jeremy and motioning him over. Jeremy shot Kate an apologetic look.

"Sorry. Pheebs calls. Must dash." He began working himself back through the ever-shifting crowd. "Good luck, Scotland Yard!"

Realizing she had forgotten to introduce herself, Kate called back, "It's Kate. Detective Sergeant Kate Wakefield! If you remember anything else, or if you ever need to talk, ring the Yard and ask for me!" But this last surely went unheard because Jeremy, in pursuit of the pregnant Phoebe, was gone.

Kate's conversation with Jeremy Bentham cost her that first opportunity to speak with Sir Duncan. When she turned back to where Sir Duncan had been, there was only the horse-faced woman, whinnying in the ear of some new victim. The crowd's detritus—to which Kate decidedly belonged—had been left behind. The young and fashionably disheveled, including Kyla Sloane, had followed in Sir Duncan's wake.

Also gone, Kate discovered as she awkwardly hoofed it from one side of the ballroom to the other, was Hetheridge and Lady Margaret. Kate's mobile, tucked in her tiny clutch, could not find a signal within the cavernous ballroom. Frustrated, Kate asked a bartender—the same impassive bartender who'd served her Prosecco—where she could find a landline. He pointed to the red-carpeted staircase. On the next floor—she was informed in a tone suggesting anyone who was anyone would already know—she would find a phone, a powder room and a valet capable of assisting with more complex needs.

"Cheers, mate," Kate told the bartender, allowing her East End bray to come through. She did not follow Hetheridge's example of an extravagant tip.

Climbing the stairs alone, Kate was more than a little suspicious she'd been the butt of a disgruntled server's joke. But as she emerged on the next floor, she saw an antique telephone stand bearing an incongruously modern phone. Snatching it up, Kate dialed Hetheridge's mobile from memory.

It rang four times. Then a recorded BT voice told Kate the number was not available, and to please try again later.

Kate muttered a few choice curses. Hetheridge, like the apatosaurus and the tyrannosaurus, switched off his mobile at public events, considering it rude to take a call when otherwise engaged. Contemporary human beings, including herself and DS Bhar, kept the damned things on, to get their damned calls, especially in damned difficult situations ...

"May I help you, madam?" a rather strangled voice inquired.

Kate put down the handset. A slender, uniformed valet with the face of a trout stared at her, eyes bulging, lips pursed like he wanted an excuse to toss her out.

"Too right. I need to pee. Where's the bog?"

"Madam." Emotionless, the valet pointed to an alcove covered by a tapestry hung from large brass rings. "Just there."

So much for trying to rattle him. Striving not to look disappointed, Kate thrust back the tapestry and sailed into the room. She hoped to find the facilities ridiculous, worthy of a blistering complaint. Instead, what she found was almost a religious experience.

A triple vanity in beige marble stood before an enormous gilt-edged mirror. Three woven baskets sat on the countertop, one filled with soaps, another with rolled hand towels, a third with tampons. Three subalcoves, divided by smaller yet still magnificent tapestries, awaited Kate. Peeking into the first, she found both a toilet and a bidet. It appeared the rich needed no locking stalls. A tapestry curtain on brass rings was sufficient; good breeding protected the sanctity of the loo.

When Kate exited, she expected another confrontation with the fish-lipped valet. Surely he expected her to emerge loaded down with soap, hand towels and a month's supply of tampons?

No. The valet was nowhere to be seen. Kate glanced at the landline again. No use continuing to call Hetheridge, and if Lady Margaret had a mobile number, Kate didn't know it. Kate thought for a moment. And then, instead of heading back downstairs into the ballroom, she wandered deeper into Lady Isabel Bartlow's home.

The first door she encountered led into what appeared to be a salon or study—Kate wasn't sure of the precise term. It held a small desk, a bookshelf and a dozen wall-mounted plaques and commendations issued to Lady Isabel's father or grandfather. There was no visible dust, but the room smelled disused.

The second door Kate encountered led into a broom cupboard. The third, to a small kitchenette outfitted with a dorm fridge, wine chiller, hotplate and lots of cabinetry. The fourth door opened onto an outdoor terrace overlooking the house's dark inner garden. Lit by two frosted glass globes, the terrace was furnished with a wrought iron table, two chairs and a small hooked rug. Enticed by the scent of fresh night air —October air, which always seemed imbued with wood smoke and a hint of frost—Kate wandered to the balcony's rail. For what seemed like a long time, she leaned against the chilly wrought iron, pushing her face into the breeze. Breathing deeply, she stared, mostly unseeing, into the darkness.

"What are you doing here?"

Kate's head whipped around. Her heart pounded so hard it threatened to leap out of her mouth. The voice was not accusing.

It was courteous, charming. But Kate's heart beat fast and hard, all the same.

"Forgive me. That came out altogether wrong," Sir Duncan Godington stepped onto the terrace. "What I meant to say is, how did a creature like you find yourself here? With this sort of crowd? With these people, who aren't your sort at all?"

There was nothing condescending in the question. At least, not toward Kate. Rather, it sounded as if Sir Duncan intended disrespect toward the vast majority of his half-sister's guests.

"I'm a friend of Lady Margaret Knolls," Kate said, sticking to the angle Hetheridge had chosen for her. "She thought I'd enjoy myself here tonight."

Sir Duncan regarded her steadily. He took one step closer. Then another. Kate was startled by her own visceral reaction. At close range, surrounded by the fresh October night, Sir Duncan was not handsome. He was beautiful.

"You know you don't belong here," he murmured. Pausing only an arm's length from Kate, he allowed his gaze to travel up her body—hips, waist, cleavage. Then he found her eyes, holding them as he continued to speak, like a trainer bent on mesmerizing a beast. "You're too authentic. Too real."

Kate didn't know what to say. Part of her was frightened. The rest was too charmed to respond, to launch into a line of questions, to do anything but gaze upon his face and his tall, well-proportioned physique.

"I think you're from Scotland Yard," Sir Duncan continued with a slow, conspiratorial smile. "Perhaps on the arm of that ghastly policeman. His father was a friend of my father's—and if that isn't condemnation across the board, I don't know what is. Lord Hetheridge, isn't it? Are you his protégé?"

Mention of Hetheridge's name brought Kate back to herself. It was like being immersed in a realistic dream—and then having the strong, unmistakable suspicion she needed to awaken.

"I did some research on you, Sir Duncan," Kate said. "To the press and the police, you've always spoken of your father with the utmost reverence. This is the first time you've ever said anything remotely unflattering about him."

Sir Duncan's smile widened. "Ah. But the trial's over. I've been acquitted. Can't be tried for the same crime again."

"True. But suppose another trial is looming? One involving Emmeline Wardle's murdered guests? Clive French and Trevor Parsons?"

Sir Duncan gave an elegant shrug. "Everywhere I go, my dear, I find tedious policemen desperate to saddle me with unsolved murders. Last year, in the south of France, I was meant to be a rapist/killer who cannibalized his victims. The year before that, in the United States, I was thought to have committed anarchist bombings. The year before that, in Scotland, I was believed to have strangled two old women for what amounted to twenty pounds." Sir Duncan put his head to one side, studying Kate frankly. "Now I have the misfortune to own a house next door to the site of a double murder. No doubt you were dispatched to inquire if I have any psychosexual fixations with the axe."

"Do you?" Kate tried to make it a challenge.

"None whatsoever. Were I to murder two university students at random, surely I could find a better way? Something with more style and panache than an axe buried in the skull?"

"Did your father and brother die with style and panache? Dismembered and mutilated, in the case of your father," Kate said. "Sawed in half while still alive, in the case of your brother."

Gaze unblinking, Sir Duncan came close enough to touch. "Which do you prefer? Truth? Or lie?"

Kate crossed her arms across her chest. "Lie."

"The way my beloved father and brother died was far from a display of style or panache," Sir Duncan recited. "It was the butchery of an unbalanced mind. But I do not believe they suffered. Their murderer, that deranged and evil person, attacked their bodies but could never harm their souls."

Kate was impressed. Sir Duncan stumbled only when he used the word "souls." He pronounced the word with an unconscious irony that most human beings, eager to believe the best of their fellow creatures, would never catch.

"Brilliant," Kate said, clapping. "Now. Truth."

"Ah, the truth." Sir Duncan's smile changed like the shifting of a serpent, its muscular coils rearranging as it took hold of its prey. "Do you recall when the ghost, Jacob Marley, visited Ebenezer Scrooge? He told Scrooge, 'You wear the chain you made in life. You forged it link by link—it is a ponderous chain!' So it was with my father and brother. They forged the fate that took them from this world. One can only hope they enjoyed the dénouement as much as ... well. As their destroyer did."

"But you killed the butler, too?" Kate asked. She wanted to be shocked—she should have been shocked—but mostly felt nothing but curiosity. It was curiosity that endured, even grew, as a detective wandered further into the excesses of human depravity. The ability to be shocked faded with each foray into the dark.

"Philip Jergens was your beloved family retainer, as you called him, time and time again," Kate said. "I can accept that you hated your father and brother. There's always hatred in families. But the old butler. Why did he have to die?"

"Because he was loyal to them," Sir Duncan said. "Completely loyal, and thus undeserving of mercy." Still without anger, without passion of any kind, Sir Duncan said, "Now you tell me. How could I have possibly done it? How could I have managed such an act, in such a tight timeline, in the manner the Crown prosecutor suggested?"

Before Kate could answer, Sir Duncan began shrugging out of his black silk jacket. "How could I have rushed from the airport to my ancestral home," he freed one arm, "committed triple murder," he freed the other, "fled headlong to my apartment and resumed my decadent life?" He held out the jacket to Kate with a gentle, and gentlemanly, smile.

She stared at it, cold to the bone but unable to accept.

"All without witnesses," Sir Duncan continued, jacket still offered between them. "And not a shred of physical evidence to connect me to the crimes. How did I pull it off?"

"You weren't alone. Your friends helped you," a familiar voice said from the doorway. "You've always had acolytes to do your dirty work, all your life. And once the act was finished, you bound them to you in a web tighter than anything Scotland Yard could hope to unravel."

CHAPTER FIFTEEN

"Ah. And here is the ghastly policeman, in the flesh." Sir Duncan inclined his head at Hetheridge. "What a pleasure!"

"Indeed." Hetheridge crossed the balcony to Kate's side. Taking Sir Duncan's jacket as if he were the intended recipient, Hetheridge draped it over Kate's shoulders with a proprietary flourish, positioning himself between her and Sir Duncan.

"By God, it's Lord Anthony Hetheridge, is it not?" Sir Duncan shook Hetheridge's hand. "Izzie called you a tired old wreck, but I disagree. You don't look a bit worse than you did at my trial."

"I'm flattered you remember me at all," Hetheridge said, smiling. "I was far from a major player in your trial, except near the end. The day that unfortunate stalker of yours was collared wearing women's clothes, as a matter of fact. And by then, the die was cast."

"Oh, never fear, Lord Hetheridge, I remember you well. I was only just telling your companion here ..." Sir Duncan stopped, swiveling back to Kate. "How inexcusably rude. I forgot to ask your name."

"I'm Kate." She worked to keep her tone light. Hetheridge's

appearance had shattered her concentration. Now she felt a bit off-balance, especially with Sir Duncan's weighty black jacket settled on her shoulders. It smelled of some woodsy cologne—familiar yet sexy. The kind of scent a woman instinctively liked. Trusted, even.

"Kate." Sir Duncan seemed to taste the name as much as say it. "Forgive me. I was so captivated by you, I dove right into the conversation, ignoring the necessary superficialities. Call me Duncan." His gaze shifted back to Hetheridge. "I was telling Kate that your father was a great friend of my father's."

"I'm afraid that doesn't say much for Sir Raleigh's character," Hetheridge said.

"I told Kate precisely the same thing about the late Lord Hetheridge," Sir Duncan laughed. Something seemed to thaw within him, subtly altering his face and carriage.

"All kidding aside, Tony—may I call you Tony?—I'm glad you came tonight, and not just because you brought this astonishing creature along. Now—back to your theory. By all means, tell me more about myself. You think I masterminded the triple murder? That I talked my mates into bloodying their hands in my service while I … what? Buggered off to establish an alibi?"

"You didn't bugger off. You wouldn't have missed it for the world," Hetheridge said. "At the very least, you sat back and watched while your friends slaughtered your father, brother and butler to your specifications. But I don't think so. I think you did all the major work yourself. Your friends were merely needed to keep lookout, hold down flailing limbs, ensure a smooth exit from the scene and so on."

"You wound me." Sir Duncan flashed that famous cannibal grin, the one the tabloids loved so much. "But Lord Hetheridge, if you'll recall, the jury not only exonerated me. Those jurors seemed appalled, frankly, that I was even accused. Why on earth would I commit such heinous acts?"

Hetheridge didn't answer. He merely kept his gaze locked with Sir Duncan's.

"Am I mentally ill?" Sir Duncan asked. "Do you consider me a psychopath?"

"No."

"A sociopath?"

"Indeed, I do not."

Kate was surprised. And to her chagrin, Sir Duncan inclined his head toward her.

"That was Kate's first thought," he said. "Rather obviously, too, if you'll forgive me for saying so. But she's not the first. It's a nice modern catch-all term for many a violent offender. Why not apply it to me?"

"In my experience," Hetheridge said, "speaking not as a psychiatrist, but merely a detective, true sociopaths are tone deaf, as it were, to the nuances of human relationships."

Sir Duncan folded his arms across his chest. His platinum cufflinks, each with a large G, flashed at Kate. "Tone deaf?"

"Yes. Mind you, sociopaths experience many of the same needs we all do," Hetheridge continued. "They attend schools, maintain jobs. I believe they can even love, in the way little children love—a combination of wanting and demanding. But sociopaths have no conscience, no innate sense of responsibility toward others. They cannot believe other people have separate lives beyond the sociopath's own needs and expectations. Sociopaths are incapable of empathy, though the more intelligent ones are frequently able to fake it. And that's the key."

Sir Duncan raised his eyebrows. "Is it?"

"Yes. I've been a policeman for a long time," Hetheridge said. "This much I know. Keep a sociopath off-balance long enough— put him in a complex social situation with no time to work out his feigned responses in advance—and he'll inadvertently reveal himself."

"Is that so?" Sir Duncan shot Kate a pleased look. "So Tony, do

I understand you correctly? You endorse my command of nuanced human relationships? You consider me—normal?"

"I do not consider you normal," Hetheridge said. He hadn't moved from Kate's side; he had, in fact, moved fractionally closer. "I consider you exceptional, Sir Duncan. Especially at offering flattery so well aimed, the recipient barely suspects what you're about. And when flattery seems inapt, you use insults to probe for soft spots. As you did with me a moment ago. And with that policeman's effigy downstairs."

"When you break down my approach, it sounds terribly artificial," Sir Duncan sighed. "How can you be sure I'm not the cleverest, best-prepared sociopath you've ever met?"

"Because I've seen you in extremis." Hetheridge paused, allowing that to sink in. "Though I doubt you had the slightest notion I was there. When Tessa Chilcott was shifted from New Scotland Yard to Parkwood Psychiatric Hospital for remand, I was there at the scene. I saw you cry out to her."

Sir Duncan's smile faded.

"You called her name," Hetheridge continued. "Tried to get her attention. Tried to speak with her. But she wouldn't respond. As they pushed Tessa into that van, I saw you collapse. Crumple into an empty doorway and weep, face against the bricks. No cameras to mug for. No jurors to convince." Hetheridge paused again, gaze locked with Sir Duncan's. "As I said, I am a detective, not a psychiatrist. Yet I believe I know what I saw. Simple, garden-variety guilt. And no sociopath alive feels that."

"What happened to Tessa was a mistake. On her part, and on mine." Before Kate's eyes, Sir Duncan's demeanor changed subtly again, his voice roughening with a new intensity. "I could tell you more, but you don't seem to require many answers from me. So please, Tony, do go on. Tell me your version of how the triple murders occurred."

"Mind you, it's only a theory." Hetheridge's tone was mild. "But judging from what we learned of your past, I think your mother, Lady Godington, died a natural death. Or at the very least, one you weren't involved in. When your father took your governess as his new mistress, it struck you as the very worst sort of betrayal. We know you were a physically strong, remarkably intelligent young boy. Fully capable of killing the governess for taking your mother's place. Probably you smothered her as she slept. And I doubt anyone ever suspected you, or guessed a little boy might be capable of such an act.

"Once you graduated university," Hetheridge continued, "you went off to the third world to do green activism and wildlife conservation. Statistics from those countries proved virtually useless to us. But I noticed something interesting during your final months in Borneo. A man was found dead on the outskirts of Kuching. He had a reputation as a successful poacher. He appeared to have been sawed in half, either by sword or machete."

Sir Duncan's grin reappeared. "What a bloody shame."

"Indeed. We know you made two trips home before returning permanently to England. I think during that time, you gathered your friends to you, told them your plans for your father and brother, and enlisted their aid. The triple murder went off almost without a hitch. A few traces of forensic evidence here and there, but nothing your brief couldn't argue away. Your hair strands at the scene meant nothing—you admitted to visiting the house that day. Blood tracked on the lawn and splattered on a hedge didn't point definitely to you. Even the traces of blood found in your Range Rover didn't move the jury. They bought the defense's theory, ridiculous as it was, that a sloppy lab might confuse your own blood, from a small wound, with the blood of your father or brother. Naturally, your brief knew all this, and much more, ahead of time, because a detective foolishly confided in his girl-friend, Tessa Chilcott. And she brought every scrap of information back to you and your team.

"Now here," Hetheridge paused. "Here is an area upon which

I'm unclear. Did you go so far as to send Ms. Chilcott to befriend, even seduce, a detective on the case? Or did she undertake that seduction on her own, to help you?"

Kate waited, determined to keep her face blank. She didn't know which answer Paul Bhar would have preferred—or indeed, at this late date, if he still cared. But remembering Tessa Chilcott as pictured beside Sir Duncan in that long-ago society column—a painfully thin young woman with masses of thick dark hair—Kate found herself wanting to know the truth.

Sir Duncan did not answer. He merely waited, transparently expectant, for Hetheridge to finish. The fire that flashed briefly at the mention of Tessa's mental breakdown was gone again, or safely under control.

"I suppose the truth doesn't matter now," Hetheridge said at last. "Ms. Chilcott's early contribution to your defense sealed your acquittal. Afterwards, you were seen together, out on the town. Then she was arrested for stabbing a woman to death—a perfect stranger, chosen at random on the street. The police report said Ms. Chilcott appeared unable to comprehend the gravity of her actions. I must tell you, there was some talk in the Met that she put on an act of madness to avoid conviction, but I never believed that. I think the truth was rather darker."

Hetheridge paused. Sir Duncan did not interrupt. Kate sensed the pull of energy between the two men, felt Sir Duncan's unspoken warning. But if Hetheridge was aware, he continued nevertheless.

"I think Tessa Chilcott loved you. Loved you enough to participate in the vengeance you wrought against the three people you hated most. Perhaps as long as you were under arrest, and thus in danger, she was able to put aside the knowledge of what she'd done. But after your release, she fell apart. Descended into true psychosis. I think she killed that stranger to prove to herself she could be like you. A person for whom murder is just another choice. When Tessa discovered it wasn't, her mind snapped. And to my knowledge, she's shown little progress toward recovery, even after years of custodial psychiatric treatment."

"A person like me," Sir Duncan repeated softly. "But if in your estimation I'm not a psychopath or a sociopath, what am I? What's the clinical term these days?"

"A very old one," Hetheridge said. "In my early days on the job, I wouldn't have hesitated to apply that word to you. Nowadays ... suffice it to say, I don't know what you are."

Sir Duncan's gaze shifted to Kate. She found herself pinned again by the intensity of that stare, by his physical presence. Intellectually, it was impossible for her to find such a person attractive. Yet on some level, the man kept forcing her body to react.

"Will I tarnish myself in your eyes, my dear Kate, if I reply to Tony's accusations?" Sir Duncan sounded amused.

Kate shrugged. She was furious with herself for that visceral attraction. Furious, mystified and once again questioning her own sanity—as she always did when a completely inappropriate man provoked her familiar, self-destructive response.

A cold breeze swept across the balcony, reminding Kate of whose coat was draped across her shoulders. Shrugging free, she held it out to Sir Duncan.

"Where shall I correct you?" Sir Duncan asked Hetheridge, sliding into his jacket with effortless grace. "On only a few points. I did not kill a poacher in Borneo. I killed eight poachers in Borneo. A minimal loss for the human race, to be sure.

"As for why Tessa killed that stranger ..." Sir Duncan lifted each sleeve, adjusting his cuff links. "I've thought about it so many times. I don't know. But I'm certain she was psychotic before she did it, and therefore not to blame.

"But am I to blame, for befriending her, for trusting her, for allowing her into my inner world?" Sir Duncan, almost a head taller than Hetheridge, leaned close, too close for polite society. "I would say—yes. Nothing can help her. Not money, not solicitors, not doctors. Which means I must live with my guilt. And I can honestly say that of all my dark deeds, my role in Tessa's disintegration is the only one that causes me shame."

"As it should." Hetheridge stood his ground, unblinking. "It's not every man whose association can drive a normal woman stark raving mad. Tessa Chilcott strikes me as terminally thick. Before you taught her how to commit murder, you might have warned her not to try it at home."

Sir Duncan's upper lip curled back. His fist went up almost faster than Kate's eye could follow. Once again, her body reacted differently than her mind—throwing herself in front of Hetheridge, right arm shooting up to block the punch that never came.

Sir Duncan stared at Kate. They both must have looked completely ridiculous, each with an arm raised. Kate, highly rated in martial arts and self-defense, slowly drew her arm back to her side. She'd fought many times, in many ways, but never in a rented ball gown and teetering high heels.

Sir Duncan stepped back. He was cold again, perfectly composed. Putting his head to one side, he studied Hetheridge, then Kate, then Hetheridge again.

"What is this?" Sir Duncan murmured. "Tony. I assumed dear Kate was merely your colleague. Is she in fact … yours?"

Hetheridge gave a short, unpleasant laugh. "Old wreck I may be. Yet I haven't been reduced to dating plods off the beat."

"I suppose not. Roddy Hetheridge and his fox killers would have a field day. Now," Sir Duncan said. "This conversation has been fascinating, but I really must return to my other guests. Tell me, Tony, have I said or done anything to allay your suspicion I had something to do with the double murder in Chelsea?"

"All in good time." Hetheridge sounded perfectly serene, as if the other man's aborted attack had never occurred. "I trust if the

Met formally requests your assistance with our inquiries, you shall make yourself available forthwith?"

"Only if my brief informs me I have no other choice. I did not put the axe to those children's skulls. Believe me. Now have the good taste to get the hell out of my sister's house." Without waiting to see them comply, Sir Duncan turned, exiting the terrace without a backward glance.

Kate watched, tense all over, until certain Sir Duncan was truly gone. Then she turned back to Hetheridge. To her surprise, she found him standing with eyes closed, taking deep breaths.

"What is it? Are you all right?"

Hetheridge's eyes opened. "Sorry about that. Just regaining my composure."

"What? Why?"

"Because that man frightens me to my very bones. I don't suppose you felt the same?"

"Not really," Kate admitted. "Maybe when he lost control and started to hit you. Proof positive Sir Duncan's not a sociopath?"

"Indeed. And still nurses protective feelings for Tessa Chilcott, a detail that may someday prove helpful. I must say," Hetheridge continued, pinching the bridge of his nose, "during most of the interview, you looked positively besotted. If Marks & Spenser sold a Sir Duncan poster, would you pin it to the ceiling above your bed?"

Kate felt her cheeks go hot. "I haven't been reduced to dating plods on the beat," she retorted, doing her best Lord Hetheridge. "Feeling guilty for that?"

"Not a bit. I don't want Sir Duncan thinking you mean something to me. I don't want him thinking of you at all."

"How did you find me up here, anyway?"

"That bartender. The one you scolded me for overtipping. Quite an obliging fellow. Told me all about you venturing upstairs in search of a loo and never coming down again."

"So you created an informant. I suppose that's why you tip so big?"

Hetheridge's hand curved around Kate's waist, pulling her close. "I tip so big because I can afford to." Face to face, lips close to hers, he asked, "Do you need a drink as much as I do?"

Her heart was beating fast again. Why on earth did Hetheridge have to look so good in evening dress? It had been a long time since a man had held her this way. Too long.

"I do believe Sir Duncan threw us out."

"Not here. I know someplace better." He put their mouths together, kissing her softly, slowly, until her lips parted. Then he pulled back, something almost as predatory as Sir Duncan in those ice blue eyes. "Come with me."

CHAPTER SIXTEEN

Tipping the valet, Hetheridge waved him away, opening the car door for Kate himself. She was growing more accustomed to navigating the world in formal dress, he saw. She seated herself in the Lexus as elegantly as any lady born to a life of parties, fetes and limousine rides. Yet as Hetheridge slid behind the wheel, he spied Kate twisting her hands in her lap. Her nails were painted red—a departure for a woman who usually wore only clear polish—and chipped on the right, as if she'd nibbled them while his back was turned. Why? Even Sir Duncan had been taken by her. Psychoanalyzing such a man might be impossible, but he was no snob and no fool. Kate was warm and alive, her lush curves barely contained by that ball gown, blond hair escaping her chignon and curling along the back of her neck. True, Lady Isabel's party had been filled with beautiful women—slender, youthful and dressed to the nines. But only Kate possessed such heat in her hazel eyes; only Kate could be knowing yet not jaded, keenly observant but not cruel. And she had the most perfectly formed lips Hetheridge had ever seen.

He touched the nape of her neck. She made a little sound as his fingers tangled in those curls. Then he closed his mouth over hers, careful not to go too fast, half convinced she would pull away and bolt from the car. Instead Kate slid her arms around him, pulling him closer. He closed his eyes. In that moment Hetheridge forgot Sir Duncan, the case, even the Lexus itself. The driver idling behind them had to sound the horn twice to make him break away from Kate.

The valet was waving Hetheridge forward; the driver of the Fiat behind him was supplementing the horn with his middle finger. Cursing, Hetheridge put the Lexus in gear. Soon they were back on the road, Lady Isabel's house and Mayfair shrinking in the rearview mirror.

Hetheridge didn't engage the car's audio system; he had no interest in music, had almost forgotten such a thing existed. He felt Kate's hand slide up his trouser leg, tracing a light pattern on his thigh before creeping further up. It took everything he had to maintain the car's forward motion. Kate looked pleased with herself, smiling the way women do when they have a man under complete control. All Hetheridge could do was smile back. And drive faster.

For a quiet drink, the Nautilus Hotel was his second choice. His first, an impossibly romantic bistro called Julian's, was closed for renovation. But the Nautilus was always open, twenty-four/seven, Christmas and Easter and every day in between. There were no velvet ropes and no valet. The hotel, built in 1940, did not advertise and had never been touted as a tourist destination; top travel guides mysteriously, uniformly rated it as a place to avoid. At the Nautilus, patrons self-parked, registered under any name they liked and relaxed in the lounge—MP and girlfriend, pop star and groupie, tart and vicar. William and Kate had shared many a late night in that bar, as Hetheridge well knew. Diana and Dodi had also been known to check in, once upon a time. The hotel offered few amenities but unparalleled discretion.

Hetheridge kept his hand on the small of Kate's back as they moved toward the bar. Most of the leather-topped stools were taken, so Hetheridge helped Kate onto one of the few free seats, standing just behind her to order. As they waited for their drinks, his mind catalogued his surroundings. It was every detective's inner failing, a mental avalanche of details—two exits, no windows, a house phone behind the bar and a prison tattoo on the bartender's forearm. Bleach soaking the bar rags, fresh pint glasses clinking as they were unloaded, tiny flames dancing in the tabletop lanterns. And Kate, eating her entire strawberry before taking the first sip of Prosecco, well aware he couldn't tear his gaze away from her mouth.

Or from any part of Kate. Her hair had fallen loose on one side; her heels sat empty on the floor. The longer Hetheridge looked at her, the less he heard the giggles of underage girls in the corner or noticed the rent boy chatting up his married punter. The tsunami of mundane faded away.

Before long, Kate's slender flute glass was empty, the strawberry reduced to a ragged green cap. Hetheridge knocked back his own single-malt Scotch without tasting it. Sinful—one might just as soon drink rotgut—but he hadn't selected the Nautilus because he was feeling saintly.

He checked in under his usual alias—"Roderick Hetheridge and Companion." One fine day Randy Roddy would make yet another hypocritical speech about his "solid English values" and some reporter would finally uncover a trail of one-nighters in posh London hotels. Then perhaps Roderick's beleaguered wife would finally gather the courage to leave him, no matter how fervently her eternally unzipped husband promised to change.

Kate, still barefoot with heels in hand, rested her head on Hetheridge's shoulder as they took the lift up to their room. He kept his arm about her waist, watching the floors slide past the lift's old-fashioned iron gates. When the attendant pulled it open —like the doorman he was careful to make no eye contact, muttering only a half-audible "sir"—Hetheridge passed the young man a folded bill, making sure Kate didn't see the denomination. Why had he bothered using Roderick's name here? No member of the Nautilus staff would ever give it up. Not even *The Sun* provided sufficient incentive to make them crack when the perks of employment were so good.

Hetheridge swiped his plastic card in the room's electronic lock, opening the door and letting Kate slip past. He was perfectly content to follow. The unconscious swing of those hips was mesmerizing.

The room was modest—writing desk, television, half-bath. And a bed. Tossing her heels on the floor, Kate went to the window and drew back the curtains. As she looked down at the street, still bright and busy, Hetheridge doused the room's single lamp. Shrugging out of his suit jacket, he dropped it on the bedside table. Next came his tie—undone, off. Putting his hands on Kate's shoulders, he kissed the back of her neck, pressing his lips against one warm, fragrant blond tendril. For a moment she trembled in his grasp, again like a wild creature threatening to bolt. Hetheridge tightened his grip.

"I love you," he whispered. "God knows I love you."

Kate turned in his arms, kissing him fiercely, and everything else he'd planned to say melted away.

"I kept thinking you'd come by. After I went home from the hospital." Kate was curled in Hetheridge's arms, cheek pressed against his bare chest. "But you never did. Except to pick up Henry for his fencing lessons."

"I considered it."

"Bet you were afraid we'd have to talk about it."

His hand was tangled in Kate's hair, fingertips tracing her scalp in a way that made her shiver. "About what?"

"You almost getting yourself killed."

Hetheridge made a dismissive sound.

"What, then? Why'd you leave me to recover at home alone like a pariah?"

"I didn't. I directed Mrs. Snell to send you a plant."

"She did. It had slugs." Kate raised herself on one elbow. "Truth, Tony. Why?"

"Because you'd just miscarried. It hardly seemed like the time to pop round with a bouquet of flowers and declare my intentions."

Kate rolled her eyes. "I thought you'd changed your mind about me. I thought you regretted—well. Everything. And when you told me about tonight's party ... even told me what to wear, like I might show up wearing red sequins and chewing bubblegum ..."

He retaliated by caressing her neck and shoulders. "I told you. I wanted you visually optimized from an undercover standpoint. That's all."

"Undercover." Kate sighed, pushing the sheet aside to take full advantage of the massage. This rendered her quite the opposite of undercover. And provoked such a strong physical response in Hetheridge, he suddenly doubted he was sixty.

"I don't know what was undercover about it," Kate continued. "Sir Duncan and Lady Isabel expected us. Set up that effigy. They even—oi!" Kate sat up, playfully covering herself with hands and arms when Hetheridge snapped on the bedside lamp. "What'd you do that for?"

"I'm old. I require better light to see you," he said placidly.

"Tony." The covering hands and arms fell away, rendering Kate perfectly, gloriously nude. "If we're going to do this, you have to quit carping on your age. I can count. And I'm not going to talk you off the ledge twice a week because you're a little older than me."

Hetheridge didn't bother to correct her, unless by "little" she actually meant twenty-seven years. Instead he let his hands travel, cataloguing her curves until she giggled.

"*Are* we going to do this?" she demanded, placing her fists on her hips with mock severity.

"Yes. Which brings me to this." Reaching for his suit jacket, Hetheridge located the square bulge in the inner pocket. Before Kate could say a word, he'd opened the silver-plated jewel box. Too fast for her to speak—but not too fast to see the horror in her eyes.

"Oh." Kate put a hand to her throat. She stared at the vintage ring—the cushion-cut diamond paired with identical sapphires—as if it were a piranha or a dirty bomb. "I—I can't. I can't."

He was too experienced a policeman and interrogator to let his inner despair show. "Why not?"

Kate gaped at him. "Because I can never be Lady Hetheridge."

Steeling himself, Hetheridge sat up, the boxed engagement ring still in his hand. "Why not?"

Kate let out a pained laugh. The sound rescued Hetheridge, saving him from true anger, from true hurt. The moment he heard it, he understood instinctively, no matter how long it took his brain and spinal cord to catch up.

"Because everyone will crucify you." Blinking rapidly, Kate took a deep breath. "Your family. The press. The Yard. Everyone. You'll lose everything. Your heir—Roddy Roddington or whatever he's called—will haul you into court, don't think he won't. He'll say some young chippie from the wrong part of London exerted undue influence. The Yard will sack us both, or sack me and reassign you. And the press?" She gave a high, hysterical laugh. "Can't you just see it? Lord Hetheridge loses his mind over a prostitute's daughter! Now a lovely Christmas lunch looms— the Hetheridges, the prostitute mum-in-law, the retarded brother-in law and the mentally ill aunt!"

Hetheridge waited. He was no longer much aware of the jewel box in his hand. He was, however, aware of the tears Kate fought so hard to conceal. Finally he pressed the bed sheet into her hand. She wiped her eyes.

"I shouldn't have called Ritchie retarded. We don't mean it bad," Kate said with a shaky smile. "In our family, we've always used the word. But I'm trying to stop because it bothers people nowadays. Makes them sad."

"No one loves Ritchie more than you," Hetheridge said, placing a hand against Kate's cheek. "Except possibly Henry."

"Ritchie's my big brother," Kate shrugged. She wiped at her face with the bed sheet again.

Hetheridge snapped the jewel box shut. With effort, he controlled himself—his impulse was to chuck it into the wall, but instead he placed it gently on the bedside table. "So your answer is no."

"My answer is never!" Casting the sheet aside, Kate straddled his chest in a way he might otherwise have found unbearable. "You live inside the privileged bubble, Tony, but you're a good man. A wonderful man. I won't be the one to destroy your life. To taint everything and make you hate me in the end."

"Kate." Catching her face in both hands, Hetheridge pulled her close, almost close enough for a kiss. "Promise me. It's just the title? Just the Peerage?"

She nodded, eyes brimming. "It is. Otherwise, my answer would be yes. I love you, Tony. I love you."

"Then that's enough for me. For now, at least." Hetheridge allowed himself one glance at the jewel box. Then Kate was rubbing against him, hungry for fresh satisfaction, the sort he knew he could deliver with lips and hands, possibly more. When she doused the lamp, he pinned her beneath him, passing the rest of their time at the Nautilus without words.

CHAPTER SEVENTEEN

Detective Sergeant Paul Bhar turned up at New Scotland Yard several times on Saturday, logging extra hours to avoid his mum. Sharada was deep in the grip of what Bhar privately thought of as "author meltdown." In the early days of her romance novelist career, many events could elicit author meltdown: a one-star review, a week of low sales, an editor's demand for fresh rewrites. Now his mum's worst moments seemed triggered by only one thing: Facebook.

"I've unfriended them all," Sharada sniffed. "All sixteen of them."

Bhar passed her a fresh Kleenex. "I'm sure they didn't mean to say you can't write for toffee. Did one of your writer friends actually say, verbatim, Sharada Bhar can't write for toffee?"

"They are not my friends." Sharada blew noisily into the tissue. "I have unfriended them. And if they don't message me in the next twenty-four hours and beg my forgiveness, I will block them. *Block* them," she cried, dabbing at the mascara stains under her eyes.

"Mum. What did they actually say?" Sometimes he had to be stern with her, as he was with a confabulating witness.

"Regina said, 'No offense, Sharada, but you write love scenes like English is your fourth language.' And Polly commented, 'LOL!'" Sharada blew into the tissue again.

Bhar waited. When no more details seemed forthcoming, he said, "That's two. Why did you unfriend the other fourteen?"

Sharada's wide eyes went even wider. "Because they said nothing! No one rushed to my defense! No one stood up for my honor!" She pointed a finger in his face. "Have you never heard it said? Silence equals death!"

"I've heard it said. In a slightly different context," Bhar said carefully. If he laughed or smiled, he would be the one who discovered death's equivalencies. "I'm not sure it meant you should Facebook-kill anyone who doesn't chime in on a post. Maybe your other friends were away, I don't know, having a coffee. Working their day job. Living their lives."

"What good are friends if they're off living their lives when I need them?" Sharada burst into fresh tears.

Bhar stood up. Before the advent of author meltdowns, he'd never once witnessed his mum break down. When he was nine and the family pet, Furby, had been eaten by a pack of dogs, Sharada had written him a letter, purportedly from Furby, explaining the joys of the feline afterlife. When he was fifteen and his father briefly ran away with an office temp, Sharada had rented a stack of comedy films and made him watch every last one. And when his father left for good, cutting off his wife and son without a penny, Sharada had declared only fools cry over betrayal.

"In this house we weep only for people who deserve it," she'd said. "Not a single tear for those who do not."

Yet there she was, his mum, sobbing into a crumpled Kleenex like her heart would break. Clearly being an author drove otherwise normal people mad. Especially when combined with Facebook.

"Hang on," Bhar said, hurrying to the kitchen. In less than a minute, he was back with an open pint of cookie dough ice cream and a long spoon. "Here."

Sharada peeked into the carton to check the flavor. "I am too upset. I could not possibly eat."

"Sure about that?" He made as if to dig into the pint himself.

"But since you've gone to all this trouble, I will force myself." She ate one small spoonful, then a bigger one. Bhar suspected an empty carton would appear in the rubbish bin before long.

"Thank you, Deepal. You're a good son."

"Yes. Well. Thanks, Mum. But I have to dash," he lied, giving her what he hoped was a regretful look. "The French-Parsons case calls."

"I still think you should recuse yourself," Sharada said around a third mouthful of ice cream.

"Can't," he called over his shoulder, and was gone.

Checking his messages at the Yard, Bhar learned Clive French's mother Molly had been released from residential care and was willing to be interviewed in the next few days. Apparently Clive had been her only living relative; most of her healthcare seemed to be coordinated by social services, her landlord and neighbors. It was Molly French's landlord who told Paul that an immediate interview was out of the question.

"She's not a well woman. Just got sprung from the bleeding nuthouse. And between you, me and the wall, they might have kept her a bit longer," the landlord said. "Poor old Molly won't comb her hair or take a bath. Took my wife to convince her to put some proper clothes on instead of going about in her night-gown all day."

"I see. Is there no one else to take care of her?"

"No one but Clive and now he's dead as a post, isn't he? And the bloody Met won't release the bloody body. Molly French never had too much strength, mind you, and she's already been put through more misery than one woman should ever have to bear. Now her boy's dead and she can't even bury him."

"I understand your concern," Bhar said. "But I'm not the enemy. My only goal is to get justice for Clive French."

"Is that right? Good on you." The landlord's gruff tone might or might not have been sarcasm. "Come round Tuesday at two o'clock. Don't expect to stay more than an hour. Don't expect no high tea, either."

Bhar's other lead, Phoebe Paquette, answered his call on the second ring. "Oh, of course, anything I can do to help. I'm home all weekend. Just doing a bit of decorating. Pop round right now, if you like."

"That's very kind. Where do you live?"

"Shepherd's Bush. May I ask—why did you choose me? The officer who took my statement the night of the murders didn't seem terribly impressed. He looked ready to fall asleep the whole time I was talking."

"I'm sure he was just overworked," Bhar said, knowing full well the officer in question was him. "As for why I chose you. Well. Another witness mentioned your name. Thought you might have insights into why Clive French or Trevor Parsons was targeted. That witness must remain confidential, of course, but—"

"Emmeline Wardle." Phoebe let out a sudden laugh. "She probably told you I'm the murderer. You aren't coming over to bang me up, are you?"

"Not unless you want to confess right now."

"Good, because I'm pregnant. What you might call ready to pop." Phoebe laughed again, loud and jarring. "Don't want to give birth in a cell."

Bhar reached the flat in Shepherd's Bush by midafternoon. After interviewing the Wardles in that white fairy tale castle, he expected a bit more than what he found—a brick walk-up with barred windows, a pokey foyer and gloomy front room.

"Oh, it's you! Mr. Sleepy Copper! Fancy a cuppa before I start nattering on?"

"I don't need caffeine. I'm quite refreshed," Bhar smiled.

"Brilliant. Well—what do you think? Home sweet home. Not much but it's all mine!" Phoebe Paquette showed Bhar around her front room, pointing out knickknacks here and there. "This house is my first major purchase. Still can't believe my name's on the lease."

"Home ownership is wonderful," Bhar said automatically, wondering if Sharada would ever permit him to move out. Of course, if his only recourse was a flat quite this grim, he'd prefer living at home, where his clothes never wanted pressing and his meals appeared as if by magic.

"Hah! You don't look terribly impressed. But I like the neighborhood, and the fact is, I had to move out. Mum and Dad went a bit doolally over this bit of news." Phoebe patted her pregnant belly. Dressed in a white cotton blouse and black leggings, her blond hair swept back in a ponytail, Phoebe looked too young to know where babies came from, much less expect one of her own.

"I'll be redoing the lounge in sky blue with white crown molding," she continued, pointing. "All the metal fixtures will be stainless steel. Very modern. Won't it be fab?"

"Fab," Bhar agreed. Anything would be an improvement over the current décor—burgundy wallpaper, stained carpet and a blackened hearth. "Lucky you could afford this place. Not many uni students could."

Phoebe grinned. "If that's your way of asking about my cash

situation, it's rather sad at present. But I have a trust fund. And after a bit of a legal battle, I got enough money released to buy this place and fix it up. Once I turn twenty-two, I'll be master of my own fate. Until then, it's a waiting game," she said, leading Bhar into the kitchen. The cabinetry was old and battered, but the walls had been recently painted. Two brand new appliances—a stainless steel refrigerator and cooker—looked wildly out of place.

"I'll admit, it's a bit small," Phoebe sighed. "But if I'd stayed at home, Mum would still be badgering me to give up the baby. And I won't."

"If you don't mind my asking—when is the baby due?"

"In three weeks." Phoebe managed to look ecstatic, terrified and amused all at once. "My hormones are all over the place. If I say something awful, or seem tone-deaf, chalk it up to hormones. What I asked you earlier—I'll bet that sounded really inappropriate." She emitted that laugh again, even louder and more jarring in person.

"What you asked?" Bhar repeated, trying not to frown. Phoebe's laugh was nails on a chalkboard.

"If you were coming to arrest me. Based on Emmeline's recommendation," Phoebe explained, leading Bhar up the stairs, which were surprisingly steep. "I mean, she doesn't like me. I don't like her. But I can't believe even Emmy White Lines would accuse me of murder."

"Emmy White Lines?"

Phoebe held up a finger. "Oi. Let me catch my breath." She panted for a moment, then started climbing again. "If I turn up in the antenatal unit ahead of schedule, it will be due to those fecking stairs. My bedroom's to the left." She pointed. "But there's nothing to see in there, officer. That horse left the barn eight months ago." Another laugh. "But come on, have a look at my next big thing, my pride and joy."

Bhar followed Phoebe into the nursery, where butter-yellow

walls were decorated with a thin floral stripe. A crib waited in the center of the room, already made up with a yellow blanket and filled with stuffed animals. A pleasant-looking young man with neat brown hair stood halfway up a stepladder, installing a new ceiling lamp with what looked like a Swiss Army knife.

"Sure that's safe?" Bhar called.

The young man paused. "Oh. Detective Bhar. Hallo." Climbing down from the ladder, Jeremy held out the folding toolkit so Bhar could see which implement he'd been using. "This model has three blades, plus a corkscrew and a Phillips head screwdriver. I never go anywhere without it. Not since I became Phoebe's handyman on call. Anyway, I reckon I'd better reintroduce myself. I suppose you meet new suspects every day."

"Jeremy, we're not suspects," Phoebe said. "You mustn't say things like that—it sounds bad. I've already scared Detective Bhar half to death with my laugh. He thinks I've gone round the bend. But it's just hormones!" Phoebe gave Bhar a cuff on the forearm. "Detective Bhar, this is my friend Jeremy Bentham. And no, he's not the dad-to-be. Just my Rock of Gibraltar."

Jeremy blinked. "He didn't ask if I was the dad."

"He's a policeman. He's going to ask us about everything. Jeremy?" Phoebe twisted her ponytail around a fingertip. "Would you hate me if I said I wanted curry again tonight?"

Jeremy smiled, transforming from merely cute to almost handsome. "Of course I won't hate you."

"I don't suppose …" Phoebe trailed off, still tugging on her hair.

"Now?" He frowned. "What if Detective Bhar wants to question me, too?"

"I'm only here to interview Ms. Paquette," Bhar said, putting on his most reassuring smile. Jeremy looked unconvinced.

"But Pheebs, I have a better memory than you," Jeremy said. "What if you forget something? Or say something wrong?"

She raised her eyebrows.

"Fine. Where's your bag?" the young man sighed.

"Downstairs. There should be enough cash in the inner pocket. If not, take my bank card."

As soon as Jeremy had gone, Phoebe visibly relaxed. "Don't be shy. Have a seat in the rocking chair."

Bhar did so, expecting Phoebe to sink onto the pouf near the crib. But she remained on her feet, pacing.

"Don't get me wrong," she said, circling the room in a slow waddle. "Jeremy is a sweetheart. The best friend a girl could ever want. But he can be a bit—clingy. The minute I told him you were coming by, he refused to go home. I knew if I didn't invent an errand, we'd never be able to speak privately."

"Is that important? For Jeremy not to hear us?" Bhar strove to look and sound neutral.

Phoebe blew out her breath. "He doesn't like to hear me talk about Trevor. The father of my baby, in case you're not one of the sharper detectives." She patted her stomach again. "Trevor and I used to date. I got pregnant and decided to keep the baby. He buggered off. Before long, he was dating Emmeline. Needless to say, that didn't exactly endear Trev to me."

"Emmeline claims you hated him."

Phoebe shrugged.

"*Did* you hate Trevor Parsons?" Bhar's notebook was out, pen ready. Sometimes he regretted the necessity of taking notes—for many witnesses, the sight of a notebook had a chilling effect—but unlike Hetheridge, he wasn't willing to gamble on memory alone. Nor would he dash off cryptic LOL-speak emails to himself, as Kate did. Bhar's notes were always perfect.

"I'm not sure I've ever really felt that. Hate, I mean." Drifting over to the window, Phoebe parted the curtains and stared into the street. "I was in love with Trevor for a while. That's the part Jeremy just can't get. Trev and I were great together, it was really special. Then I got pregnant and Trevor wanted to pretend like he never laid a finger on me."

"That would be sufficient to make most women hate him."

"But I understand why he panicked. Trev wasn't ready to be a dad. He expected to go into a pro athletics career and didn't want a wife and kiddie holding him down. I knew all that, and I chose to have the baby, anyway."

"Was Trevor prepared to support the child?"

Phoebe hugged her stomach protectively. "I think so. He knew if I took him to court, I'd win. And he was already sick of Em. He told me so just two weeks ago. We met in a caff for lunch and he said he was ready to give her a push if things didn't get better."

Bhar copied that into his notebook. "Under the circumstances, I'm surprised Emmeline invited you to her Halloween party."

"Yes. Well." Turning away from the window, Phoebe went to the empty white crib, picking up a stuffed teddy and fussing with its paws. "Emmeline invited Jeremy and Jeremy invited me. I accepted just for another chance to see Trev. See if he'd made a decision about leaving Em. We slipped away for a little. Had a beer together ..." She stopped, giving Bhar a mischievous look. "Don't tell Jeremy. He's a complete Nazi when it comes to me and my healthy pregnancy."

"How did it go?"

"He tried to stall me," she sighed. "I got angry. Told him he couldn't keep hiding his head in the sand. Or between Emmeline's legs." Phoebe tossed the teddy back into the crib. It landed face down.

Bhar pretended to jot down far more than he actually did, working to buy himself time. Once the silence finally made Phoebe restless—when she began to toy with the settings on the Fisher Price baby monitor—he asked, "What about cocaine? Was it just a party favor? Or the real reason for the party?"

"The reason." Phoebe's voice was flat. "I don't do coke

anymore. Haven't since I found out. But most of the guests were higher than kites."

"Emmeline Wardle seemed reasonable when I interviewed her. But the night of the murders she screamed herself hoarse, then got herself arrested. Her piss test is still pending, but I'll have it soon enough. She was coked out, wasn't she?"

"Emmeline Wardle can be tolerable. Emmy White Lines is a crazy, out-of-control cow." Phoebe's nails-on-chalkboard laugh followed. "Especially when her partner in crime isn't around."

"Partner in crime? Do you mean Kyla Sloane?"

"Who else?" At last Phoebe sank onto the pouf, shoulders sagging. "Kyla and Emmeline have been besties since nursery school. Sad to watch them throw it all away for a man. But we females are always mucking up the works running after the boys, aren't we? Kyla walked in on me and Trev alone together. He had his arms around me, so of course, she didn't wait for an explanation. She went straight to Emmeline." Phoebe snorted. "And Emmeline didn't believe her. She accused Kyla of wanting Trev for herself."

"Did she?"

"Not that I could ever see," Phoebe shrugged. "But Emmeline went nuts. Next thing I knew, they were rowing about Sir Duncan and Kyla's obsession …"

"Wait," Paul cut across Phoebe. It was poor practice to talk over an interviewee, but he couldn't help himself. "You don't mean Kyla Sloane was having an affair with Emmeline's neighbor? With Sir Duncan Godington?"

Phoebe emitted that laugh again, off-key and more cringe-inducing than ever. "Of course not! Why would you think that?"

Bhar cast about for a reasonable answer. The truth was, he didn't know why he'd said that. Only that Tessa Chilcott had been on his mind a great deal of late. "My colleague saw them together recently. At a society gala."

"You mean Izzie Bartlow's party?" Phoebe rolled her eyes.

"London society is one big incestuous circle. We all talk to each other. It doesn't mean a thing—certainly doesn't mean we're dating. But remember Tessa Chilcott? The woman who went mad for Sir Duncan?" Phoebe leaned forward confidentially. "Kyla is Tessa's half-sister."

CHAPTER EIGHTEEN

"How do you—are you sure?" Bhar fought not to look as surprised as he felt. "I never—Tessa—" He stopped, taking a deep breath. "Ms. Paquette, I was involved in the Sir Raleigh Godington murder case. I've met Tessa Chilcott. I don't recall her having a younger sister."

"I don't think they were close. Kyla isn't even the one who told me. Em told me during one of her coke binges. She was furious with Kyla over something silly and decided to spill Kyla's big secret."

"And you never told anyone?"

Phoebe shrugged. "I wasn't sure I could believe it. But after Kyla caught me with Trevor, I decided to find Em and do some damage control. I found them upstairs, hissing in a full-on catfight. Em said Kyla was in love with Trev. Kyla said it wasn't true. Em said Kyla was as crazy as her sister. Kyla was so furious, she chucked that heirloom vase." Phoebe smiled. "Em went wild. Half of all that screaming she did was over the vase, not Trev. And Kyla ran into the back garden. Probably to ring Sir Duncan, since I imagine Tessa isn't licensed to drive again yet."

"What?" Bhar was certain he'd misheard Phoebe. "What do

you mean, Tessa isn't licensed to drive? She's been committed into residential care."

"Well, then, the doctors must be permitting her home visits, eh? Kyla told Em she didn't need her, which is bollocks. Kyla's always been under Em's protection at uni. No one tried to take the mickey by teasing her too much because Em wouldn't have stood for it. And Em said, and I quote, 'Go home to your nutter sister. You're worse than she ever was.'" Phoebe smiled. "I think Kyla's charmed life in our hallowed halls has finally come to an end. One sec. Need some lippie stuff."

Going to the white-lacquered tall boy, Phoebe withdrew a key chain from the top drawer. Attached to the key chain's main ring was a shiny silver ball. Seating herself back on the pouf, Phoebe unscrewed the ball into separate halves, revealing a pot of lip balm inside.

"Sorry. Dry lips. Acne spots. Stretch marks. Who knew being pregnant sucks the life out of you like an alien parasite?" Dipping a finger in the pot, Phoebe coated her mouth with clear gloss before screwing the silver halves together again.

"I've seen one of those somewhere," Bhar said, mind still on Tessa. The idea of her making home visits was too much for him to process. And did she really have a half-sister? Or was it just a rumor borne of Kyla's uncanny resemblance to Sir Duncan's most famous alleged accomplice?

"Lots of the girls at uni have them. Some of the boys, too. Clive French had one, now that I think of it, clipped to his backpack."

"Speaking of Clive ... one challenge in the French-Parsons case is determining a motive that fits both victims. Emmeline told me Clive French was selling schoolwork—papers, quiz answers, things like that. She says he might have crashed her party to collect on unpaid debts. Did you ever witness that sort of behavior from him?"

"Once or twice." Phoebe rattled her keys, shifting them from hand to hand. "Listen. You might as well know the truth. I bought a chemistry paper from Clive last month. But I didn't owe him any money, I was all paid up. Buying a university paper—that isn't the sort of thing Scotland Yard actually arrests pregnant women for, is it?"

"Of course not. The only thing I care about is the identity of the killer. Or killers," Bhar amended. "Apart from the row Emmeline and Kyla had over Trevor—apart from the thrown vase—did you witness any other violent behavior? Any potentially explosive interactions?"

"Well. I did hear Trev call Em a cow and Kyla a slag. Kyla screamed that she hated everyone. Em said what she said about Tessa and *bang* went the vase, smashed into a million pieces. Emmy said she was going to kill Kyla over the vase, but I think we can chalk that up to—well, chalk dust." Phoebe pantomimed sniffing an imaginary line. "Someone told Jeremy they saw a stranger outside. Jeremy told me he'd go have a look. Later—the next day—he told me he'd checked the front and back, and no one was there."

"What time was this? When Jeremy checked the premises outside the townhouse, I mean?"

"You'll have to ask Jeremy," Phoebe said. "Once Trev died and Emmy started screaming, everything went a bit cuckoo, you know? Besides, I think the intruder story was just a silly rumor. The kind of thing people spread around Halloween."

Bhar regarded his notes for a moment, purely to give himself breathing room. In truth, his eyes saw the page but registered nothing.

"So," he began at last. "Plenty of people seem to have disliked Clive French. As far as Trevor Parsons goes, at least three people disliked him—you, Emmeline and Kyla. Is there anyone else who might have wished Trevor ill?"

"I don't think so. I mean, I'm sure Trev was in debt to Emmy for party favors. And heaven knows she needs the money, but

Trev would have paid her eventually. Brought in new buyers, too, since he was always surrounded by wannabes. Em's strong—anyone who's ever seen her compete in gymnastics knows that, she's almost as strong as Kyla. But strength aside, assuming Em had the guts to murder a man with an axe—two men—I can't believe she'd kill a good customer. Not now, anyway."

"A customer?" Bhar blinked. "As in …" He started to ask, "Sex?" but that seemed too far-fetched to say aloud. "And what do you mean, 'heaven knows she needs the money'? The Wardles are rolling in it. I've seen their main home."

"What do you mean you've seen it? It's gone," Phoebe said. "All the Wardles have left is the townhouse, and it's next on the block. Their old manor in Belgravia was bulldozed months ago to make room for something modern."

"Right. Hang on. Let's start from the top." Bhar put his pen and notebook aside. "Why does Emmeline Wardle need money? Her father's a frozen foods baron. They live in a big white mansion in Holland Park."

Phoebe emitted her loud cackle. "Oh! I thought since you were the police, you knew everything. About all of us. Hah! Allow me to assist with your inquiries. As far as Em's dear old dad goes, he's losing his shirt. Global recession, you know. Word is, he'll liquidate what little he has left and move to the States. Try to start over with frozen chicken."

Arkansas, Bhar thought, remembering his phone conversation with Kate and the question he'd neglected to ask. He was hazy on U.S. geography, but wasn't Arkansas mostly farmland?

"And the Wardles' house in Holland Park? Are they losing it?"

"It's not theirs. If you mean Euro Disney, as we call it, that house belongs to one of Mrs. Wardle's friends. I'm sure she thought it would make an intimidating setting for sweet little Emmy's interview." Phoebe raised her eyebrows. "Were you impressed?"

"Unduly," Bhar muttered. "So. Back to the party. You said the point was cocaine. Are you telling me Emmeline Wardle was the dealer?"

"Not really. That would be too much like getting her hands dirty. But Em provided the venue and took a cut. That's what I hear." Tossing her ponytail, Phoebe gave her pregnant belly another pat. "Sorry. Hormones make me so foggy. Can't remember who said it."

"Of course not." Bhar studied the young woman's face for as long as he dared. Was she as straightforward as she seemed? Or perfectly, brilliantly manipulative? And was a man who'd been taken in by Tessa Chilcott capable of discerning the difference?

"Is it safe to say, when Emmeline sent me to interview you, she thought you didn't know about her method of earning extra income?"

"Nope. Everyone who went to the party knew she'd teamed up with one dealer or other," Phoebe said. "Em just assumed I wouldn't dare mention it to you. But I've had to put up with Em since she was eight years old. Every school I attended, every summer camp, every birthday party, she was always there, throwing a tantrum and getting her way. Now her day in the sun is almost over. Once I have full access to my trust fund, I'll be able to buy and sell her."

"Will you?" Though Bhar had made a few enemies at the Met, he doubted he'd ever find himself in such a position. "Buy and sell Emmeline Wardle, I mean?"

"I don't know." Phoebe unscrewed the silver ball to apply a fresh coat of lip balm. "We never know what money will do to us until we hold the cash in hand."

When Bhar arrived home that evening, an empty pint of cookie dough ice cream lay in the rubbish bin. Calm and composed, Sharada made him dinner with a minimum of conversation, staring into space while he worked his way through yellow rice, butter chicken and aloo mutter. A less attuned son might fear Sharada was still obsessing over the rift with her Facebook writers' group, but Bhar knew that blank, dreamy look all too well. His mum was going through the motions of dinner with him because she felt it was her duty. As soon as he finished and the dishes were cleared, she headed to the computer to begin typing up whatever was happening behind those long-lashed black eyes.

After an hour trying to locate something bearable to watch on television, Bhar regretted properly outsourcing Phoebe Paquette's accusations to the detective inspector in charge of the case's Incident Room. Several tasks had been logged in the case's Action Book:

Determine ownership of the white "Euro Disney" mansion in Holland Park;

Evaluate the financial viability of Mr. Wardle's frozen foods company;

Locate Kyla Sloane's original birth certificate;

Confirm or deny any relationship between Kyla Sloan and Tessa Chilcott.

Bhar possessed the detective skills, computer access and tenacity to accomplish all those tasks himself. Hetheridge preferred for his detectives to focus on the big picture while letting subordinates check and double-check the details. But that didn't mean Bhar couldn't securely log into his New Scotland Yard workstation from home and check for new developments.

Emmeline Wardle's urinalysis was back. Not surprisingly, the test was positive for both alcohol and cocaine. Phoebe Paquette had been truthful about that particular detail, even if all the rest was still in doubt.

Bhar scrolled through the rest of the witness list, looking at photographs until he found the one he sought. Kyla Sloane. Yes, she was pretty—exactly his type. Once upon a time, Tessa Chilcott had been much like Kyla. Not in that society-page photo with the newly acquitted Sir Duncan by her side, looking wan and fragile. And certainly not in her mug shot, with matted hair and staring eyes. But the very first time Bhar met Tessa, at a New Year's party packed with people he didn't know, Tessa had been like Kyla: lovely, fresh and hopeful.

Dateless and determined to ring in the New Year in possession of at least one phone number, Bhar had approached Tessa—slender and elegant, with long-lashed eyes and a cloud of dark curls. She was looking down at her feet, fidgeting inside a pair of shoes with pointed toes and tall heels. As Bhar watched, Tessa kept trying to reposition herself, searching for a more comfortable way to stand. Finally she looked up, saw him watching her and stopped fidgeting, smiling so beautifully he was left speechless.

"Funny about my feet. They just won't fit these shoes."

"Well. Um. Er." Bhar had cleared his throat. "Surely it's the other way round? Shouldn't your shoes fit your feet?"

"D'you think?" Tessa regarded him doubtfully. "The size is right, and they come very highly recommended. But my feet are wrong somehow."

Three months after that first meeting, Bhar had expected to marry Tessa. He knew she was elusive, changeable, never quite within his reach. But he'd been certain he could win her over, make her his own, make her happy. And he'd gone on believing that until the day she rang him to say she loved Sir Duncan Godington and was returning to his side.

"I'm sorry," Tessa had wept, voice so distorted he'd known her tears were genuine. "You're so kind. So perfect. I can't be with you. I just can't."

Fourteen months after that first meeting, Bhar had tried, unbeknownst to Sharada or anyone else, to visit Tessa at Parkwood. Ward sisters had escorted her into the visiting room. Gaze downcast and hair scraped back in a bun, Tessa had been dressed in a soft track suit without zippers or buttons. As her eyes lifted, Bhar put on the smile he'd practiced before the mirror.

Tessa screamed. Not his name, nothing but "No!" over and over again. Blundering backward, stumbling over the plain institution-style table and chairs, Tessa had cowered in a corner until the ward sisters successfully dragged her away. The same thing happened on his second and final visit. Bhar had left uncertain if Tessa rejected him personally, or simply fled an unknown visitor in her deranged state. He never decided which interpretation he preferred.

In those days, Bhar's disgrace at the Yard and the very real threat of dismissal—the series of simple-minded assignments, the daily gauntlet of cold shoulders and contempt—had been a blessing. If the Bhar family had incorporated any British adage into its DNA, it was "Keep calm and carry on." His father, rocked by midlife disillusionment, had carried on with his mistress into a brand new life. His mum, humiliated and frightened by her husband's defection, had carried on into a modest but highly satisfying career. And Bhar, golden in both his didactics and his field performance, had fallen so low he'd been forced to decide. Sweep up the last bits of his dignity and bugger off to a different branch of the civil service—or swallow his pride, take his lumps and carry on.

That was a key difference between him and DS Kate Wakefield. He knew enough of her history, despite her rather secretive nature, to guess she had stumbled into police work. A more typical life course for a woman with her upbringing was to leave school early, have a baby or two and settle down to a life of telly and the dole. Instead, Kate had confounded the entire sociologic blueprint of her existence. After their last case, even the Met's Jurassic top brass had begun seeing Kate as a hot property. By contrast, Bhar was a has-been, a former up-and-comer who'd torpedoed his own career out of naiveté and a wild desire to impress the woman he loved.

Bhar blinked at his computer monitor. He wasn't looking at Tessa Chilcott. No. This was Kyla Sloane—dark and delicately pretty, but with a sharpness to those fine eyes that Tessa had always lacked. His mum had worried because to her, all young women looked alike—threats to her beloved son's future happiness. But Kyla wasn't really so much like Tessa. Kyla had the air of a survivor. And besides—Bhar had evolved beyond his early preferences. When he finally settled down, his bride would possess the perfect combination of looks, sexual combustibility and cash. And if he never hit on such a trifecta of feminine perfection, he was content to spend the rest of his life rebuilding his career.

He had logged out of his Met workstation and drifted over to an Internet gaming site—he was quite good at video poker— when his mobile rang. It was DI Owen Wasserman, weekend manager of the French-Parsons incident room.

"On a date, Paulie, my lad?" Wasserman always sounded cheery.

"Of course. Having it off with Stella Artois and my right hand. Wotcha?"

"You poor sick sod," Wasserman chuckled. "You can't handle what I got. Tried ringing My Lord, but he's not answering. Harvey the manservant says he's 'away.'"

"I heard he flew Mrs. Snell to Las Vegas for a quickie wedding," Bhar said. It was the sort of speculation they all enjoyed about "Lady Hetheridge," as Mrs. Snell was unaffectionately known around the Yard.

"Never. I heard he's doing the dirty with Chop-Off-Your-Bollocks Kate."

Bhar forced a laugh. But that was a little too close to the truth to let stand. "You've got it all wrong, as usual. Our Kate's a lesbian. Only goes for birds that look like Posh Spice."

"Sure. And you're a poof dating blokes what look like David Beckham. Can we get on? You want to hear this bit o' game-changing info, or shall I just ring *The News of the World* and have done with it?"

"Tell me." Bhar was already consulting his PIN generator, imputing the random passcode that currently gave him access to his Met workstation once again.

"Did you know the Wardle house on Burnaby Street has been sold? A rush job, but held up in court for another day or so. Who do you think bought it?"

"Paul McCartney."

"Sir Duncan Godington," Wasserman intoned, adding a few quiz show *dings* as if Bhar had guessed correctly. "And did you know the Wardle house had two CCTV cameras?"

"I did. Both were mounted about three meters up. And looked knocked about."

"They was. Some clever git hit 'em with a stone or summat. The front camera gave FSS nothing but lovely pictures o' the constellations. Suitable for framing or wrapping fish. But the camera in the back garden, where Clive French died ..."

"Tell me," Bhar said. Something in Wasserman's tone made the hairs on the back of his neck rise.

"Don't take my word for it. See for yourself." Wasserman told Bhar which file to access.

The image was digital but taken from so far up, several key details were sacrificed. Bhar saw an indistinct figure on the ground that had to be Clive French, right where the police discovered him.

"Oi! This could be gold. Don't hold back, Wass! Did you get pics of the murder?"

"Nope. Out of range. Everything this camera got came after the murder. Keep looking."

Not far from Clive's corpse stood a compressed figure with long dark hair. Bhar had little doubt it was Kyla Sloane. That, however, was the sort of supposition unlikely to gain purchase in a court of law. After all, no part of the female's face was visible.

"Look at the bloke in the foreground," Wasserman said impatiently.

Bhar studied the tall man with blond, light brown or gray hair. From the camera angle, his face was visible, but too shadowed to identify.

"Mystery man?"

"Oh, ye of little faith. Shall I apply a bit o' facial recognition software?"

"For all the good it will do," Bhar said. Most of the time, CCTV camera images were too compromised by their height and broad scope to render the positive ID needed for a murder case. The sort of facial geometry such computer software relied upon —the distance between each eye, between the top of the nose and the bow of the upper lip, etc.—was hard-pressed to function on foreshortened, shadowed CCTV pictures.

"Hah!" Wasserman crowed in Bhar's ear. "Now who might that be, standing bold as brass at the scene of the crime?"

Bhar bit his lip. He couldn't say the name. Sir Duncan Godington.

CHAPTER NINETEEN

I t was too cold and windy for tea in Wellegrave House's
walled garden, so Chief Superintendent Hetheridge's
manservant, Harvey, served Hetheridge, Kate and Bhar in
the small salon. With the curtains drawn back, the floor-to-
ceiling windows allowed the trio to take in autumn's last hurrah
while discussing the French-Parsons case in comfort.

"It will take a bit of time to officially determine whether the
Wardles are as desperate for capital as Ms. Paquette asserted,"
Hetheridge said. "But unofficially, I already have confirmation
that it is true. Mr. Wardle overextended himself during the global
banking crisis and now stands to lose everything." Hetheridge
poured himself a second cup of tea. The silver tea service, a
rather monstrous Victorian relic from the Hetheridges of yore,
was so highly polished, he could see his own distorted reflection.
When he dined alone, he preferred his white ceramic service,
purchased on holiday in Japan. But Harvey would never dream of
subjecting Hetheridge's rare guests to such simplicity.

"Unofficial means we're once again treating Lady Margaret's
opinion as fact, doesn't it?" Bhar rolled his eyes. "It can't be good,
always turning to that old bat for gossip. How do we know she

doesn't just have it in for Emmeline's dad? Lady Margaret always struck me as a bit of a man-hater."

"Oh, please. Lady Margaret doesn't hate all men. Just you." Kate buttered her toast with vigor. "Anyway, it explains why the Wardles are trying to sue the Met over that vase. The silly thing was all they had left. Though I do plan on asking Kyla Sloane why she smashed it."

"Phoebe told us why," Bhar said. "During a catfight with Emmeline over the apparently irresistible Trevor Parsons."

Kate made a scornful noise. "Yes, of course, Phoebe Paquette. Now there's a disinterested witness. The woman Trevor Parsons knocked up, making accusations and even stapling motives onto her rivals. Both of whom she's hated for years." Delving into Harvey's homemade blackberry jam, Kate spread a thick layer atop her butter-soaked toast. "I don't necessarily doubt Kyla threw that vase. But if she did, why aren't the Wardles suing Kyla? Besides—Kyla seemed so well controlled. It was the first thing I noticed about her." Kate took a bite of toast.

"Back to your evil ways, I see. Butter and jam. Given up on slimming?" Bhar put on a mock-sympathetic look, as if ready to hear her confession.

Kate took her time chewing. "I heard you prefer slim girls," she said at last, "so I'm stuffing my gob as fast as I can."

"Is that a fact? Well. Just so happens *I've* heard—" Bhar stopped. He didn't seem to know how to continue, his look of triumph fading away.

Hetheridge, a forkful of eggs halfway to his mouth, also halted. So did Kate. No one spoke.

Kate shot Hetheridge a quick, guarded glance. Bhar did the same, meeting Hetheridge's eyes for a half second. Then he turned back to Kate, giving her what he no doubt hoped was a nonchalant shrug.

"I've heard nothing but sunshine and daisies," he finished woodenly.

"Brilliant. Can't tell you how relieved I am." Kate pushed her plate away.

Hetheridge cleared his throat. He'd used this trick many times before—the loud, theatrical interruption always produced the desired response. Kate and Bhar snapped to attention.

"I enjoy gossip and rumors as much as the next man. Particularly if that man pries into secrets and lies for a living." Leaning back in his chair, Hetheridge regarded his junior officers steadily. "I believe there will need to be a reckoning between the three of us, and soon. But just for now, just for this discussion, let's focus on Clive French and Trevor Parsons. At the end of the day, capturing their killer is more important than office gossip. Agreed?"

"Agreed," Bhar said.

"Of course," Kate said.

"I've read every pertinent bit of data provided by the Incident Room manager," Hetheridge continued, gesturing toward the table's center. Between the tea service and the rashers of bacon, Harvey's bowl of yellow chrysanthemums had been replaced with a stack of affidavits, photocopies and printouts, all pertaining to the French-Parsons case. "According to FSS, there were no useable prints on the axe handles, just a lot of partials, which may date back to when they were on offer in the hardware store. Therefore, the killer probably wore gloves.

"DCI Jackson and two DIs spent a good deal of time cross-referencing statements to try and determine who was last seen with Trevor Parsons. The consensus is Emmeline Wardle and Kyla Sloane."

"Nothing about Quinton Baylor?" Bhar asked.

"Not according to DCI Jackson's report."

"Like I'd ever hang my hat on anything *he* signed off on," Kate snorted.

"Noted." Hetheridge repressed a smile. "At this point, I'm still not convinced Emmeline Wardle is Murder Boy, as Kate calls our killer. Kyla Sloane, we'll discuss in a moment. Of the male party-goers, it must be noted that Quinton Baylor has two motives for killing Trevor Parsons, as he's taken Mr. Parsons' place in two arenas—on the rugby pitch and in Ms. Wardle's affections, at least for the time being."

"Phoebe Paquette isn't spotless," Bhar said. "We only have her word that she and Trevor Parsons were on the verge of getting back together. Something to ask Kyla Sloane about. And Jeremy Bentham has a motive, too. He obviously plans to marry Phoebe, assuming she'll have him. If he knew Phoebe and Trevor were close to patching things up ..." Bhar shrugged, trailing off.

"But why would anyone kill Clive French?" Kate asked.

"That does seem to be the sticking point. Suggesting the act itself was the point, not the victims. Bringing us back to Sir Duncan," Hetheridge said. "And despite the rather stunning fact that he was indeed on the Wardle premises during the time of the murders, I don't like him for MB, either."

"Why?" Bhar looked startled.

"Because Sir Duncan told me he did not put the axe to those children's skulls. His precise words, more or less. He told me, and I believed him."

Kate, too, appeared incredulous. Not for the first time, Hetheridge was tempted to chuckle at his subordinates' transparent dismay. They were still young enough to pounce whole-heartedly on the biggest, shiniest element, often missing smaller glimmers in the background.

"I doubt Sir Duncan ever felt remorse for any of his crimes," Hetheridge continued. "Not for the eight poachers in Borneo and not for his father, brother or family butler. But when Sir Duncan mentioned the axe murders, he looked disgusted. At the very least, disapproving." Hetheridge turned to Kate. "Would you agree?"

"I don't know," Kate said. "Can't say I've formulated a unified theory of Sir Duncan Godington. I only know he's very smart, very confident and very ... well, full of himself."

"So naturally, the ladies love him." Bhar sounded more than a little bitter.

"Probably." Kate replied seriously. "My point is, he's no typical killer, acting on impulse and then confessing to the first copper on the scene. Sir Duncan is a born manipulator. I wouldn't take his word on anything."

Hetheridge rifled through the stack of case-related documents, assuring himself that what he needed wasn't there. It would be possible to answer his next question by quietly asking another detective to handle the inquiry. But doing that would humiliate DS Bhar more than asking the man outright.

"About Tessa Chilcott. Are we quite certain she remains in full-time residential psychiatric care?" Hetheridge asked Bhar. "No daytrips or weekend breaks? No transfer to a part-time facility? I trust you understand what I'm getting at." He held up the relevant CCTV photo, tapping the image of a faceless female with long, dark hair. "No appearances in a Chelsea back garden, far-fetched as the notion might be?"

"I'm sure that's impossible." Bhar pushed his plate aside, dropping his white linen napkin on top. "But after I saw that picture, I made a formal inquiry. She's made significant progress since I last checked in. Three times now, she's been allowed visitation with her family. The first two visits were supervised, and lasted forty-eight hours. The most recent visitation, in the custody of her family, lasted a full seven days."

"When was it?" Hetheridge kept his voice neutral.

Bhar let out an explosive sigh. "All right. About two weeks ago. So yes, Tessa was away from Parkwood the night of the murders. But she—" He stopped, struggling to moderate his tone. "From what her case manager told me, Tessa is always doped to the eyeballs and never left alone. The idea that she could pop into the Wardle Halloween party with an axe in each hand and kill two random men ..."

"Even though she walked down a London street with a knife in her coat and killed a random woman?" Kate asked. "Sorry—I'm not trying to be cruel, I'm really not. But we have to look at this objectively. You know a defense counsel would play up an idea like that for all it's worth."

"Let's not theorize about a future defense counselor just yet," Hetheridge said. "Since you checked in with Tessa's case manager, DS Bhar, tell me this. Has she had any visitors of note in the last six months?"

"Her mother, once in the last eighteen months," Bhar said stiffly, obviously still offended by Kate's remark. "Sir Duncan, three times in the last eighteen months. A person listed as Kyla Chilcott six times in the last three months," Bhar said. "And of course, Kyla's original birth certificate confirms her relationship to Tessa. Sloane is her mother's maiden name."

"I don't blame her for changing it," Kate said. "It's tough enough in school these days." She was nibbling her toast again.

"A changed name," Hetheridge said slowly. "That reminds me. I should put a PC on it, checking the legalities of all the party guests' names. Just to prevent another surprise in this age of remarriages, sex reassignment surgery, etc."

Bhar and Kate stared at him, speechless.

"I have heard of such things," Hetheridge added, irritated by their incredulity. "My old mentor used to say, inattention to detail is the criminal's best friend. We already have one suspect with a new name. Why not check for another? In the meantime, a picture is forming ..." He drew in his breath. "Specifically, of Kyla and Sir Duncan committing these murders. But why? Why kill Clive French, the boy no one liked, and also Trevor Parsons, the popular athlete? Why on the same night, in the same way? In a venue with potentially dozens of witnesses, should any part of the murders go wrong?"

"Madness?" Kate suggested. "Killing two random people for —" She seemed about to say, "for sport," then stopped. "For no reason except to kill them?"

"Well, that's Sir Duncan's motivation, isn't it? Bloodshed for the sake of bloodshed?" Bhar didn't keep the bitterness from his voice.

"Is it?" Hetheridge held Bhar's gaze until he knew he had the younger man's full attention. "Sir Duncan's only passion is nature conservation. His prey in the jungles of Borneo? Eight poachers. Men who slaughtered endangered great apes for the equivalent of a pound or two ..."

"So *he* says," Bhar interjected.

"And at home, Sir Duncan's crimes were quite personal. I make no excuse for them. I merely state they were not random. As Kate already pointed out, Tessa Chilcott's crime was random, in public, in view of several witnesses. Either the product of utter derangement, or a twisted cry for help, or both. My point," Hetheridge said more firmly, sensing Bhar's rising emotion and determined not to let it derail the discussion, "is I find it hard to accept that Kyla Sloane, or Chilcott, or whatever her legal name, has been so mesmerized by the influence of her elder sister and Emmeline Wardle's neighbor, she murdered two schoolmates for fun."

"Maybe it wasn't for fun," Kate said. "Maybe she had other reasons, and just turned to Tessa and Sir Duncan to work out the practicalities."

"What do you mean?"

"Well, Tessa killed someone and was put away for the foreseeable future. Sir Duncan killed several people and got off. Maybe if Kyla had reason enough to hate both Clive French and Trevor Parsons, she decided to get rid of them. And she wanted to hear about the nuts and bolts of murder from a person who succeeded and a person who failed."

Hetheridge turned that over in his mind. "Did she strike you as so cold? So perfectly balanced, to murder two men with an axe after polling the experts?"

Kate considered. "She struck me as controlled for a twenty- or twenty-one-year-old. For a girl who's always run with the right crowd. Who's never been in trouble. But she broke when I mentioned the smashed vase. I mean, she's not cold to the marrow."

"So now instead of Tessa, it's Kyla who strolled into the party carrying two real axes, and no one said a word?" Bhar asked.

"Someone did." Kate finished off her buttered toast and jam. "Probably in a backpack. Most of the males had them, they're everywhere these days. But since Kyla and Emmeline organized the party, they could have brought the weapons in earlier— maybe several days earlier. You're the one who discovered both girls are athletes—swim team and archery, right? They aren't exactly weaklings."

Bhar sighed. "These are great intellectual theories, as far as purely intellectual theories go. Has FSS sent us any evidence that ties into it?"

"Yes and no." Hetheridge referred back to the pile of papers. "The CCTV data from W. C. Marsden has been reviewed. Recall that both axes were new. One still bore its price sticker. Two days before the murder, they were purchased by someone the clerk cannot recall. Having spoken to the clerk myself," he sighed, "I imagine it's difficult for the young man to remember anything, given his obvious penchant for smoking cannabis before a shift. But the shop's camera, at least, provided a photo of the customer in question."

He held it up. As always, the shot was high and wide, detailing most of the merchandise aisles. In the foreground stood the clerk, two axes sitting near the cash register. The customer, dressed in trench coat and sunglasses, had long dark hair very much like Kyla Sloane's. Or the figure photographed near Clive French's body, assuming they weren't one and the same.

"She paid in cash, I assume?" Kate said.

"Of course," Hetheridge said, frustrated by the way she hardly dared look at him after Bhar's abortive declaration. Yes—soon they would need to have it out, the three of them. But after the French-Parsons case wrapped, and not before.

"Paid in cash, but wasn't smart enough to cover her hair or wear a wig?" Bhar shook his head, sounding uncharacteristically peevish. "You know, if I didn't know any better—if she wasn't pregnant—I'd swear Phoebe Paquette had a hand in the murders. Something about my interview with her, some piece of it, was off —I promise you, it smelled bad. I just can't put my finger on what."

"Well, this lady buying the axes definitely isn't pregnant," Kate said dryly. "But there were lots of girls at the party. Could be Emmeline Wardle in a wig. Could be a friend of the killer, someone unrelated, sent to run an errand. Sir Duncan isn't the only person with loads of helpful friends."

"And it could be Kyla Sloane, well aware that such a vague picture is no positive ID. Especially if she's under Sir Duncan's tutelage," Hetheridge said.

"I thought you believed he wasn't involved," Bhar said. "That he found the French-Parson murders disgusting."

"Oh, I do believe Sir Duncan didn't wield the axe. As for his disgust—yes, I'm convinced it was real. And yet. I've been mistaken before. Best not to close off any avenue too soon."

"Anything else from FSS?" Kate asked.

"Yes. Three half-ounces of cocaine were found in the Wardle townhouse in three different locations," Hetheridge said. "All in the same type of container, which may help identify the dealer. This." Digging under the papers, he came up with a sealed plastic bag. Inside was a metal keychain attached to a round silver ball with a seam in the middle.

"I found one in the private dining room," Kate said.

"Yes. Another was found in the media room. And another, in the attic where Trevor Parsons was attacked."

"Phoebe Paquette had one of those," Bhar said, eyes widening. "She said lots of girls at uni have them. According to her, Clive French had one, too, clipped to his backpack. Of course, hers just had lip gloss inside."

"All three of these were filled with cocaine," Hetheridge said. "And the fact that Clive French possessed at least one intrigues me. Most motives boil down to love, money or both. We haven't uncovered much love, so at this point, my working hypothesis is money."

"The Wardles are in dire financial straits," Kate said.

"And Clive must have needed money, since he was collecting on old debts," Bhar added. "Emmeline Wardle was determined not to claim him as a friend. Phoebe claimed she was working with a dealer. Do you think it could have been Clive?"

"If Clive French was running two illicit cash schemes instead of one, that would double his chances of getting murdered," Hetheridge agreed, taking a belated sip of his tea. It had gone quite cold.

"So let's talk this through," Kate said. "Kyla meets Clive in the garden. He demands money, but he's a little guy, not very intimidating. She's tired of being harassed, so she kills him, then panics. Tries to move the body—hang on, do we have confirmation that she really did move the body?"

"Yes." Hetheridge uncovered the corresponding report. "Three strands of Clive French's hair were found in the wheelbarrow, along with traces of his blood. No doubt there was far more, initially, but someone tried to wash out the wheelbarrow with the Wardles' garden hose. More blood traces were found beneath the bonfire. FSS estimates it burned for less than a quarter hour before it, too, was doused with water."

"All right. Kyla kills Clive in the garden," Kate repeated, starting again. "She panics. Moves the body with the wheelbarrow. Sets fire to the spot where Clive died. In a full-blown panic, she rings Sir Duncan. He turns up, calms her down. Says stop tampering with the evidence and just say you're the person who found him. So—what? Does she say, hang on, Trevor Parsons just infuriated me, better kill him, too?" Kate shook her head. "No. There's no way I can imagine Kyla racing from the back garden into the house to kill Trevor."

"Can we turn it around?" Bhar asked. "Suppose Kyla killed Trevor first? If she really was obsessed with Sir Duncan, maybe she wanted to get his attention? Lure him out of retirement with something spectacular and newsworthy, like a double axe murder?"

"Jeremy did mention something about that at Lady Isabel's party," Kate said. "That Sir Duncan has so many followers, if you really want to get close to him, you have to stand out. Be interesting."

"But it still doesn't work," Bhar protested. "Why would Kyla kill Trevor Parsons? Leaving that aside, even if she *did* do it, how did she rush out to the back garden, kill Clive, set the fire and call Sir Duncan, all before Trevor staggered down those stairs? I saw Jackson's report. There's a good consensus among the witnesses that Kyla ran into the house with the news about Clive around the same time Emmeline started screaming over Trevor."

"Kyla working with another killer, then?" Hetheridge suggested. "Kyla and Phoebe?"

"Why would the latest girlfriend team up with the disgruntled ex?" Kate asked.

"God knows. Some kind of hell-hath-no-fury scenario, I assume," Bhar shrugged.

"Which doesn't take money into account at all." Hetheridge found himself leaning precariously far back in his chair. Carefully, he eased forward again until all four legs were back on the floor. "Paul. You had someone check into Phoebe Paquette's finances? Made certain she isn't worse off than she seems?"

"Yes, and it's just the opposite," Bhar said. "She's set for life, once her trust fund comes in. Maybe Trevor thought that's why he could just walk away. Even if he made a nice pro rugby career, it's unlikely Phoebe would ever need money. She really will be able to buy and sell the Wardles, just like she claimed."

"So what do we have?" Hetheridge said, as much to himself as to Kate and Bhar. "A family who needs money. A daughter dealing cocaine in partnership with a person unknown. A best friend who may have been sleeping with Trevor Parsons. Trevor's wealthy pregnant ex. Two young men, Quinton Baylor and Jeremy Bentham, each with sufficient reason to want Trevor gone for good. And Sir Duncan, right next door." He sighed. "Something crucial is missing. But no matter how we approach the evidence, Kyla Sloane is the closest thing to a unifying factor. Along with the photograph from W. C. Marsden and the evidence that she moved the body."

"So what comes next?" Kate asked. "I know we'll need permission from the assistant commissioner before we can bring in Sir Duncan for questioning. Put a toe out of line there and the sky will fall."

Hetheridge nodded. "Legal is already discussing whether the enhanced image alone is enough, or if it might be considered too subjective. Especially in the absence of any corroborating evidence, like fingerprints."

"A first interview with Molly French, then," Kate suggested, "to try and determine if her son was dealing drugs? Or a second interview with Kyla Sloane?"

"Neither." Bhar held a CCTV image in either hand—the W. C. Marsden customer in his left, Sir Duncan and the faceless brunette in his right. "I have a feeling I should try to talk to Tessa one more time."

CHAPTER TWENTY

As Harvey cleared the dishes, Bhar went into the next room to ring Parkwood Psychiatric Hospital. In most cases, visiting hours were strictly observed, but a Scotland Yard detective with a warrant card could move heaven and earth, even on a Sunday afternoon.

"Should we be concerned?" Kate asked Hetheridge.

He raised his eyebrows, giving her that infuriatingly serene look he often put on just before pulling rank, or using his Peerage connections to pulverize all opposition. "I trust Bhar to behave responsibly. I doubt anything Tessa says will be admissible in court, but if she's lucid, she might give us some insight about Kyla we can use to our advantage. Besides, we'd be remiss not to follow up on the fact that Tessa was visiting her family when the murders occurred."

"Oh, pull the other one. You know what I mean!" Kate barked, irritated by the amusement in his eyes. "Bhar practically told us we're being gossiped about. And it's sure to get worse."

"Of course. Devilish hard to keep secrets among detectives."

"Well, then, how are we going to sort this? Should I make up a boyfriend? Should you dig up a suitable lady friend to squire around the West End?"

"Kate." Drawing her close, he kissed her—softly first, then with more heat. "When it comes to the Yard, unwritten rules outnumber the written and I know the playbook by heart. I promise, I won't gamble with your career."

"I know that." She shook her head, amazed he could misunderstand her on that score. "But what about *your* career?"

"My career with the Met has been long and distinguished," Hetheridge said evenly. "But it will not continue indefinitely. Let me worry about how and when it ends."

"I thought you wanted to share everything with me."

He kissed her again, cupping her face in both hands. "You know I do. Don't tease me on that point, Kate."

"I'm not teasing you," she said, startled by the note of emotion in his voice. "I just want to be sure you—"

"Kate. I know you've always had to look after others, including Ritchie and Henry. But you don't have to look after me."

From the doorway, Harvey said in a loud voice, "Why, Detective Bhar, I'd thought you'd left us!"

Kate pulled away from Hetheridge as Bhar slunk in, trying to enter the salon feet first and eyes last. If he'd been wearing a hat, no doubt he would have tossed it in before taking the first step.

"It's all arranged. I'll go to Parkwood, interview Tessa and ring you both afterward."

"No need," Kate said briskly, snatching up her bag. "There's an unpleasant task I've been putting off, and this seems like just the time to tackle it. You know my nephew Henry lives with me. Well, I need to have a little talk with his mother—my sister, Maura. It's time to set some limits on how much contact she can have with him until he gets older, or she gets better."

Bhar blinked. He didn't have to reply for Kate to know he felt sucker-punched.

"Parkwood's a good facility." Looking Bhar in the eye, Kate spoke as matter-of-factly as possible. "But the simple fact is, I hate it. After an hour there, I want to peel my skin off. But the effect Maura's having on Henry gets worse every visit. As his guardian, I have the right to stop visitation. And I intend ..." She bit her lip. "I *think* I intend to do it. So. Mind if I tag along?"

Suspicion disappeared from Bhar's eyes, replaced with something else—possibly gratitude. "Fine. But I'm warning you. I already have evidence of the last time you befouled my car."

"Won't shed a single hair," she vowed.

Bhar followed Kate into Parkwood via the hospital's north entrance, up a stone-flagged path beneath two hornbeam trees. This path, which Bhar had never used, led up to a narrow, black-lacquered door. Chiseled in the lintel stone above the entry was the year 1897. An engraved brass plaque bolted to the door read: VISITORS.

Pushing open the door, Kate led Bhar into a small foyer that smelled overpoweringly of lemon cleaner. "Maura's earned a lot of privileges. She can have visitors any day of the week. Most mornings after breakfast, she's out on the lawn, taking the sun and lighting one fag after another."

Checking his inner coat pocket, Bhar realized he'd left his pack at home. "Oi. I'd kill for one of those right now." The act of holding a cigarette would at least give his hands something to do. Otherwise he had to keep them in his pockets so Kate wouldn't see how they shook.

"No problem." Kate indicated a vending machine in the corner. "But first let's check in at the desk."

As Kate obtained their visitor badges, Bhar bought a pack of Marlboros. Breaking the seal, he put his nose to the pack and inhaled deeply, energized by the scent of tobacco. Then he was ready to follow Kate onto the wide green lawn.

The midafternoon sun was bright. It was far warmer here than in Hetheridge's walled garden. Patting down his coat, Bhar realized he'd forgotten his lighter, too. Unlit cigarette in hand, he glanced about miserably, ignored by ward sisters and orderlies. Finally, a passing young man offered him a light.

"Cheers, mate." Taking a deep drag, Bhar smiled at the genial, rather spotty-faced young man. He wore blue jeans and cheap trainers that had seen better days. No visitor's badge was clipped to his white T-shirt.

"My pleasure." The young man ambled away, settling contentedly into a deck chair as Bhar watched. The resident seemed well-adjusted and friendly, too. Did he dare hope Tessa had undergone such a transformation?

Scanning the lawn, Bhar caught sight of Kate on the far side. Two striped deck chairs faced an empty garden bed, already cleared for winter. Ensconced in one chair, a woman sat smoking. Kate, looking far less comfortable, had to perch sideways to face her sister.

Bhar approached slowly, uncertain if Kate truly wanted him within earshot during the conversation. If she was aware of him, she gave no sign. It was Maura Wakefield who looked up suddenly, eyeing him from head to toe.

"Well, if it ain't Paki the Blackie. You banging my sis?"

"Maura." Kate's tone was dangerous.

"Not meaning it racist or nothing." Maura pronounced the last word "nuffink." "Been out with Pakis, I have. Got an all-round appreciation for the male species. You a copper, too?"

"DS Paul Bhar," he said, leaning down to offer his hand. Taking it eagerly, Maura gave him a bold smile. A missing canine and molar left a gap in that smile's upper left side. Maura was heavier than Kate by two or three stone, with deep grooves along each side of her mouth. Her hair was more gray than blond, and her forehead was stacked with lines. Nevertheless, Bhar could see the shadow of Kate in her sister's face.

"My Henry's mentioned you." Pronouncing her son's name without the H, Maura wagged a finger at Bhar. "Forgot to say you were dead gorgeous. Maybe you'll be round to pick up the pieces when Katie's sugar daddy gives her the push?"

Kate sat up straighter. "That's exactly what I've come to discuss with you, Maura. I realize Henry's your son, but you have to be careful what you say to him. If he tells you about my friends, or my boyfriends, you shouldn't make comments that would upset an adult, much less a young boy."

"Will you listen at that?" Maura winked at Bhar. "Miz Poshie Received Pronunciation come to tell me I better watch myself. Like enough people aren't running my life at present, thank you very much. Like I don't have to follow a hundred bleeding rules if I ever hope to get out of here. And now me little sis has come to tell me what to say to me own son. Just what sent him into a bloody tailspin this time?"

"I don't know," Kate said stiffly. "He won't tell me. The last couple of visits, he went straight to his room, locked the door and cried. It was days before he was back to his old self again."

"Because he misses me," Maura roared, sitting up so suddenly Bhar took an involuntary step back. "Because he only gets his mum, *his real mum*, for an hour a month! Then it's back to limbo with the paid nurse and that retard and you, when you aren't shagging your wrinkly old toff!"

"That retard is our brother." Kate's voice was cold.

"Think he knows that? Think he knows his arse from a peat bog? He should be in an institution. Heaven knows, if there was any justice, he'd be here and I'd be living with you till I was back on me feet. But for that to happen, you'd have to give two nits about me, wouldn't you? You'd have to sponsor me, not leave me to claw me own way up. But I won't be sick forever, Katie! I'll be out soon, just you wait!"

Kate stood up. "I hope so, Maura. I hope so."

"Katie always did think she was better than the rest of us," Maura told Bhar. "Kissing the teacher's arse, hoarding money and dreaming up ways to leave us behind. Now she's turning me own son against me. Katie! You think you're helping Henry with *fencing lessons* while some rich old man vacations in your knickers? You're giving Henry a taste of all the things he can never have! Ruining him for life in the real world!"

"I'm sorry." Kate was backing away. "I'll still come and see you. And I'll let Henry come back someday. When you're better."

Bhar followed Kate back toward the hospital building. She moved swiftly, keeping her head up and her back straight as Maura shrieked, "Katie! You think I like it this way? You think I like staring at this rubbish garden every fecking day of me worthless fecking life?"

To Bhar's intense relief, Kate did not want to discuss what transpired on Parkwood's lawn. He knew that made him a coward, but that wasn't exactly news. If Kate turned to him for sympathy or—God forbid—started to cry, Bhar feared he might cry, too. And smoking, that most soothing of bad habits, wasn't allowed inside the hospital proper. He had to shove his hands in his pockets again, lest they resume shaking.

When they reached Tessa Chilcott's unit—a heavily secured area where residents had no cigarette machine and no lawn to walk on—Kate approached the ward sister with warrant card in hand. After a brief word with the unit's medical director, they were conducted to a waiting room. After almost half an hour, a sister appeared to escort one or both of them to the visiting room.

Kate turned to Bhar. "Should I stay out here, or go in with you?" Her tone was so neutral, so devoid of judgment, his eyes went hot and his vision blurred.

"In," he sighed, trying to blink unobtrusively. "I don't think I can do this without you."

CHAPTER TWENTY-ONE

The visitors' room was more or less as Detective Sergeant Kate Wakefield expected. In the last few years, there had been a movement in public health facilities to "normalize" common areas as much as was practical. Unfortunately, given only limited funds, this meant little; such spaces had evolved from fluorescent-lit rooms with stark white floors and reform school furniture into fluorescent-lit rooms with striped lino floors and hotel-surplus furnishings. Today, someone had gone so far as to add a watercolor seascape (bolted to the wall) and a bowl of fake Gerbera daisies. Most visitors would still find it depressing, but Kate appreciated the effort. At least one brave soul at Parkwood still had hope, either that residents would recognize an attempt at homeyness, or those obligated to visit would be comforted by the gesture.

Kate sat down at the table nearest the door. After a moment, Bhar followed suit. He didn't seem to trust himself to speak. The wall clock—cage-faced like clocks in gyms and prisons—ticked loudly. After what felt like forever, a ward sister escorted Tessa Chilcott into the room.

Kate wasn't surprised to find Tessa had changed from her

society-photo snap. Her cloud of dark curls had been cut into a rather nice bob. She wore no makeup or jewelry, but her short fingernails appeared recently manicured. Their soft petal pink matched the color of her Velcro-fastened track suit.

"First thing I did during my last visit home was get a manicure," Tessa said, noticing Kate's gaze and spreading her fingers for closer inspection. "Visited a hair salon, too. You never realize how much those things mean to you until you can't have them. You're from Scotland Yard?"

"Yes. DS Kate Wakefield." Kate waited for Tessa's gaze to lift from her fingertips. "DS Paul Bhar, you already know."

"Of course. Glad you didn't get the sack, Deepal." Tessa's voice had the slow, underinflected quality Kate associated with powerful medication.

"I was never in real danger. Too few Asians at the Yard as it is."

Kate leaned back in her chair, ostensibly to get comfortable, but really to get a glimpse of Bhar's face. He was smiling gently. His voice sounded warm and natural.

Good on you, Kate thought with a surge of admiration. *Muddle through this and I'll buy the first round tonight.*

Tessa studied Bhar, neither believing nor disbelieving. Despite her detached way of speaking, her body language reminded Kate of a battered woman. During her days as a uniformed constable, Kate had met many. Often they responded to a male officer's questions just as Tessa did now—slumped in pretended nonchalance, one hand braced around the opposite forearm, awaiting a blow that might come at any moment.

"Deepal. I know you won't believe I could ask you this," Tessa said at last, "but could I have a fag?"

Bhar shook out a cigarette, giving the ward sister an appealing glance. Pinched-faced and suspicious, the sister nonetheless produced a lighter. As Bhar passed the lit cigarette to

Tessa, their fingers brushed. Bhar smiled encouragingly. Tessa flinched.

"Thanks." Tessa exhaled cigarette smoke daintily, like the socialite she'd once been. Remembering the brutality of the murder this woman had committed—the victim's twenty-eight stab wounds, her nearly severed head—Kate was surprised. Her sister Maura, who in her prediagnosis days had been twice banged up for assaulting boyfriends, still seemed more physically dangerous than Tessa.

"So," Tessa continued. "You can't both be here just to talk to me. What's Duncan meant to have done this time?"

"There was a double murder in Chelsea," Paul said. "It happened in the townhouse next to Sir Duncan's. 14 Burnaby. Two University College students, Clive French and Trevor Parsons, died violently. Besides the proximity to Sir Duncan's home, the method is similar to the presumed machete used on Sir Duncan's father, brother and servant."

"And there's one other detail," Kate said. "Something we need to clear up."

Tessa stiffened a fraction more. "Yes?"

"The murders occurred on 20 October. Your case manager tells us you've made great progress in the last several months. So much that after two brief supervised visitations, you were allowed seven days with your family. Since you were at liberty on 20 October, I'm afraid I must ask: where were you between the hours of six and ten that evening?"

Tessa gave a weak laugh. "If you talked to my case manager, I'm sure she told you. I didn't get my full seven days. I was packed up and sent back for bad behavior."

Kate glanced at Bhar, trying not to look as surprised as she felt. *That* was a detail he'd neglected to share.

"She told me you'd slipped out of your father's house," Bhar said. "Took the tube to Chelsea. A citizen found you wandering and drove you back to your family. They rang the hospital and your therapist insisted you return to Parkwood immediately."

"Yes. I broke the behavioral contract. Dr. Feingold called it a 'grievous breach of trust,'" Tessa said, imitating a man's low voice. "Have you spoken to my dad about this?"

"Not yet," Bhar said.

"Please don't. He was so disappointed in me. And when he saw Duncan ..."

"What?" Kate sat up straighter.

Tessa took a long, triumphant drag off the cigarette. "Oh, yes. I may be daft, but I can still get around Chelsea blindfolded. I made it to Duncan's house. He was furious with me for jeopardizing my recovery." She rolled her eyes. "Took me back to my dad's himself. Not that Dad appreciated it. I think he wanted to commit murder himself, from the look on his—"

"Tessa," the ward sister interrupted. "You know I'll have to report all this to Dr. Feingold. If you're fantasizing about seeing the gentleman again, you need to come clean to these detectives now."

"*The gentleman*," Tessa repeated. "They won't use Duncan's name around me. As if that will help me forget. So to more properly answer your question—I was on the tube around six in the evening. Arrived at Duncan's around sevenish, maybe, I'm not sure. He had me back at my dad's house by eight. Is that enough of an alibi to take him off your list?"

"No," Kate said, wondering if anything Tessa told them was true.

"Right. Well, then, let me see if I can help." Tessa put on an unconvincing smile. "Start with the victims. What did they do to Duncan?"

"Nothing we know of," Kate said. "Sir Duncan denies being acquainted with either. So far we've uncovered no proof to the contrary."

Accepting the red plastic ashtray the ward sister passed over,

Tessa rested her cigarette in it, hand hovering protectively as if someone might take it away. "Were the victims dismembered?"

"No. Each young man was killed by a single blow to the head," Bhar said. "Preliminary forensics estimate the first murder happened sometime around six or seven in the evening—the other, up to an hour later."

"Lots of blood?" Tessa asked in that dull, medicated tone.

The ward sister scowled. Bhar looked equally taken aback by the nonchalance of Tessa's inquiry.

"Not really," Kate said. "The victims died of shock and massive brain trauma, not blood loss."

"Then it couldn't have been Duncan." Tessa brought the cigarette back to her lips.

Kate exchanged glances with Bhar. He looked equally blank. "Why?"

Tessa regarded Kate silently for several seconds. It was the sort of appraisal only one woman could give another—usually in the presence of a man who completes the triangle. Just when Kate expected Tessa to demand what place she, Kate, occupied in Bhar's life, Tessa chose to reply.

"When Duncan was seventeen, he read an article about a primitive tribe in New Guinea or somewhere, I don't know, that ritually slaughtered captive enemies and bathed in their blood. Duncan adored the idea. Left the country to get away from it, from the temptation of doing it to people who ... hurt him. Went to do charity work for a wild animal rescue group and ended up giving in to the temptation. Bathing in blood."

"Animal blood?" Bhar asked. But Kate knew the answer before Tessa spoke.

"No, never," Tessa said. "He loves animals, especially elephants, lions and great apes. They're like he is."

"He told me he killed some poachers," Kate said.

"*You* spoke to Duncan?" Tessa's voice rose. "When? Did he mention me?"

"Tessa," the ward sister said repressively.

Kate looked at Bhar. That careful smile was now frozen on his face. His hands were clenched in his lap.

Tessa closed her eyes. After several seconds, she opened them again, bringing the cigarette back to her lips. "Dr. Feingold says I can never have contact with Duncan again." She uttered a small laugh. "I'm not even supposed to talk about him anymore, except in therapy. I'm surprised I'm permitted to discuss him with you. Don't you have computers and police profilers to help you?"

"We needed to establish your whereabouts," Kate reminded her. "Beyond that, a guest at the party where the murders occurred has become a prime suspect. Your half-sister, Kyla Sloane."

The moment the words were out, Kate regretted lapsing into the "gotcha" style of dropping key information she frequently employed with suspects. Tessa looked like she'd been slapped.

"Jesus." Tessa ground out the cigarette with sudden violence. "Jesus, Jesus."

"Does Kyla know Sir Duncan well?" Bhar asked. "Do they have some sort of relationship? We know he's always had lots of young friends. Followers, really ..."

"You mean like me." For the first time Tessa stared directly into Bhar's eyes.

"Yes."

"Kyla was just fourteen when Duncan went on trial. She was fascinated by him, and I'm sure she would have done anything he asked. Just like me," Tessa admitted, gaze locked with Bhar's. "Help him plan. Buy his supplies. Even act as lookout while he ... took a bath. Duncan didn't have time for Kyla back then. She was too young. Now ... now I suppose she might be enough of a person to finally interest him." Tessa uttered those last words as if they caused her physical pain.

"Do you think Sir Duncan has taken your little sister under his wing? Does he require his closest friends to prove themselves by personally committing a murder?" Kate wondered if she had hit on a solid motive at long last. "Is that what he did to you, Ms. Chilcott?"

"Of course not. Duncan never asked me to kill anyone. I did it on my own." Tessa looked mournfully at the remains of her cigarette, smashed far beyond relighting. "Only once did he ever ask me to do something I didn't want to do. I hated it. It was nothing like I thought, and it hurt like the devil." Tessa stared into Bhar's face. "But yes, Deepal. Because Duncan asked me to, I did it, all the same."

The emotion in Bhar's dark eyes was alarming. Hastily, Kate tossed out the only other question on her mind. "During your unsupervised home visit, what did you talk about? You and Kyla, I mean?"

"Duncan." Tessa's voice went flat again. "She asked me if he was guilty. Poor little thing. I said no, of course not. Assured her it was all a mistake."

"Right." Kate shot another look at Bhar. He seemed incapable of speech, so she continued for both of them. "You do realize you may have pushed your little sister into his arms? Given her an excuse to trust him at her worst possible moment?"

Tessa didn't seem to hear that. "Can I have another fag?"

Kate passed one over. After the ward sister lit the cigarette, Tessa said, "There's a lady here with a condition, I forget what it's called. Sometimes she wakes in the night and starts screaming that there's a stranger in bed with her. But it's not a stranger. It's the left side of her own body. Except she doesn't recognize it anymore. It's no use trying to reason with her. If you point to her left side in a mirror and say it's connected to her right side, she just says no. She thinks there's a stranger grafted onto her, and she wants free of that stranger more than anything. The docs can't make her accept her left side. All they can do is quiet her down. That's how it is with me." Tessa released a lungful of smoke. "I wake up in the night and think, no, this isn't me, this isn't my life. When I look in the mirror, all I can say is no, no, no. I want peace from it, from the stranger grafted onto my soul. But in a place like this … peace isn't an option."

"Tessa." The ward sister stood up. "I've taken note of that statement. You know I have to report all types of suicidal ideation."

"Of course. Which is why I'll not be allowed belts or steak knives anytime soon. Are you finished with me, detectives?" Tessa asked.

Bhar seemed unable to answer, so Kate spoke up. "For now. But did I understand the point of your story? Kyla doesn't matter? Just you?"

Tessa shrugged again. "My sister came to me for reassurance. I gave it to her. If she used that reassurance to do something foolish, well … things are tough all over. Deepal," she said as Kate and Bhar rose to leave. "Would you do one more thing for me?"

He cleared his throat, offering her a perfectly believable smile. "Of course."

"Next time, don't come. Send somebody else."

CHAPTER TWENTY-TWO

Detective Sergeant Kate Wakefield was disappointed by Detective Sergeant Bhar's refusal of a drink. He didn't seem to want anything—not alcohol, not darts and pig snacks in some raucous pub, not even to return to the Yard to check and see if any new case details had broken.

"Need to pop round Tesco. Get my mum some more ice cream. She's gutted over her books."

"Bad reviews?"

"Something like that." Bhar kept his hands at ten and two and his eyes on the road.

"You know, I've always wanted to meet your mum. See the woman behind the man. I mean, someday you'll be a man," Kate said casually. It was the sort of comment usually guaranteed to spark a volley of insults and one-upmanship. Bhar didn't seem to hear.

"Or you can just drop me at the guv's." Sighing, Kate plucked a long, golden hair from her disobedient mane, tossing it on the dashboard within Bhar's line of vision.

"I'll do that." Bhar's gaze remained trained straight ahead.

"Paul. Can I tell you something?"

Bhar made a noncommittal sound.

"My mum was a piece of work. My sister—well, you saw. She's not well. I've never known her when she wasn't like that. An emotional vampire. If I ever allow it, she'd drain me dry. But you know what my secret weapon is?"

His eyes flicked toward her, then back on the road again.

"Selfishness. Parts of my life are only for me. As long as I hang on to my selfish side, Maura can't destroy me. If I ever decided helping her was more important than helping me—or Henry, or Ritchie—I'd be lost. Maura would chew me up and spit me out, just like everyone else who's ever got close to her."

"You don't have to worry about me." Bhar sounded brusque, even a little insulted. "You don't see me sobbing my heart out over here, do you? Only fools cry over betrayal."

Kate started to reply, then thought better of it. The irrepressible jokester she knew was gone, replaced by a stiff-necked stranger. They traveled the rest of the way back to Wellegrave House in silence.

Steering his Astra up Hetheridge's long gravel drive, Bhar parked as close to the entrance as possible. Just as Kate was about to disembark, he touched her arm.

"Hey. Kate."

Door already open, she looked over her shoulder at him.

"Be careful."

"You mean—with Tony?"

"In general. I've ..." He broke off, smiling a little. "I've got used to you."

"Oh." Kate took a deep breath. "You, too. Watch yourself. Because just between you and me—the next person to muck with you is in for a royal arse-kicking."

"Just hope I'm conscious to see it." For the first time, Bhar seemed to notice the blond hair on his dashboard. Seizing it between thumb and forefinger, he tossed it at Kate. "Tomorrow I plan on interviewing Kyla first, then Molly French. You in?"

"Of course." Kate waved at the Astra as Bhar sped away. He hadn't been warning her against Hetheridge, she decided. Just wishing her safe in general. And if that wasn't the very essence of every copper's prayers, what was?

≈

"Oh. I hate to say it. But I need to get home soon." Kate enjoyed the feel of Hetheridge's arms around her. As she'd noted long before their first coupling, he was surprisingly well-muscled and broad through the chest, making this sort of embrace particularly satisfying. It was unusual for her to feel so relaxed, so tempted to stay the night. Apparently what older men lacked in repeat engagements, they made up for in stamina and skill.

"I know. Should you ring Henry and Ritchie? Make an excuse?"

"Unless I get up and dressed in the next ten minutes," Kate said, pressing her cheek against his light mat of chest hair. "Ritchie's carer is there, so it's not like they're home alone. But they worry. Well—Henry worries. Somewhere in the back of his mind, he remembers Maura abandoning him. He was only four years old, and alone for two days before the neighbors found him. He says he doesn't remember, but I'm dead certain he does."

Hetheridge's hand stroked the back of her neck. "I've been thinking you might adopt him one day."

"Maura won't allow it. She hasn't lost all parental rights. Today she even claimed she's close to release. I need to check with her doctors, but with my luck, it's true." Kate sighed. "Unofficial is better."

"Not better for Henry."

Kate lifted herself. The bedside lamp's soft illumination was sufficient for her to see his face. "Oi. Guilt trip? Really? For that, I let you lure me into your bed?"

Hetheridge chuckled. "Henry is a very traditional young man.

An old soul. He wants to belong somewhere. That's why visits with Maura send him crying. He wants you for a mum. And the assurance only a legal bond can create."

"For a man with no children, you have very particular views about childrearing," Kate said tartly, then remembered. "Oh. Sorry. I keep forgetting about Jules."

"I know. So do I. I need to do something about that," Hetheridge sighed. "In her case, I have no notion where to start. Henry is far easier. He's a good lad. A smart lad."

"But still a target for bullies. Now that I know you advised him to fight, I keep waiting for that phone call. The one where I get told what a rubbish guardian I am."

"I was bullied at school," Hetheridge said. "Quite viciously, as a matter of fact. And that was a very different time, when professors felt it was their duty to ignore such harassment and let only the strong survive. Being bullied as a youngster is no measure of future happiness or success. Henry will do just fine. You'll see."

"I think he will," Kate said, sliding up for a long, warm kiss. She adored the way Hetheridge moved his mouth, the way he cupped her face between his hands as if she were the most precious thing he'd ever held between them.

"Do you think …" she began, breaking away, and was suddenly afraid to continue.

"Think what?"

"Think you could be Henry's godfather? Officially, I mean? That would give him a bit of stability."

"Well. A godfather's role, outside of the American Mafia, is to instruct a child in matters of religion." Hetheridge cleared his throat. "I fear I'm not religious at all. Belief in a benign creator is largely incompatible with police work. Particularly if you specialize in murder."

"I know what a godfather is," Kate lied, embarrassed that she could have lived so long without truly understanding the term. "I just meant—a mentor, but with a more official name. Someone

Henry could count on. Someone dedicated to helping him become a man."

"I think you mean a stepfather," Hetheridge said.

Kate sat up. Straddling his chest, she let him take her in, enjoying the feel of his gaze upon her. Hetheridge used his eyes like he used his mouth, caressing her so thoroughly, she felt like an almost perfect female specimen. "Tony. If I'm not marrying you, I'm not marrying anyone. So a stepfather for Henry is off the table."

"Kate." Using his thighs, Hetheridge seized Kate and flipped her sideways, putting her on her back and himself astride her. It was a self-defense move he performed poorly in the officer's gymnasium and brilliantly in bed. And judging by the feel of his body against hers, a repeat engagement was entirely possible. "If you aren't marrying anyone else, I've already won half the battle."

Hetheridge's manservant, Harvey, drove Kate back to her building around two in the morning. He promised to have her car delivered soon after. Kate, yawning and more than a little embarrassed, kept up a brave smile through the drive to the East End. Surely her neighbors had grown accustomed to the occasional limousine or silver sports car turning up in front of her building?

"I grew up in Manchester," Harvey said suddenly as they drew close to Kate's home. "Rather doubt you could tell by how I speak."

"No," Kate admitted.

"I trained to be an actor. Nailed the Received Pronunciation. The rest was a bit more difficult. As a second choice, I thought life as a domestic would be fine. And I always hoped to serve someone like Lord Hetheridge. A man of quality. Not just breeding but true quality." Harvey flashed a quick smile. Tall and gaunt, he always smelled of lilac, no matter what time of day or night. His manner of speaking was gentle and flowing. Not so much feminine as lyrical, as if every declaration was half a song.

"Lucky you found him, then," Kate said politely. She'd never wanted to serve anyone, much less an aristocrat. Often the twists and turns of her own life were a surprise even to her.

"Yes. I'd be so pleased if Lord Hetheridge settled down at last," Harvey said, guiding the Bentley up alongside the curb. "These days, sixty is the new forty. I'd be overjoyed to see him take the correct sort of wife."

"And what's that? The correct sort?" Kate asked, cold.

Harvey's deep-set eyes sparkled as he released her door lock. "Someone he chose. Someone like you. I could clear your way, Detective Sergeant Wakefield. As Baroness Hetheridge, you'd never want for guidance. Never make a public misstep. Not with me to help."

Kate caught her breath. She had no idea what to say.

"Just think about it," Harvey continued. "And know if you decide to say yes—well. You'll have at least one ally."

Nodding, Kate picked up her bag and stumbled out of the Bentley. By the time she reached her building's lobby and looked back, the car was already sliding away.

"You look half-undead," Bhar told Kate as she slid into his Astra a mere seven hours later. "Not quite a vampire. Just unclean enough to shrink from sunlight." He grinned. "Is that it? Did you spend last night in the devil's embrace?"

Kate slipped on her Chanel sunglasses, bought from an unshaven man in the Petticoat Lane Market who said they'd fallen off the back of a truck. "Never mind about me. What about you? Get your mum that Tesco ice cream?"

"I did. But it proved unnecessary. Mum's writing a new

romance and on top of the world. Didn't even ask me about the case, which is a very good sign."

"This isn't another one like *The Lordly Detective*, is it? I had the feeling that was loosely based on our guv."

"You never mentioned you read my mum's stuff."

"'Course I do. Got a Kindle, don't I?" she grinned, wishing she'd enjoyed a full night's sleep in Hetheridge's arms instead of returning to her own bed to toss and turn. "Most of it was pretty silly. Except the sex. The sex was bloody brilliant."

Bhar made a pained noise.

"Sorry, I forgot—your mum only had sex once, to conceive you. Moving on. Did you call ahead to tell Kyla Sloane we were coming?"

"I did. She still lives with her father, Edward Chilcott. I've actually been to the house, but it was a long time ago."

"How did she react to the news we want to re-interview her?"

"Like she was forearmed." Bhar's grip on the steering wheel tightened. "I can't help but wonder if Tessa rang her. Or convinced another resident to do it for her, since she seems to be on lockdown."

"We'll need to be on guard for that possibility," Kate said. "Paul—are you sure you're up for this?"

The look he sent her said it all. Kate, in no mood to dance around his feelings any longer, let out an infuriated huff.

"Paul! You've met Maura. You know how screwed up my family life is. And don't you dare pretend to be clueless about me and Tony, because I'd bet half my salary he's already come clean to you. I'm not saying you're unfit for the job. I'm only asking— are you up for interviewing Kyla Sloane? Knowing who she reminds you of?"

"You think I'm weak," Bhar muttered.

"No. I think you're human," Kate said. "And I'll cover for you if you need it. Just like I know you'd cover for me."

"You don't know that."

"Really?" Twisting her hair in both hands, Kate fashioned it into what she hoped was a passable early morning bun. "How many people have you told about Tony and me? It would be the end of my career. But guaranteed to advance yours."

"I owe the guv. I'd never turn on him."

"Oh, but you'd sell me out. Is that it?"

Bhar shrugged.

"Fine. Here's a juicy tidbit. DCI Vic Jackson still has it in for me. Whisper in *his* ear that I'm shagging the guv. I dare you."

"Kate, you bloody well know I'd never sabotage your career!"

"And I'd never call you weak. Just cover for you if you're not up for a particular interview. So." Kate paused. "Are you up for this particular interview?"

He firmed his jaw. "Yes." They traveled the rest of the way to Kyla Sloane's without another word.

CHAPTER TWENTY-THREE

The Chilcott family villa on Limerston Street had seen better days. The pale exterior could have done with a good pressure washing; the roof had lost more than a few tiles. Kate rang the bell as Bhar paced behind her, poking around empty flower boxes and dead shrubbery. The front garden was a blanket of fallen leaves.

"Who is it?" a little girl's voice called from behind the door.

"My name's Kate," Kate called, aware that if she frightened the child, they might be denied entry altogether. Suspects would capitalize on any excuse, including a startled youngster, to complain of police brutality and stall an interview. "I phoned earlier. Kyla's expecting me."

"Okay. Wait," the little girl called. Silence followed for two or three minutes. Kate was just about to push the bell again when the door opened. A slim man with a mustache squinted at Kate from behind thick glasses. A little girl, perhaps eight, hung on his trouser leg. She had black hair, almond-shaped eyes and a tongue that protruded slightly.

"You're pretty," the little girl said, grinning at Kate.

"So are you." Kate couldn't stop herself from grinning back.

"She has Downs. Are you the police?" the man asked. He looked as if he hadn't slept. Coffee stains dotted his shirt; his wool cardigan was mis-buttoned.

Kate ignored his first remark. Her own mother had often greeted total strangers with "my boy's retarded" before Ritchie could get so much as a word out.

"You like Dora the Explorer?" Kate asked the little girl, pointing at her T-shirt. "I like Diego." To the man, Kate said, "I'm Detective Sergeant Kate Wakefield. This is my colleague, Detective Sergeant Paul Bhar. We spoke to Kyla Sloane earlier this morning. We've come to discuss the French-Parsons case."

"French parsley?" the little girl echoed. "That's silly."

"Gigi, go to your room." The man's voice was flat.

"She said parsley. Don't think we have any parsley," Gigi said, releasing the man's trouser leg and transferring herself onto Kate's like a clinging vine. "You like Diego."

"Yes," Kate said, still grinning.

"If that's what it takes to get a little attention, I like Diego, too," Bhar said, squatting so he was at the child's eye level. "Maybe I look like him."

"No, you don't!" Gigi giggled.

"Gigi, I said go to your room. Now, damn it," the man thundered.

Releasing Kate's leg, the child darted into the house, squeaking in relief when someone else scooped her up. It was Kyla Sloane.

"Dad. It's me they want to talk to. Go take a nap."

"Nap," Gigi said, hiding her face against Kyla's neck.

"Kyla, I don't want you speaking to these people alone," Mr. Chilcott said. "We should engage counsel first. They can come back later, once I've—"

"Dad," Kyla repeated in a soft tone remarkably like her father's. "Take a nap. Take a drink. Whichever. I can handle this."

Mr. Chilcott's shoulders slumped. "Right. Of course. Detectives ... come in."

As her father disappeared into a back room, Kyla negotiated with Gigi, trying to convince the girl to watch an animated film while the adults conversed upstairs. Kate used the time to examine the villa as unobtrusively as possible. The walls, mostly bare, were in want of fresh paint. In several places framed art or photographs had been taken down, leaving gouges behind in the plaster. The furnishings, although top quality and almost surely bespoke, were minimal—one sofa, one chair and a coffee table. If not for Gigi's picture books and dolls scattered throughout, the front parlor would have looked depressingly bare.

"Your mum has a phrase for this," Kate whispered to Bhar, noting the tiny TV set. "In her books, when folks live at a posh address but hardly have a pot to piss in ..."

"Impoverished gentility," Bhar said close to her ear. "Guess the Wardles aren't the only family in need of a few quid."

"Everyone tell Gigi bye!" Kyla announced, putting in a Pixar Blu-ray and turning it on. Kate and Bhar made their goodbyes—it took longer than expected because Gigi kept forgetting her part of the bargain and trying to follow them upstairs—but eventually they were alone with Kyla Sloane in her bedroom.

"I know the kitchen would be nicer. I could offer you a bit of coffee or tea. But I didn't want Gigi bursting in every five minutes. Or Dad, for that matter." Kyla's room had no desk or chairs, but she indicated the neatly made bed. "Have a seat."

"We're fine," Kate said. Like the Sloane's front parlor, the room was sparsely decorated. Books were stacked on the floor and arranged along the windowsill. A laptop sat on the bedside table, a cheap prefab item that looked odd next to Kyla's cherry wood sleigh bed. The walls were covered with pages from *Vogue*, *W* and *Elle*—runway models, perfume ads and interviews with successful spokesmodels.

"Are you a model?" Kate asked, hoping to hit the right tone, somewhere between curious and admiring. Apparently she failed, because Kyla folded her arms across her chest, her neutral expression turning to stone.

"Is that part of your official inquiry, detective?"

"Not at all." Bhar stepped forward. "You simply seemed suited to the career. That and your choice of decorations …" he shrugged, smiling. "I interviewed dozens of guests on the night of the murders, but I don't think you were one of them. I'm—"

"Deepal Bhar," Kyla cut across him. "I know who you are. We met, remember? Twice, when I was sixteen."

Bhar blinked. "I'm sorry. I don't recall …"

"Not surprised. You had your head pretty far up—well. Up in the clouds, so to speak. Twice you came here to collect Tessa. I was downstairs both times. We chatted about cinema."

"Did we? I …"

"You don't remember." Kyla's calm expression betrayed nothing. "It's all right. If you'd been eyeing me instead of Tessa, you would have been a creep. So—you're still with Scotland Yard?"

Bhar nodded.

"Good. What Tessa did to you was awful. But she's sick. You know that." Kyla seemed to unclench by will alone, forcing her arms to her sides and putting on a helpful expression. "What would you like to know?"

"First question." Kate knew that if either she or Bhar was going to maintain the upper hand in this dual interview, it would have to be her. "Why did you move Clive French's body?"

Kyla's face paled and her pupils dilated. "It was … a bad night," she whispered.

"I'll say. You loaded him in the wheelbarrow and lit a bonfire on the spot where he died. Did you kill him yourself?" Kate demanded. "Or were you just covering up for the person who did?"

"Tell us," Bhar urged Kyla with surprising gentleness. "Start at the beginning. Early in the evening, you had a row with

Emmeline over Trevor Parsons. Did you have a relationship with him?"

"No!" Kyla cried, eyes widening. "Trev was Emmeline's. I'm her best—I *was* her best friend. We have nothing in common now, but for years we were everything to each other. I'd never let some guy come between us. Especially not a guy like Trevor."

"What sort of guy is that?" Kate asked.

Kyla made a derisive sound. "Thick. Conceited," she said. "There are guys like Trev on every street corner. Most aren't as good-looking, or as gifted at moving a ball up the field. Otherwise, they're exactly the same."

"So Trevor Parsons never laid a finger on you, and vice versa," Kate said.

"I just said that."

"Then what was the row about? Between you and Emmeline?" Kate insisted.

Sighing, Kyla went to her bag, digging out a pack of Marlboros and a lighter. Opening the window, she lit a cigarette near the screen, directing the smoke outside. "Gigi has a touch of asthma. Don't want to make it worse. Anyhow ... Trev always had a wandering eye. You've met Phoebe Paquette?"

"We have," Bhar said.

"Trev got her pregnant and legged it. Phoebe's a cold one—don't kid yourself, she's no prize. But she didn't deserve to be left to raise Trev's baby alone. When Trev took up with Em, I reckoned she could keep him in hand. I was wrong. Not an hour into the party, I went to the kitchen to bring out another tray of snacks and there's Trev getting fed a sandwich by Phoebe. He'd just put his arms around her when I broke it up."

"What happened next?" Bhar prompted.

"What do you think? Phoebe said she needed the loo and waddled off. Trev slunk away like nothing happened. I tidied up the kitchen in a sort of fog. Stashed the sandwich and beers while I tried to decide if I should to tell Em or not. It was none of my business," Kyla said. "Still. If I'd been in Em's place, I would have wanted her to tell me. So I did."

"And it blew up in your face," Kate guessed.

"Of course. I tried to be discreet, but Em was—well. A wee bit out of control, if you want the truth. Then Trev turned up and accused me of lying because he'd turned me down. And Em believed him." Kyla broke off, laughing incredulously. "After we'd been friends for so long. After sharing so much. She knew about my sister Tessa, how she fell in love with Sir Duncan and fell apart. I knew about her own family skeletons."

"The Wardles are bankrupt," Bhar said. "And Emmeline's been selling cocaine to help keep up appearances, at least for herself."

Kyla nodded, directing another plume of smoke out the window. "But in the end, when it came down to Trev's word or mine, she believed Trev. Said I was mad, as mad as Tessa. So I picked up the amphora vase. I knew what it meant to Em's family. I knew it was all they had left. But in that moment, I just didn't care."

"So you pitched it," Kate said.

"Pitched it at Em's head. Lucky for her, I missed. The vase shattered on the floor."

"What happened after that?" Bhar asked.

"Em called me names. So did Trev. They both stormed off in different directions and I went outside to get some air. That's when I found Clive."

"Dead?" Bhar prompted.

Kyla blinked. "Of course he was dead. Why would I kill Clive?"

"I don't know. I don't even know why you moved his body," Kate said. "Were you planning to transport him off the premises in the wheelbarrow? Dump him a few streets away?"

Kyla took another drag off her cigarette but said nothing.

"Here's my theory," Kate continued. "You ran into the back garden, just like you said. You found Clive's body and realized the game you'd been playing with Sir Duncan had suddenly turned quite real."

"What?" Kyla looked from Kate to Bhar and back again.

"When you found out Sir Duncan had moved next door to your best friend, you decided to meet with him. Maybe so you could confront him over your sister. Maybe because you idolized him as a child," Kate said, warming to her theory even as it coalesced in her mind. "I've met Sir Duncan. He's very seductive. Hypnotic, even. Did you tell him about the people who'd let you down? Emmeline, who cared more about a tosser like Trevor than a lifelong friend? Clive, who was pestering you for money? Because you did owe Clive money, didn't you, Kyla?"

For the first time, the young woman seemed completely rattled. "Yes, I owed Clive money. Over two thousand pounds. He was doing my assignments in maths and chemistry while I skived off to do photo shoots. I'm trying to get a modeling portfolio together. A way to support myself that will pay enough to help all of us. Gigi will always need special care and Dad—Dad's lost everything. If I can't keep us from losing the house, he may even lose the will to live."

"Fair enough. And Sir Duncan wouldn't part with his own dosh, but he was willing to get rid of your enemies, is that it?" Kate asked.

"What? I never asked Duncan for money. I wouldn't take it if he offered! I barely know the man!" Kyla cried, stubbing out her cigarette with a violence that reminded Kate of Tessa.

"Then why do the Wardle house CCTV cameras show you and Sir Duncan standing near Clive French's body?" Kate persisted. "What was he doing at the scene of the crime? Providing disposal tips? Or just moral support?"

Kyla's hand went to her mouth. For a moment, Kate thought the young woman would burst into tears. Then she stumbled to the bed and sat down, not speaking for several seconds.

"Are you going to arrest me?" she whispered, voice shaking.

"Ms. Sloane. Kyla." Bhar's tone was so carefully neutral, Kate wasn't sure if he was fighting sympathy or rising anger. "Tell me the truth. Without it, there's no way I can possibly help you. Did you kill Clive French or Trevor Parsons?"

"No." Kyla's voice was steady again.

"Do you know who did?"

She shook her head.

"After what happened to Tessa," Bhar continued, still in that painfully neutral tone, "what made you seek out Sir Duncan? Why go within a hundred meters of him?"

"I met him at Parkwood," Kyla said softly, not meeting their eyes. "Waiting to visit Tessa. He was so kind. He actually listened to me, which is more than most people do. I wasn't just a pretty face to him."

"Of course you were just a pretty face to him. You were *Tessa's* pretty face," Bhar snapped. Kate, alarmed, put a hand up, willing him to remember who was the good cop and who was the bad in this particular scenario. At the same moment, her mobile rang. It was the "emergency" tone she'd assigned for Ritchie's carer and Henry's school.

"Everyone, calm down. Take a break," Kate said, hoping her suspicions about the call didn't prove correct. "I'll just step outside the room to answer this."

~

"Well?" Bhar appeared in the hall just as Kate disconnected.

"How is she?" Kate whispered, nodding at Kyla's bedroom door.

"Bricking it. Didn't say a word to me. Just stared into space. I hope—hope she doesn't go the way Tessa did." Bhar pointed at Kate's mobile. "What about you? Problem?"

"Yes." Kate sighed, fighting a wave of bitter frustration. How could she ever advance in her career if her family life kept interrupting? "The bullies cornered Henry during lunch again. Except this time, someone told him to stand his ground and fight. So he did."

Bhar gave a low whistle. "That took guts. Is he hurt?"

"I don't know. He's in the school infirmary. I'm under orders to get there, now."

"Do it," Bhar urged. "I'll take over. If the guv is free, he can accompany me to Molly French's house. Help me make sense of what Kyla's said."

"She's more or less already admitted she's guilty," Kate said. "Guilty of obstruction at the very least. You have to place her under arrest."

"I know. But not until I've got as much as I can before the lawyers descend. Go on," Bhar repeated, jerking his head toward the stairs. "Rescue Henry. Catch up with me and the guv at Mrs. French's, if you're able."

～

After Kate departed, Bhar took another five minutes alone in the hall before reentering Kyla Sloane's bedroom.

"My colleague was called away," he said, relieved to find Kyla looking mutinous rather than vague. With that set to her features, she looked nothing like Tessa, except for relatively minor details like height and hair color. "I shouldn't have said that. About you being nothing but Tessa's pretty face to Sir Duncan. It was … inappropriate."

"You're talking about yourself. Not Sir Duncan," Kyla sighed. "Don't feel too bad. My dad's just like you. He wants to forget about Tessa. To put her away in a compartment and move on with his life. But he can't. Not so long as I'm around, and he has to look at me."

Bhar felt himself beginning to blush. Fortunately, his complexion was so dark, he doubted Kyla would be able to tell.

"I believe you about the fight with Emmeline. The vase. How you rushed into the back garden to get away. I believe you found Clive dead and panicked. Tried to cover it up. Was that for Sir Duncan's benefit?"

Kyla nodded. "He'd been so kind to me. Even tried to give me money, but I wouldn't take it. So he gave me modeling agencies to try. Agents I could send headshots to. When I found Clive, I thought … I thought every terrible thing I'd ever heard about Duncan was true. And he'd end up in Parkwood, just like Tessa. I —I went wild. I dragged Clive into the wheelbarrow. But even though he was a little guy, he was heavy—so heavy. I couldn't get far before I needed a breather. Then I saw the blood on the ground and set the bonfire. But the wind kept picking up. I was afraid I'd set the whole garden on fire. So I called Duncan, and he came over. Talked sense into me. Told me to touch nothing else, run into the house screaming and say I'd just found the body. He said if I kept calm enough, no one would be able to prove I'd moved things around."

"And you did it? Right then?"

Kyla nodded.

"Sir Duncan was in the back garden when you ran into the house? And Trevor Parsons came down the stairs with an axe in his head?"

"When I came in, Trev was already on the floor. Em was already screaming."

"So Sir Duncan was in the garden with you at the exact time Trevor was being killed."

"I guess so," Kyla shrugged. "I never thought about it. Even though I panicked when I saw Clive, I knew in my heart Duncan never killed anyone. That's why he got off. It was all a mistake."

"A mistake?" Bhar snapped. "Kyla, listen to me. Sir Duncan might not have been convicted, but let me assure you, he's killed at least a dozen people. He's a monster!"

"No, he's not! I've met monsters," Kyla cried. "You might not

226

have them in your world, but they're around every corner in mine! You think Em's mum cares about anything besides money? You think a muscle-bound jerk like Trev ever loved anyone but himself? Look at Phoebe Paquette, hooking up with a coke dealer just to have some guy—any guy—at her beck and call! He's the coldest creep I've ever met!"

"A coke dealer?" For a split second, Bhar thought he'd heard Kyla wrong. "You mean—Jeremy?"

Kyla stared at him. "My God! You don't know anything, do you? Jeremy dealt the coke! Clive was the courier! He gave out free tastes in those stupid little key chains! When I told Em I wanted nothing to do with Jeremy or his business, that was the beginning of the end for us. All downhill from there."

Bhar digested that. He would have to ring Hetheridge. But he had one last question to ask.

"Kyla. Did Jeremy dislike Clive or Trevor? Hold a grudge against them? Hate them, even?"

"That's what I'm trying to tell you," Kyla said. "All you can see is Duncan, but Jeremy's the real monster. He has no feelings at all."

CHAPTER TWENTY-FOUR

A fat man with a grizzled beard waited outside Molly French's third-floor flat. Despite the late October chill, he wore a bowling shirt, shorts, plastic sandals and black socks that came up almost to his knees. He sat in a deck chair with a cricket bat balanced across his lap.

"Police?" he called as Hetheridge and Bhar approached.

"Indeed. I'm Chief Superintendent Hetheridge. This is Detective Sergeant Paul Bhar." Ignoring the cricket bat's implicit threat, Hetheridge put out his hand. The fat man shook it like a prize-fighter completing the preliminaries before he came out swinging.

"Let me tell you summat. That lady," the fat man pointed at Molly French's door with his cricket bat, "has lived a life about as sweet as a cow pat from the devil's own satanic herd. Her poofter son went and got himself killed. And she's dying, if you don't know. Got colon cancer. Won't finish another six months, to hear the doctors tell it."

"We had no idea," Hetheridge said. "You are …?"

"The bloke what owns this building. Lonnie T. McGraw," the man said, pronouncing his name slowly and distinctly, like a curse. "I've run off the *Sun* twice and the *Daily Mirror* five times. Plus that little uncover bugger, whichever rag he's from. Always turns up with a bouquet and a big phony smile. How long do you reckon you'll be in there?"

"Half hour. Hour at the most," Hetheridge said.

"Fine. I need a good long sit on the bog. Hate to leave Molly alone. 'Fraid she'll do herself harm. There won't be no last holiday in Hawaii for her now, and it's a right awful shame. What's she got to live for?"

"Mr. McGraw," Hetheridge said as the landlord rose from his deck chair. "One of my subordinates may join us later. Young, blond female. DS Kate Wakefield. If she attempts entry, please don't swing the cricket bat at her head."

"Noted," the landlord grunted, leaving the bat lying across the deck chair's seat. "While I'm gone, give me the same courtesy and don't send poor Molly crying. Yesterday she wept so much over her boy, she threw up." McGraw shook his head. "Sodding stupid poofter. Couldn't stay alive another six months. Couldn't do that much for his poor old mum."

Hetheridge knocked first, then tried the bell. By the time McGraw had shambled, bow-legged, down the stairs, a stooped woman in a dressing gown opened the door.

"You're the police." Her hair, uncombed, was dyed brown with three inches of white showing at the roots. "Please come in."

"Mrs. French." Hetheridge refrained from stepping over the threshold, waiting until she gingerly accepted his hand. "Before we enter your home. I'm Anthony Hetheridge. An inspector for New Scotland Yard. Please accept my deepest sympathies for the loss of your son, Clive."

Molly French's blue eyes moistened. "Oh. Thank you. Still can't believe it. Still keep thinking I might wake and find it's all a dream." Stepping back, she waved Hetheridge and Bhar inside. "I suppose you're here to ask questions."

"I'll be taking notes," Bhar said, holding up his notebook and pen where Molly French could see it. "If I may begin—did your son have any enemies? Anyone who might have wanted to do him harm?"

"Not that he ever spoke of." Molly French fiddled with the belt of her terry cloth robe. "My Clive was a shy one. Gay, I think, but he never told me. Never seemed to fancy girls. Just his schoolwork and the computer, of course. I didn't care if Clive was gay. He was the best son a mother could hope for." Taking a deep breath, she pressed her lips together, transparently fighting back tears. "He would have flown me anywhere in the world if there was a cure. And when he heard there wasn't—when the doc said I might as well pack it in—Clive said, 'Never mind, Mum. I'll fly you to Hawaii. We'll vacation in paradise.'"

"Did your son have sufficient savings? To fly you to Hawaii, I mean?" Bhar asked.

Molly French shook her head. "Not in the bank. But he tutored other students at uni. Lots of his mates owed him money. Fees here and there that my Clive let ride. He was always generous like that. But once he had Hawaii set in his mind, he told me he'd collect or know the reason why not."

"Were the people who owed Clive money truly his mates?" Hetheridge asked gently. "Or just other students he knew through a sort of business association?"

Molly French gave Hetheridge a stricken look. "They had to be his mates. Clive was secretive, he never said much about uni, but I'm sure he had friends. Everyone has friends. Maybe even a boyfriend. I'm sure my Clive wasn't all alone in the world. There was one lad who visited him regular. I think *he* was the boyfriend …"

"Did Clive associate with a young man named Trevor Parsons?" Bhar asked.

Molly French shook her head.

"Emmeline Wardle? Kyla Sloane?" Hetheridge asked, watching as the woman's watery eyes darted from side to side.

"Not that I ever heard of," she muttered. "My Clive loved his computer, he did. If someone killed him—" She stopped. "Someone did kill him. I know that. I haven't gone mad, I know what happened. But it must have been a mistake. I can't believe anyone who knew Clive would ever—ever—"

Hetheridge started to go to her but Bhar was already there, snatching a Kleenex from the coffee table and pressing it into Molly French's hand. "If you don't mind—could we see your son's bedroom?" he asked.

"Of course. Let me—let me take my medicine first." Slow and deliberate, Molly French made her way to the kitchen. Opening a prescription bottle, she shook out two large white pills, swallowing them with a glass of water. "Now. Clive's room. This way."

Hetheridge and Bhar followed Molly French into her son's bedroom. It looked small and dispiritingly hopeful. The twin bed was made with an Avengers bedspread. The Mac on Clive's desk displayed a Thor screensaver.

"Always did love Thor, my Clive," Molly French said fondly, tracing the blond demigod's digital image with a fingertip.

"Mrs. French. Your pardon, but—what are those?" Hetheridge asked, pointing to a shoebox near the computer desk. It overflowed with silver balls, each attached to a key ring by a long metal chain.

"Oh! Key chains, don't you know," Molly French said. "They come with lip balm inside. I've always had dry lips. But if you don't need lip balm, you can chuck the pot and fill it with—"

"Hallo! Mrs. French? It's me!" a young man called.

"Oh." Drawing her robe closer around her throat, Molly French smoothed her hair with both hands. "There he is. My Clive's secret fellow. Don't let on we know." Drawing herself up, she put on a weak approximation of a smile. "In here, luv. Come on back."

Hetheridge and Bhar turned as one as Jeremy Bentham

entered Clive's bedroom. He carried a supermarket bouquet of carnations and a miniature teddy bear.

"Detective Bhar," Jeremy said, flashing a smile. His gaze shifted to Hetheridge. "Is this your superior officer? The one who arrested Em?"

"Yes. Chief Superintendent Hetheridge," Bhar said. "He's in charge of the French-Parsons case. Chief, this is Jeremy Bentham."

"Pleasure to meet you, Mr. Bentham," Hetheridge said, shaking the young man's hand. "Remarkable for you to remember DS Bhar's name."

"Not really. We've met twice before." Jeremy pressed the bouquet and small teddy into Molly French's hands. "I brought these for you. Little pick-me-up. Figured you could use it. Just came by to collect some of my ... ah! There you are, you little buggers!" he said, spying the shoebox full of key chains.

Stooping, he bent to retrieve the box, dumping its contents atop Clive's bed. "Right. Let me just count these. Clive was always losing things. If he wasn't dead, I'd have to give him a slap."

"Mr. Bentham," Hetheridge said, giving Bhar one sidelong glance. "I was told Ms. Paquette is near her time. How does she fare?"

"Premature labor. In the antenatal unit as we speak," Jeremy said, not looking up from his counting. "Thank goodness she chose her cousin as her birth partner. All that waiting would be too much for me."

"You might consider popping round to check on her soon," Hetheridge suggested. "Sometimes a new mother dies in labor. The baby dies, too. Nine months of sacrifice for nothing." He laughed. "It's actually quite funny, if you think about it."

"Hey?" Jeremy shot Hetheridge a wicked grin. "Well, sure. If they both died ... Talk about a colossal waste of time." He giggled.

"Jeremy." Molly French sounded shocked.

"I want you to know, I understand your position," Hetheridge continued, moving closer to the door as Bhar took a careful step toward Jeremy. "Most of the marriages in my family tree come down to money, connections or both. Phoebe is your golden ticket, isn't she? No more working your way up the ladder with one scheme or another. Marry Phoebe and once she has access to her trust fund, you'll never want for anything ever again."

Jeremy frowned. He seemed to be thinking as rapidly as possible, trying to reason out a puzzle fraught with emotional resonance for most, but not for him. "Most people do marry for security, as well as companionship," he said slowly. "I've proven I can be everything Pheebs needs. She just needs time to get over Trevor. She'll have more money than she can spend. It won't hurt her to go halfsies with me. And her baby will need a father."

"Of course. No one would argue with that," Hetheridge said. "Trevor Parsons was in the way, wasn't he?"

As Hetheridge took another step toward the door, Bhar moved incrementally closer to Jeremy, saying, "Phoebe told me she went as your guest to Emmeline's Halloween party. And she attended for just one reason. She wanted to rekindle her relationship with Trevor Parsons. To tell him there was still time for him to change his mind before she sued him for paternity."

"I don't understand," Molly French quavered. "What's happening? What are you all on about?"

"We almost missed the connection between you and Clive," Hetheridge told Jeremy. "Clive was determined to earn enough money to take his mother to Hawaii. His academic pursuits weren't enough. So he started working with you. Delivering samples and collecting on debts. I wonder …" Hetheridge glanced at Molly French. "Forgive me for asking this, Mrs. French, but I begin to wonder if Clive's success at blackmailing students didn't inspire him to overreach. To demand hush money from Mr. Bentham here, or else tip off the police about your thriving cocaine business."

"I know my rights." Pushing the box of key chains aside,

Jeremy stood up stiffly, like a man at attention. "I reject every allegation you've made. I want counsel."

"Mind you, I'm not concerned about the cocaine," Hetheridge said, easing forward another few centimeters. Jeremy's face remained calm, but a spot of red appeared on each cheek. His hands, still at his sides, were beginning to shake.

"And I understand why you felt Trevor and Clive needed to be eliminated. But it took me longer to work out why you did it so flamboyantly," Hetheridge said slowly, hoping Bhar was ready but not daring to split his concentration, even for a moment. "You chose a venue so big and confused that without an eyewitness or a confession, the culprit would be almost impossible to pinpoint. But perhaps more importantly, you chose a venue filled with the sort of people Sir Duncan Godington particularly values. Right next door to Sir Duncan's townhouse, even. And you wielded a weapon similar to a machete, but easier to handle for someone of your stature. Leaving me with only two conclusions. Either you meant for Sir Duncan to take the blame, or you wanted to impress him with a spectacular crime. Something to rival his own triple murder."

"I know my rights," Jeremy repeated.

"I think it was the latter," Hetheridge continued, inching still closer to the door. "Not an hour ago I received word that when you turned eighteen, you legally changed your name to Jeremy Bentham. Before that, you were Ian Burke. Twice detained for attempting to get a ringside seat at Sir Duncan Godington's trial. Once with a false ID, trying to pass for twenty-one. Once in drag. Having tried it once and nearly succeeded, you decided to purchase the murder weapons in drag, didn't you? Did you intend to resemble Kyla Sloane with the long, brunette wig, or was that just a happy coincidence?"

"Jeremy! What is he—why is he—" Molly French began.

"Shut it," Jeremy cried, seizing Molly French by the hair. For an instant his fingers clawed at her soft white throat. Then

Hetheridge was there, prying the younger man's hands away and pulling Clive's mother to safety as Bhar knocked Jeremy to the floor.

"Don't try to run," Hetheridge cried, holding onto Molly French, who was screaming and twisting like a madwoman. On the floor, Bhar got in two solid punches as Jeremy writhed, going for something in his front jeans pocket.

"Gun! He may have a gun!" Hetheridge shouted.

Something small and red flashed in Jeremy's right hand. Then Bhar screamed as a blade entered his neck and blood spurted across the room.

Hetheridge let Molly French go. As she ran screaming from the room, he advanced on Jeremy. The young man had plunged his Swiss Army knife's largest blade into the side of Bhar's neck, right where the shoulder joined with the throat.

"He's not bleeding too much," Jeremy said from the floor, one hand curled just under Bhar's chin, the other holding the knife in place. "Bet if I pull it out, he'll bleed like a stuck pig. That's a cliché. I should say … the *proverbial* stuck pig."

"Leave the blade in place, Jeremy," Hetheridge said.

"Please?" The young man grinned.

"Please."

"Get up, mate," Jeremy told Bhar. "I know your arms and legs work. Give me trouble and I'll stick you again."

Laboriously they rose as one, Jeremy panting and red-faced, Bhar determinedly blank. His lips were pressed together, but his eyes were wide and terrified. Hetheridge, who had twice faced a loaded gun, understood that terror as well as anyone.

"Now. Chief Superintendent," Jeremy's tone was still fundamentally calm, "you think you're so clever, don't you? Yes, Clive tried to blackmail me. Yes, I bought the axes in drag. Doesn't make me queer. Just careful. Clever. Like Sir Duncan. Emmeline wanted to have her Halloween party at a cinema but I convinced her to do it at the townhouse. Because I wanted to be sure Sir

Duncan had a front-row seat. To see who I am. What I can do. And he did," Jeremy grinned. "The whole world did. So. Know what you're going to do, chief? You're going to let me walk out of here. Or I'll open this wog's throat from ear to ear, I promise."

"You're going to walk backwards? With DS Bhar between you and me?"

"Why not?" To prove his capability, Jeremy swung Bhar around so the detective sergeant faced Hetheridge and Jeremy's back was aligned with the open door. "It's just a short distance for me. But a big one for you. I can kill him before you can blink."

"Jeremy." Hetheridge put all his persuasive power into his voice. "It will be difficult for the Crown to prove you killed Trevor Parsons and Clive French. But if you kill DS Bhar now, before the eyes of a top-ranking detective, you'll go to prison for life. And don't fantasize that you can run away if you manage to kill me as well as my sergeant. It simply isn't in the cards."

Jeremy's upper lip curled. "You're old. This one's hurt. Bet me." As he withdrew the knife blade, sending another spurt of Bhar's blood across the room, the cricket bat struck Jeremy Bentham's skull with an audible crack. Eyes wide and mouth open, he released Bhar, falling to his knees. When Jeremy waved the knife weakly, mouth moving like he might issue another threat, Kate hit him again even harder.

"Bet you? *Bet me.*" Kate glared down at Jeremy's inert form, McGraw's cricket bat gripped in both hands. "Twitch and I'll hit you again, you piss-headed wanker."

"Thought 'plonker' was your appellation of choice." Hetheridge fought mightily not to sound out of breath, much less frightened. He'd glimpsed Kate in the doorway, cricket bat in hand, just as Jeremy threatened to open Bhar's throat from ear to ear.

"I like to change it up," Kate said, dropping down beside Bhar. His hand was already clamped over his neck wound; she put her hand on top of his, doubling the pressure. "Backup is on the way, so stay with me, Paul. Don't faint or do anything the lads will tease you for later."

"Thought the wormy little bastard was going to kill me," Bhar said. Despite the pressure he and Kate kept on the wound, he was still bleeding significantly. Bleeding, and beginning to tremble all over with the early signs of shock.

"Detective. I need you to stay awake. Alert," Hetheridge snapped, determined not to let the younger man slip into unconsciousness. "I believe you may receive a commendation for this. How does that strike you?"

"There's only one thing I want." Bhar's voice shook.

Hetheridge met Kate's eyes, but only for a moment. "And what's that?"

"Is there some way we could keep this from … well … my mum?"

CHAPTER TWENTY-FIVE

The second meeting with Henry's school counselor went off about as well as Kate expected. Though she disagreed with virtually everything the woman said, Kate followed Hetheridge's advice and nodded and refused to be baited, only promising that Henry would do better. It gave her a grim bit of satisfaction to know that of the boys collared for fighting, Henry was the least injured. Hetheridge's fencing lessons had given the boy a bit of confidence. Standing up to his worst tormentors had given him even more. Perhaps the rest of the school year would go a bit easier for him. If so, some discipline and a few teacher-guardian meetings was a small price to pay.

After dropping Henry off at their flat, she decided to stop by the Bhar home and see how her colleague fared. The blade had dug deeply in Bhar's left trapezius muscle and nicked the carotid, requiring surgery. Now he was looking at two months of physical therapy for the neck and shoulder to regain his full range of motion.

"Come in, come in, I am so glad to meet you at last," Sharada Bhar cried, opening the door and throwing her arms around

Kate. "Deepal told me everything! You saved him! You saved my precious baby boy!"

"Mrs. Bhar." Kate couldn't stop herself from hugging the little woman back with the same fierce gusto, thrilled to see so much of Bhar in his mum's beaming face. Ordinarily Kate kept her emotions at bay as much as possible. After her brush with death during the Malcolm Comfrey case, she'd coped by resolutely refusing to feel anything, one way or another. But something about DS Bhar's resemblance to Sharada broke through that barrier, making Kate desperately happy she'd turned up at Molly French's in time to wield that bat. "I'll always pull Paul's fat out of the fire if I can."

"Fat out of the fire," Sharada repeated. "That is a good English phrase. When I was a little girl, we said something similar. We said—never mind. I am a novelist who writes in English," Sharada said firmly, as if someone had recently maligned that ability. "Wait and see. In one of my books, I will have some lady pull some handsome man's fat right out of the fire."

"Brilliant. So—can I see him?" Kate asked, resisting the temptation to tell Sharada she enjoyed her books. Getting into that sort of discussion with an author would likely spiral into a never-ending vortex.

"Of course. Deepal!" Sharada bellowed up the staircase. "Your police lady friend is coming up! Make sure you are wearing your trousers!"

"Does it hurt?" Kate asked, once she was alone with Bhar in his bedroom. Dressing gown belted over his pajamas, Bhar was seated at the computer, aimlessly scrolling through posts on a social networking site.

"Not as long as I take a pain pill every four hours. Otherwise, it burns," Bhar admitted. "Throbs, too, where the knife point hit my collarbone. Amazing how those American detectives on TV get shot in the shoulder every other week and never miss a day's work."

"We should put in a transfer request. From Scotland Yard to Hollywood."

"Or at least Bollywood. Where we could wear pretty costumes and dance from time to time, if nothing else," Bhar said. "One of my mates just called. Said Jeremy Bentham used his one phone call on Sir Duncan. The call must not have gone how he planned, because a few hours later, he killed himself in custody. Beat his head against the wall until he collapsed and died."

"I heard."

Bhar's gaze shifted back to the computer monitor, shifting from posts to chat, where he had an ongoing conversation with Model_Citizen_21. "Am I a bad person for being glad he's dead?"

"Not really. Just human."

"But is human anything to be proud of?"

Kate shrugged. "It's all we've got. Besides—you helped save Molly French's life. Defended the guv. Kept Kyla Sloane from an unjust trial and maybe even an unjust conviction. When it comes to your actions, I don't see what you have to complain about."

Bhar rolled his eyes. "It all comes back to the same thing. I let Tessa Chilcott draw me in. I said too much. And Sir Duncan Godington went free."

"Paul. I read up on the case. Sir Duncan would have gone free no matter what. The Crown didn't have enough direct evidence. The jury was completely in love with him. An acquittal was inevitable."

"Doesn't change the main point," Bhar said, grimacing as he tried to flex his left arm. "I have poor judgment. I'm not like the guv. Not like you. Whatever I think, whatever I feel—it's sure to be wrong."

Kate took a deep breath. Growing up with almost no female friends, she was terrible at playing the sneaky, subtle, emotional cheerleader. Whether she gave advice or just an opinion, she knew no way but to speak the truth as she saw it.

"Kyla Sloane isn't a bad person. Maybe she showed poor judgment, letting Sir Duncan befriend her. But the man is magnetic. You can't dismiss her out of hand for being taken in by him. Especially if he was on his best behavior." Kate paused, then tapped the computer monitor. "Is that who you're chatting with? Model_Citizen_21?"

Bhar glanced at his closed bedroom door. Then he leaned closer to Kate. "Yes. Once I'm healed, I thought I might ask her out for a coffee. Just—just to test the waters. But if my mum finds out, she'll kill me."

Kate bit back a laugh. "That's between you and Mrs. Bhar. But I'll never tell."

~

When Kate went back downstairs, she found Sharada studying what looked like a manuscript on her computer monitor. As she read it, Sharada used the mouse to scroll down, lips moving soundlessly.

"Almost done?" Kate asked.

Sharada made a startled noise. "Kate!" she cried, pressing a hand to her chest. "Oh! You startled me! I was just checking over my latest. I call it, *By His Hand Uplifted.* The story of a commoner girl who catches the eye of a duke. They fall deeply in love. She believes he seeks her out only for her physical charms." Sharada's eyes sparkled. "And so the first time he proposes marriage, she says no. Out of fear for what marriage to a commoner will do to his reputation."

"Oh. Really. Isn't that … remarkable," Kate managed, squashing the temptation to sprint back upstairs and throttle Bhar. Surely that would be unsporting, given his neck injury. She'd have to settle the score at some future date.

"Never fear. They marry in the end. The physical connection is too strong to overcome," Sharada continued with a rather earthy chuckle.

"But what about hard, cold reality after the wedding?" Kate demanded. If she couldn't rain on her injured colleague's parade, she might as well rain on Sharada's. "How does a girl from nowhere—from nothing—learn to be a member of the aristocracy?"

Sharada smiled that impish smile. "Why, the same way I learned English. Practice."

~

"This is nice," Kate murmured. It was the fifth evening in a row she'd spent at Wellegrave House. Four times she'd let poor Harvey drive her home in the wee hours. Tonight, a carer for Ritchie was engaged, while Henry was sleeping over at a mate's. Kate and Hetheridge had the entire night to themselves.

"Shall I turn on the television?"

"Didn't know you had one in here," Kate said, lifting her cheek off his chest. "Where?"

"Watch and learn." Taking a remote from the bedside table, Hetheridge pointed it at the wall. The rather nondescript piece of framed art—a pastoral oil—slid out of sight, revealing the flat screen TV behind it. Another click of the button and they were watching BBC World News. Snuggled back in Hetheridge's arms, Kate was half-asleep when the words "Foxhound Fanciers" roused her.

"Oi! Is that your git of an heir?"

"It is indeed. Randy Roddy," Hetheridge said, turning up the volume.

"It's just that foxes are vermin. Pests," Roderick Hetheridge earnestly told a reporter. "And even if they weren't, that's not really the point, is it? We're humans. We have a culture to uphold.

When I think about a world where young British men don't learn good sportsmanship by riding to hounds, it makes me want to weep."

"Makes me want to puke," Kate said. "Lord. Does he have to be your heir? Can't you pick someone else?"

"That's not how the aristocracy works, as you very well know." Hetheridge sounded amused. "Sometimes when I see Roddy on the television, I feel a bit sorry for myself. Bad as he is, at least he has a wife. He managed to trick some poor, thick girl into marrying him …"

"Tony," Kate groaned. "Do I really have to start again from the top?"

"Not at all. But assure me of one small detail. You won't marry me because you don't wish to become Baroness Hetheridge. Is that correct?"

"Correct," Kate said, pressing her face against the warmth of Hetheridge's chest. She loved the sound of his voice, even when she didn't particularly care for what he was saying.

"And that's the only reason?"

"Tony." Kate lifted her face, staring into his. "You know it is."

"Excellent. I have a solution," Hetheridge said. "I'll give up my title in favor of Roderick. As you've seen, Roddy's a bit of a pill—loves the foxhunt and is always threatening to shoot the anti-blood-sport activists. He expects to receive my title as soon as I die, and has never forgiven me for living this long. Yes, Roddy, his wife and his three strapping boys would be overjoyed at the honor. And if you'll marry me … well, it goes without saying, I'll be the happiest man alive. Letting go of my title will mean nothing by comparison. What do you say?"

Kate sat up. "Tony. You'd really do that? Give up your title to Mr. Blood Sport?"

"The instant my barrister finishes drawing up the papers, if it means you'll wear my ring and be my wife. The title is nothing to me. You're the only thing I want in this world." Cupping Kate's face in both hands, Hetheridge kissed her, slow and gentle. "Well? What do you say?"

Kate made a choked sound. "Bugger that."

"I beg your pardon?"

"Bugger you giving up your title to some fox-murderer named Roderick. If you can accept me as Baroness Hetheridge, I sure as hell can." Kate kissed him on the mouth, then pulled back, staring hard into his eyes. "I mean ... I still have questions. Will the Met allow us to work together after we're married? Are you sure you can handle Henry and Ritchie twenty-four/seven? What about ..."

"All of that is for the future," Hetheridge said, pulling her back into his warm embrace. "For now, there's only you and I."

THE END

ALSO BY EMMA JAMESON

The Lord & Lady Hetheridge Mystery Series:

Ice Blue

Blue Murder

Something Blue

Black & Blue

Blue Blooded

The Dr. Benjamin Bones Mysteries:

Marriage Can Be Murder

Divorce Can Be Deadly

The Magic of Cornwall:

Dr. Bones and the Christmas Wish

Dr. Bones and the Lost Love Letter